S·P·H·I·N·X

By the same author

S·P·H·I·N·X

D. M. Thomas

VIKING

VIKING
Viking Penguin Inc.
40 West 23rd Street,
New York, New York 10010, U.S.A.

First American Edition
Published in 1987

LIBRARY OF CONGRESS CATALOGING IN PUBLICATION DATA
Thomas, D. M.
Sphinx.
I. Title.
PR6070.H58S6   1987   823'.914   86-40277
ISBN 0-670-81415-6

Printed in the United States of America by
R. R. Donnelley & Sons, Harrisonburg, Virginia
Set in Bembo

Second printing February 1987

· Notes and Acknowledgements ·

This is the third of four improvisational novels.

While the work was in progress, Part One, *Isadora's Scarf*, was commissioned by the BBC as a television play. The published text and the text for performance are substantially different.

The quotation from Chekhov's *Cherry Orchard* in One, 2, is from the version by Elisaveta Fen (Penguin, 1951). The quotation from Pushkin's *Eugene Onegin* in Three, 2, is from the version by Charles Johnston (Penguin, 1979). Other quotations from Russian poets are translated by the author.

The introductory epigraph is from *Twilight* in *Beings and things on their own* (BOA editions, 1986), translated from Greek by its author in collaboration with Jackie Willcox.

Alexander Pushkin's unfinished story *Egyptian Nights*, a major source of inspiration, is translated in *Ararat*, Part One. The quartet is dedicated to Pushkin.

D.M.T.

· CONTENTS ·

I am politically minded. I mean, I think
about death daily and compare it with a
vastly better system: life.

KATERINA ANGHELAKI-ROOKE

P·R·O·L·O·G·U·E

"Your mind is far away . . ." The Moika
Churned beneath Pushkin's rooms, but I'd
Seen the vague outline of a *troika*;
I'd not been listening to my guide.
Charsky . . . the *improvisatore* . . .
"I'm boring you," she said; "I'm sorry."
Tartly, for I'd insisted that
I must see the museum-flat,
Closed for *remont*. "No, no! I'm only
Moved to be here." "—Of course. Well, we
Should go: a friend's asked us to tea;
An actress, widowed, rather lonely.
You'll find her beautiful, I think."
Outside, thick snow—the poet's ink—

Swirled round the tram; my mind was thronging
With thoughts of that blind date with death—
With bitter-sweet and homesick longing
Known, in lost Cornish, as *hiréth*—
How Pushkin saw the snow-white crests

Of Ararat, like Sheba's Breasts
In Haggard's book . . . And suddenly
Brown, cool-dressed girls surrounded me
Instead of crones; my youth surged through me;
I lost sight of the Hermitage;
'49 was the century's age,
Not mine . . . Until Natasha drew me
Back from those blue skies: "Look, the sphinx . . ."
The dark head catches snow, and drinks.

I meet the actress, who is pleasant,
Intelligent and beautiful;
Even so, I'm not entirely present;
Her contours of Angora wool
Are Ararat, and in their hollow
I catch an outline of a swallow.
Soon a third image comes: the white
Snow-flecks against falling night
Remind me of the week-old *Guardian*
Back in my room—irate yet bland,
Doing its best to understand
Madness and evil; plump as Mardian . . .
I hear the actress, regal, sad,
Quote Pushkin: "Don't let me go mad . . ."

O·N·E

• ISADORA'S SCARF •

Duncan is in her grave . . .
ROZANOV

Dear God, don't let me go mad . . .
PUSHKIN

· I ·

Gizeh. The sphinx. A pyramid. The image yields to:

*Red Square, Moscow. Lenin's Mausoleum. A queue. Soldiers.
Then:*

*Shaven head, gaunt face, staring eyes, in close-up. The man
speaks, through broken teeth, as if remembering how he once
lectured . . .*

HISTORIAN: We broke through the rubble into the death-
chamber. The stale, hot air of many thousands of years hit
us. I shone my torch in—and saw a sarcophagus! Alas, I
couldn't see any grave-goods. They had long been pillaged.
(*Treasures of Tutankhamun, including the throne.*) Fearfully we
entered that place of mystery and death. We approached the
sarcophagus. The glass was still intact. I looked down—and
cried out. I don't mind admitting it. For there, staring up at
me, was a living face! (*The embalmed head and trunk of Lenin,
under broken glass.*) Yet, what a face! Not the young, tender

and graceful king of the holy book; but an aged despot! All subtlety, grace, beauty, had passed away. If tender emotions had ever touched that face, they had long since vanished. (*Cut to Tutankhamun's throne.*) If his consort had ever offered him a flower, or stroked his shoulder, or poured perfume into his hand—the love of power had long since dispossessed the power of love. He lay alone. No tender Ankhesenamun shared his grave, nor would wish to. Yet what happened, that such a vapid culture (*cut to sample of Soviet poster-art*) could in only a few thousand years produce this beauty . . . (*Tutankhamun treasures*) this sense of form, this subtlety and tenderness, this harmony of male and female? Answers in one hour. Write on one side of the sheet only.

A bedroom. Pale light through curtains. A wide bed on which sleep four people. Two women and a man (between them) are entwined, naked; a second, bulky man, in trousers and white shirt, snores on his back, perilously balanced on the edge of the bed. Caption: MOSCOW. 1981. NOVEMBER. *Cut back to:*

The historian, mumbling silently. He is in a queue of lunatics waiting in line for medicine, between rows of bunks. Barred windows. Portraits of Lenin and Brezhnev. The inmates wear striped shirts, baggy underpants tied with string; they mumble or moan to the nape of the man in front. A huge, thuggish orderly strides up and down, striking out here and there with a cosh.

FIRST INMATE: (*Arm raised, as if clinging to something desperately.*) One million eight hundred thousand and fifty-five . . . One million eight hundred thousand and fifty-six . . . One million six hundred thousand and fifty-eight . . .

SECOND: I'm happy happy happy happy happy happy happy happy happy happy happy happy happy happy happy happy happy happy happy . . .

ORDERLY: There's no need to exaggerate, Happy. Is that shit

you're smearing on your arms? You filthy swine! Lick it up, lick it up! (*The cosh flails.*)

THIRD: (*An old man.*)   After we'd solved the Armenian problem, I was sent to Australia to deal with the Aborigines. It's often said a hundred were shot at Warata. This isn't true. At least a dozen of them were burnt. I myself set fire to one child . . .

FOURTH: Sections, vivisections, erections, elections, injections . . .

FIFTH: What's happened to my Earl Grey tea and muffins? This is supposed to be the best Freudian clinic in London, but the service and medical attention is appalling! I've had no psychoanalysis of my case whatever.

ORDERLY: Moaning again, Kravchenko?

KRAVCHENKO: My name's Johnson, Mr Johnson, if you don't mind. I'm employed by the *New Statesman*. I'm severely depressed, and you only make me feel worse by pretending I'm someone else . . .

ORDERLY: (*Swinging his cosh.*)   You're Kravchenko, a fucking terrorist, and a raving loonie. Learn some fucking respect.

The camera moves to the front of the queue: a female psychiatrist flanked by two nurses. The psychiatrist glances at each patient's report as he shuffles up, and barks out "Sulphur" and "Haloperidol" alternately. The Haloperidol patients swallow pills, and file off right; they shake, and their eyes glaze. The Sulphur patients are grabbed by two orderlies and a nurse injects them. These patients writhe and scream. The psychiatrist's face is likewise divided. The left half, which wears half a pair of glasses, is square and surly, with short brown hair; the right half is elongated and refined, with long grey-blonde hair.

The bedroom. The bulky, snoring man wakes, groans. Lifting his head, he sees the entangled trio beside him. He half-slips off the bed and stands up, swaying, groaning still, holding his head. He stumbles over a fallen duvet towards the door.

A living-room. He enters. A chaotic scene: bottles, glasses, record-sleeves scattered; a semi-collapsed hi-fi unit. Jacket on a chair-back. He dips a hand in a pocket, and hisses with pain. His hand, when he withdraws it, oozes blood. He finds a handkerchief in the other pocket, wraps it round the cut hand. He crawls on hands and knees, as if searching for something, and vomits on to a richly embroidered rug. He hauls himself to a sofa, and lies full-length. The phone, on a bookshelf, rings. He rises, staggers to it, lifts the receiver. After listening for a few moments, he raises his handkerchiefed paw to his mouth and speaks gruffly:

BEN: Issahakian . . . Éto Issahakian . . .

Mix to: A stage; proscenium arch. The same lunatics of the mad-house dream, but wearing shirts of a different colour, and their writhings and jerkings are more stylised, to the music of Petrushka. A red banner proclaims PETROGRAD 1917. *Backcloth —black-and-white—the Neva skyline, a cruiser (the* AURORA*).*

Two orderlies drag an inmate on-stage, and dump him on to the floor.

ORDERLY: Bastard! try to hang yourself, would you? (*They roll him up in a length of canvas, till he is trussed like a mummy. Only his terrified eyes show. His voice comes, muffled.*)

MUMMY: Dear God, don't let me go mad.

ORDERLY: (*Dowsing him from a watering-can.*) Blaspheme, would you? You won't have breath for it when this starts to dry, shitface!

VOICE OFF: Cut! (*The actors freeze; the music stops.* MEYERHOLD *leaps on to the stage: gangling, stooped, predatory; a cigarette droops from thin lips.*) Okay: gather round. (*All, save the mummy, move swiftly to squat around him.*) Yesenin, come on up. (*In the front row sit golden-haired* YESENIN *and his darkly, plumply sensuous young wife,* ZINAIDA. *The poet removes his arm from her shoulder and leaps on to the stage.*) What did you think?

YESENIN: I thought it was brilliant.

MEYERHOLD: It was terrible.

YESENIN: (*Dismayed.*) I guess you're right.

MEYERHOLD: Zinaida, what did you think?

ZINAIDA: I'm not sure. I thought when I typed it, it was the best scene in the play; but it doesn't come across, somehow. It goes over the top. Such brutality—it isn't believable.

YESENIN: But it's a metaphor for this fucking country, Zina.

ZINAIDA: I know, darling. I'm sorry.

YESENIN: No, no, you're both right. It's a lousy play.

MEYERHOLD: It's brilliant! The rest is wonderful. No problems. Do we actually need this scene? Your wife's right: not even Ivan the Terrible would have kept such a mad-house. We must also think of our audience. Shell-shocked and crippled soldiers; starving factory workers. They want to be taken out of themselves.

ZINAIDA: Yesenin's a poet, not a circus-entertainer.

MEYERHOLD: I know that, Zina darling. He's a genius. It's a stunning play. And in the present unrest, Kerensky won't dare have it taken off. But leave sulphur-injections and mummies to Jules Verne—eh, my friend?

YESENIN: Cut it.

MEYERHOLD: Good. Be here at eight in the morning.

YESENIN: We'll see you. (*Jumps down, seizes his wife's hand; exeunt.*)

MEYERHOLD: (*To the actors.*) A word or two before you go. After this one, we're going to do something really big. The biggest. I want you to start thinking about it. Not merely thinking about it—eating it, drinking it, taking it to bed with you . . . (*Close in on obsessional eyes.*) Picture this . . . A leaden grey sea. Dim midnight sun through a thin shroud of clouds. A tall young man is walking along the shore, wrapped in a black cloak. He sits down on a rock, and gazes out to sea. Then suddenly, out of that expanse of grey appears a bearded warrior in silver armour, gliding across the water towards the young man in black . . .

A gun booms, making all heads turn. Smoke rises above the Neva. A red flag is run up the mast of the AURORA. MEYERHOLD *leaps high, and all the actors spring from their squatting position straight into the air, crying "Huzza! Revolution! To the Palace!" They race off-stage;* MEYERHOLD *lingers as* YESENIN *and his wife rush back down the aisle. He gives his hand to* ZINAIDA; *all three hug, then race off; another gunshot booms.*

The stage looks empty. Then we see a roll of canvas, upright, swaying. It unwinds itself. At the last turn, it is seen to be empty.

The psikhushka *as at first.* KRAVCHENKO *in close-up, skeletal, shaven-headed and gummy, and an orderly raining blows with a cosh.*

KRAVCHENKO: My name is Johnson. Mr Dick Johnson. I'm paying a hundred quid a day to stay in this clinic, and I demand some psychoanalysis . . . I'm Johnson, Johnson, Johnson, Johnson, Johnson. (*The picture dissolves. His voice echoes over the portraits, blurred, of Lenin, Brezhnev.*) Johnson, Johnson, Johnson, Sergei, Sergei, Sergei . . .

Mix to: The bedroom. BEN's *ravaged, heavy, stubbled face leaning into the camera-lens.*

BEN: (*Softly yet urgently.*) Sergei, wake up! The phone. (*He is shaking the shoulder of the sleeper squashed between two women.* ROZANOV, *fiftyish, gaunt, black-haired, groans.*)

SERGEI: What is it?

BEN: It's Nina.

ROZANOV, *shocked awake, tries to slide towards the bed's foot without disturbing the women. But one of them—dour, square-faced—stirs.*

SONIA: *Shto éto?*

SERGEI: *Nichevó. Moi mát.*

SONIA's *eyes close.* ROZANOV *becomes entangled in the fallen duvet; gathers it round his nakedness like a toga; stumbles out.* BEN *hovers, gazing.* SONIA—*who looks about thirty—springs out; exits. A door slams. A tap runs. The second woman—a tall and slender beauty, with long raven hair—opens one eye.*

MARIE: You got dreadfully drunk.

BEN: (*His voice trembling with anger.*) So you slept with him!

MARIE: (*Drowsily.*) Well? You don't own me. What have you done to your hand?

BEN: I cut it on broken glass. You remember the bottle of lotion I took from his *dacha* . . . You promised to let me give you a massage. (*A curt, ironic laugh.*)

MARIE: Did I? I don't remember. It was very silly, to cut your hand.

A toilet flushes. BEN, *with a snarl, stalks out as* SONIA *slips past him, covering herself with her hands, and dives on to the bed. Cut to: Living-room.* BEN *enters.* ROZANOV, *fearful, covers the phone's mouthpiece; relaxes as he sees it's not* SONIA.

SERGEI: (*Speaking softly.*) That's nice of Vera. Tell her I'll be back by six. Have a safe trip. I'll look after him, don't worry. Oh, did you find someone to fix the TV? . . . This evening? That's great. Thanks, darling. See you on Friday . . . Good-bye . . . (*Puts down the phone; sinks into an armchair.*) Shit, that was a close-call! Thank God you answered it, Ben, and not

Sonia! It would have been curtains! That cunt, Olga, rang her again! Said someone had told her I was dead! And now, thanks to that crazy bitch and my poor old gullible mother, Nina's got this number! (*He covers his eyes.*) Still, her concert will make her forget it, and she swallowed our cover-story, Ben; I ran some old Armenian friends of my mother home, and stayed the night. Thanks, my friend! (BEN *glares. Fade.*)

The same room. BEN *stands by the window, staring out at scudding wintry clouds.* SONIA'*s flat is high up. The others are finishing, or have finished, a light meal. A scraping of knives.* MARIE *wears a plain black dress; she is putting on make-up.* SONIA *wears a blue kimono and has put on glasses.* ROZANOV, *in jeans and a broad-striped Finnish shirt, is turning the pages of a book: the standard English-language guide to Moscow. Languor possesses the two Russians, but* MARIE *looks fresh.*

ROZANOV *begins to speak in the solemn tones of a radio book-review. The others seem hardly to be listening . . .*

SERGEI: The hero of this novel, a Georgian called Stalin, will surely live as long as novels are read. What is most remarkable about him is that his name is never once mentioned. Spassky creates his magnificent hero entirely by implication and through humour. Thus, for example, when referring to our city during the years 1936–38, he drolly mentions a drainage canal and several bridges over the Moskva, as if that was all that was going on, then adds devastatingly, "the city was literally transforming before the eyes!"

MARIE: Would you like me to leave this nail-polish with you, Sonia? I have several bottles at home. People keep giving it to me. (SONIA *shrugs.*)

SERGEI: . . . And then, Spassky says, "But the peaceful toil of

the Soviet people was violently disrupted in 1941 . . ."
Peaceful toil! A phrase of Gogolesque irony. In that single
phrase, Stalin leaps out at us, as unforgettable as Hamlet . . .

MARIE: It would look nice on you. Green would suit you.

SONIA: Thanks.

SERGEI: . . . Another memorable character is Vsevolod
Meyerhold. Again he is mentioned only once; but that is
enough to make the heart quake with terror: "At No. 12
Nezhdanova Street the famous director Meyerhold had his
apartment . . ." Just that! But we see Meyerhold's wife,
Zinaida, formerly married to our great poet Yesenin, lying
there in her own blood, eleven stab-wounds in her body, her
throat cut, her eyes gouged out . . .

SONIA: (Bored.) Sergei's obsessed with Meyerhold.

SERGEI: The author convinces us that if we could find
the still-undiscovered killer, and his motive, we would
have solved the enigma of life itself, of Russia, the
sphinx . . .

SONIA: Balls.

SERGEI: What's balls?

SONIA: (To MARIE.) He really means it . . . Don't you? You
think there's a key to unlock everything, don't you? Every
suffering? Why your father died in the Gulag . . .

SERGEI: (Flinching.) Yes.

SONIA: There's no meaning.

SERGIE tosses the Progress guidebook to MARIE, who stuffs it, along
with make-up, into an overflowing handbag.

MARIE: I'm going to read it when I get home. I'm going to
read everything I can get hold of about Russia. I think it's an
amazing country. Don't you, Ben? (His back still turned, he
ignores her question.)

SONIA: (Bitterly.) If you think life is meaningful, why do you
make everyone you meet unhappy? One could forgive you

ruining people's lives if you thought life was meaningless.
(*A gust of wind rattles the window.*)

MARIE: Gosh! did you feel the floor move?

SERGEI: All these tower-blocks are poorly built. Rushed up
in the thirties. During the peaceful toil. This is a ghost-
house. Probably two or three people in this flat went to bed
one night and weren't here in the morning.

MARIE: My mouth feels terrible. I'll be glad when I can brush
my teeth.

SONIA: Have an apple.

MARIE: They look wonderful. (SONIA *pushes the bowl across
with her foot.* MARIE *picks one; bites.*) They are!

SERGEI: Ben? An apple?

BEN: (*Curtly.*)   No thanks.

MARIE: I don't know why you're being so unpleasant. It's
Sonia who should be unpleasant. You haven't even said
you're sorry for falling on her stereo, throwing up on her
lovely rug.

SERGEI: He's feeling rough. It's my fault. We haven't given
you a very nice send-off, Ben. You should get a tetanus-jab
as soon as you reach New York. Knife-cuts can be risky.
(SONIA *lights up, offers him a cigarette as an afterthought.*) No, I
must become ascetic again.

BEN: (*Whirling round.*)   So you guys had yourselves a good
time last night!

SONIA *gives a slight headshake towards* ROZANOV.

SERGEI: Ben, nothing happened last night. We just tumbled
into bed beside you and fell asleep.

BEN: Naked!

MARIE: It was a warm night.

BEN: Bullshit!

SERGEI: We tried to take your clothes off.

MARIE: But you're so heavy.

BEN: Jesus, you *admitted* you slept with him!

MARIE: (*Reasonably.*) I slept with him, yes. We did sleep together, all four of us. Except you kept waking us with your dreadful snores.

BEN *whirls to the window again.* SONIA *rises and approaches him. Taking her cigarette from her lips she lays a smoke-curling hand on his shoulder.*

SONIA: Ben, nothing happened. We just fell asleep.

BEN: Really?

SONIA: Really. What do you say—scout's honour!

BEN: (*Sighing.*) Okay. I'm sorry. (*She squeezes his shoulder, returns to the sofa.* ROZANOV *glances at her admiringly.*)

Bedroom. ROZANOV *clicks off a battery-razor and hands it to* BEN.

BEN: Thanks, pal. (*Switches on; the razor delves into neck-folds.*)

SERGEI: It's useful when I stay overnight. Not that I've done that too often lately.

BEN: I'm sorry about all that shit I started throwing.

SERGEI: Forget it. I understand how it must have looked. But it really wasn't like that.

BEN: I know that now.

SERGEI: You've seen how it is between Sonia and me. Sex is a distant memory . . . I can understand why she's bitter. And if it weren't for my little boy . . . (*He sighs.*) But I lost my daughter; I can't lose Sasha . . .

BEN: They're both nice ladies. I hope you work it out.

SERGEI: It's hopeless. Unless that fucking Olga was right and my time is up . . . Death would simplify my life.

BEN: (*Looking uncomfortable.*) She's just crazy, like you said.

SERGEI: All the same, it's a bit spooky, don't you think? (*Looks at his exhausted face in the mirror.*) A blind woman, getting from somewhere or other the idea that I'm dead!

(*Chuckling uneasily.*) Mind you, I soon would be, if Nina found out I had a mistress! Or an ex-mistress . . . Still, your visit's cheered her up. I hope the Stolichnaya promotion goes well, my friend.

BEN *switches off the razor;* ROZANOV *takes it and stows it in a drawer.*

BEN: Thanks . . . Look, Sergei, this is probably nothing, but when I first picked up the phone I thought I heard your wife say "Sonia".

SERGEI: (*Sinking on to the bed.*) What exactly did you think she said?

BEN: (*Sitting beside him.*) "Can I speak to Sonia." Something like that. But she was pretty agitated, and you know how bad my Russian is.

SERGEI: But I wonder what you did hear . . .

BEN: Could it have been something to do with *son*, sleep? Maybe she was saying, "I'm sorry, were you asleep?"

SERGEI: (*Relaxing.*) You're right! It must have been something like that! She was perfectly okay, once she found out I was all right. Annoyed that I was not back, and rushing to catch her plane; but perfectly okay.

BEN: It's my Russian.

SERGEI: (*Standing up, mopping his brow with a handkerchief.*) But you did a fine job translating those two poems, Ben. You must translate some more and come back soon! With Marie!

BEN: There's no hope of that.

SERGEI: She's really given you nothing on this trip?

BEN: Nothing.

SERGEI: She's the bitch-type, my friend. When you get to your hotel you want to throw her on the bed, hitch her dress up, and tell her you've had enough of her prick-teasing.

BEN: I couldn't do that.

SERGEI: Do it! She likes the rough stuff, I'm sure of it. What good has gentleness done?

BEN: None. (*He stands.* ROZANOV *puts his arm round his shoulder and they move towards the door.*)

The bedroom still: MARIE, *seen in the mirror, is adjusting her coat-collar, checking her make-up.* ROZANOV, *behind her, embraces her.*

SERGEI: It was wonderful, darling! You brought us together again. Come back some day soon! I'll get you a visa; I'll show you the Caucasus, the Black Sea . . .

MARIE: I'd love to.

SERGEI: Wonderful! And do something for me . . . (*He whispers in her ear. She moves away from him.*)

MARIE: I could never do that. Anyway, we don't have time.

SERGEI: Find time. Improvise! The guy's been decent to you, hasn't he? Give him something to remember for the rest of his life. Pull him on to the bed . . .

BEN, *irate, appears in the doorway.*

BEN: We'll miss our plane if we're not careful.

MARIE: I'm coming. (SONIA *appears.* MARIE *embraces her; the Russian woman responds stiffly.*) Thanks, Sonia. It's been a wonderful experience.

SONIA: *Nichevo.*

SERGEI: Or in the plane!

MARIE, *smiling, hugs him;* ROZANOV *pumps* BEN's *hand, bound in tape; the American winces. Fade.*

The bedroom, empty. Sound of goodbyes, off. A door shuts. ROZANOV *follows* SONIA *back in.*

SONIA: You could have driven them. Don't you have to get home for Sasha?

SERGEI: Someone's looking after him. I want you. Come to bed. (*Tries to embrace her; she pushes him away.*)

SONIA: Get off. Nothing has changed. Last night was stupid, I was drunk. You shouldn't have brought them. (*Lights a cigarette.*)

SERGEI: Just lie with me for a moment.

SONIA: I have to get dressed; I have to be at the hospital by four. (*She allows him to draw her on to the bed; she sits up, puffing smoke.*)

SERGEI: Oh? What's that for?

SONIA: Just routine. A cervical smear.

SERGEI: (*Smiling in understanding.*) Ah! Your doctor's Tretkov! You said last night you had to take a party round the Tretyakov!

SONIA: I don't remember.

SERGEI: You always lie so creatively! (*Their reflections in a mirror: his hand on her breast under her robe; mix to: their naked bodies reflected, as they make love gently; the light dimmer.*) Do you love me, Sonia? Tell me you love me . . .

SONIA: (*After a silence.*) I love you . . . Oh, I love you . . . (*He moans, whether from joy or pain.*) It's eternal, isn't it? Till death, and even beyond . . .

SERGEI: Yes . . . Yes! I don't mind if Kolasky made love to you the other night. Nothing and no one else matters . . . Did he make love to you?

SONIA: (*Irritably.*) Why must you talk? No, he didn't. That's long over. (*Cut from the mirror to their actual forms.* ROZANOV *shudders and they are still. She pulls herself up, reaches for a cigarette and lights it. His eyes are closed.*) You should find someone young; a girl who can excite you without words.

SERGEI: *You* do that. I simply meant, no one else matters . . . We'll be in Armenia by the weekend. It will be warm and sunny there still. And Ararat will be pure and fresh . . .

SONIA: Armenia won't change our situation. I must shower. (*She gets up, smoking still. Against his drowsing face on the pillow we see Mount Ararat, its twin peaks snow-covered. When his eyes open, he sees* SONIA *in trousers and sweater, her glasses on, and applying a quick touch of lipstick.*) I'll see you, then, shall I?

SERGEI: Thursday evening?

SONIA: Is that when she gets back from Leningrad?

SERGEI: Yes.

SONIA: You'd better ring me first. I may be busy. (*She puts on a white scarf.*) Make sure you slam the door shut.

· 2 ·

Darkness. Late afternoon. The interior of a car; ROZANOV *at the wheel. We see from his viewpoint: the windscreen churning rain, hazy lights of passing traffic, suburban tower-blocks. Military music crackling on the car-radio; he twists the knob and settles on Fauré's* Pavane.

SERGIE: (*Voice over.*) The Editor, *Pravda*: Dear Comrade—I write to ask if any of your readers know the whereabouts of an important relic of Marx-Leninism, the scarf worn by Isadora Duncan, the famous dancer. (*Cut to a bare stage flanked by portraits of Marx and Lenin; a woman in a diaphanous dress, one breast bared, and a red scarf, dances expressively.*). As is well-known, Duncan's dancing celebrated the glorious freedom ushered in by the October Revolution. The scarf in question strangled her in 1929 by becoming entangled in a car's wheel. (*The scarf lying in a ditch.*) It then became the property of her former husband, our great poet Yesenin. (*The "golden youth" of* ROZANOV's *dream picks up the scarf and strokes it sorrowfully.*) Later, Yesenin hanged himself with it. (*The scarf, tied into a noose, is plucked from a beam by* ZINAIDA, *who weeps and is comforted by* MEYERHOLD.) It passed to his ex-wife, the actress Zinaida Raikh, and her husband, the great director Meyerhold. Zinaida was wearing it in 1939 when, after the closing-down of the Meyerhold Theatre, she was brutally murdered by unknown hands in their Moscow flat. (*The scarf lying on a carpet in a pool of blood.*) An investigator compassionately gave the scarf to Meyerhold, who was in custody, and he was wearing it when he was shot in the neck, in a cellar of the Lubyanka, a few months later. (*The scarf, in blood, drilled by a bullet-hole, on a cellar floor. Cut to* ROZANOV *driving, his face in close-up, his eyes half-closed.*) The historic scarf passed to Yesenin's son, Alexander Volpin, but was taken from him at a *psikhushka* some ten years ago, for fear that he might harm himself with it. Where is it now? With its knife-rips and bullet-hole, its mixture of blood and red dye, its madman's spittle, it should be instantly recognisable. (*Cut to the flailing wipers, passing lights.*) Its silken fabric binds together the whole glorious history of our epoch. It should have pride of place in the Lenin Museum, an ikon of—

The car has veered on the road; blinding lights straight ahead; twist of the wheel, screaming tyres. Cut back to ROZANOV, *sweating, pulling himself together, concentrating. He turns off the radio.*

The Volga turns into a glade of birches, and stops outside a wooden house; downstairs lights on. He climbs out, walks towards the door. Fade.

The living-room of ROZANOV's *dacha. Lamplight. Antique chest, samovar, etc. Framed sketch of Pasternak; large colour-photo of Sergei's wife, Nina, sitting at a harp: a woman with long grey-blonde hair.* ROZANOV *sits over a chessboard with* SASHA, *aged about seven. The boy checkmates his father.*

SASHA: (*Severely.*)   You weren't concentrating.

SERGEI: I'm sorry, Sasha. I'm very tired.

SASHA: Even Auntie Vera lasted longer than you.

SERGEI: Did she?

SASHA: Yes, and she's terrible. (*He starts to set up another game.*)

SERGEI: No. No more! It's bed. Mummy would kill me if she knew I'd let you stay up so late.

SASHA: But I need the practice. It's the school tournament tomorrow.

SERGEI: Then you must get some sleep. Or your bronchitis will come back and you'll lose.

SASHA: Can't I watch the Dynamo match?

SERGEI: No, you can't. The TV's unwatchable anyway, at the moment. Someone should be calling to fix it. Take a drink up with you and get undressed. I'll be up in ten minutes. (*Sullenly* SASHA *stands and walks to the door.* ROZANOV *switches on the TV, turning the volume-control to nil. A football-match, the image flickering up constantly, from a broken vertical-hold. He throws himself in an armchair.*)

Hallway. Dim light. Stairs, small table with phone; coat-rack, boots, galoshes. ROZANOV *comes quietly downstairs; checks in a notebook, picks up the phone and dials.*

SERGEI: Olga? (*Faintly, a cry of joy and relief.*) Of course I'm fucking alive! Why the hell did you think I wasn't? (*Fairly long pause.*) Jesus . . . that must have been Ben, a stupid American. His Russian's very poor; I went out for a while last night, and he must have told your husband I'd passed away . . . No, we certainly *can't* meet again—I just wanted to stop you from bothering my wife or my friends. (*A doorbell rings; he glances aside.*) It's kaput, Olga. Goodbye. (*Puts down the phone and goes to the door. He opens it to a gorilla-like man in overalls, carrying a toolbag in one hand, a large stuffed-full carrier-bag in the other.*)

CALLER: Comrade Rozanov?

SERGEI: Yes.

CALLER: Slobodkin. Your wife said you were having problems.

SERGEI: Ah! Wonderful! Yes, it's very bad. Come in!

The gorilla marches in. ROZANOV *leads the way into the living-room and hovers by the TV.*

SERGEI: A drink?

SLOBODKIN: I won't say no. (*As* ROZANOV *goes to the cabinet,* SLOBODKIN *drops his bags, puts his hands on his hips and watches the football uninterestedly.*) I'm sorry I'm so late.

SERGEI: Don't apologise, my friend. It's wonderful to get someone to come so quickly.

SLOBODKIN: I had a couple of rough jobs in the city. And on top of that I got held up on the way—there's been a bad accident. Thanks . . . Cheers!

SERGEI: Cheers!

SLOBODKIN: Then I had to stop in the village to ask where you lived.

SERGEI: Well—I'm very grateful.

SLOBODKIN: (*Nodding at the screen.*) You've got a bad picture.

SERGEI: Terrible.

SLOBODKIN: Nothing works properly.

SERGEI: There's a play on I particularly wanted to see.

SLOBODKIN: I don't get much time for watching. I'd better get at it.

SERGEI: It keeps (*he gestures*) bobbing up.

SLOBODKIN: Well, we'll soon find out what's wrong. I've just come from a real stinker. That's how I like 'em. (*Puts down his empty glass.*) Where's your bathroom?

SERGEI: (*Eyes fixed on a sweep upfield.*)   Up the stairs, straight ahead. Help yourself.

SLOBODKIN *picks up his tool-bag and exits.* ROZANOV *backs to the armchair, sits, drinks. After a time he raises his head, hearing a series of flushes, together with a couple of thumps. He frowns, stands up. A clomp of feet, then the workman enters, also frowning.*

SLOBODKIN: It seems okay to me.

SERGEI: What do you mean?

SLOBODKIN: It flushes all right.

SERGEI: Why shouldn't it?

SLOBODKIN: Your missus said it didn't. And *you* just said so.

SERGEI: Aren't you a TV mechanic?

SLOBODKIN: No, a plumber.

SERGEI: Good grief! (SLOBODKIN *pulls out a slip of paper;* ROZANOV *glances over his shoulder.*) Ah! I see what's happened! You want *Rezanov.* Gleb Rezanov, at the House of Creativity! I'm *Rozanov!* (*Roars with laughter.*)

SLOBODKIN: Shit. And your missus doesn't work at a dry-cleaners?

SERGEI: Afraid not! (*Indicates the carrier-bag.*) You were doing a deal with his wife, I guess?

SLOBODKIN: (*Crestfallen.*)   Yes.

SERGEI: Well, have another drink. Then I'll direct you. It's not far.

Re-fills the plumber's glass, and his own. Their eyes are drawn to the scuttling footballers. Fade. The screen re-appears. The frantically-rising screen is now filled by a woman in late-Victorian costume.

ACTRESS: . . . and then, worse luck, I fell in love with someone else. We had an affair, and just at that very time—it was my first punishment, a blow straight to my heart—my little boy was drowned here, in this river . . . (*Cut to* ROZANOV, *slumped in the chair, his eyes almost closed, the vodka-bottle empty. He pulls himself to his feet, and lurches towards the set.*) And then I went abroad, I went away for good, and never meant to return, I never meant to see the river again . . . ROZANOV'*s hand clicks her off. He switches off the lamp. A gust of wind, then silence. He lurches to the door, opens it.*

Bedroom. Twin beds. ROZANOV *fastens his pyjama-jacket and crawls between the sheets. He sips milk, puts on reading-glasses, picks up a book and browses. He settles for looking at the photo illustrations: Meyerhold's obsessed face; then scenes from his productions: the* art nouveau *of Petersburg, the brash circus-like style of the twenties, finally the petrified tableau of life-sized dummies, in* Government Inspector, *from the late thirties. He closes the book, lays it aside, removes his glasses, glances round the room while he finishes the milk. The room is full of shadows. The window rattles in a gust of wind; the curtains blow; he jumps as a framed photo of Sasha falls over on the dressing-table. A pair of tights is draped over the chair-back. Night-music begins: Bartók's* Music for Strings, Percussion and Celesta. ROZANOV *switches off the bedside-lamp and huddles down.*

Luminous phantoms appear and disappear: a grey cat jumps on to the bed . . . Nina, the woman of the harp, sits brushing her greying hair . . . The same, but blonde-haired, youthful, miniskirted, leans over him seductively. A tabby cat jumps up . . . A woman, angry and crying, stands belting her coat; a little girl, distressed, in coat and hat, clutches her. The woman picks up a luminous suitcase . . . The same woman, but younger, sits on his bed hooking panties over high heels; skirt and blouse of the 60s; standing up, she hoists the panties over stocking-tops and suspenders, lets the skirt fall back; leans to accept a luminous cigarette, strokes a luminous tabby kitten . . . The cigarette is the last to fade. Darkness. The music dies away.

The murky wings of a theatre. A cigarette droops ash, droops from the lips of MEYERHOLD—*who looks, and is, twenty years older than in* ROZANOV's *earlier dream. Stage-hands hold life-sized dummies, wearing frock-coats and gowns of the age of Gogol. Theatrical voices off; laughter. An actor dressed as a law-officer pushes past* MEYERHOLD. *We hear:*

ACTOR: The Government Inspector is here. (*Horrified gasps.*)

MEYERHOLD: Get ready . . . Lights!

The murk deepens. We hear, more than see, figures tiptoeing, rustling, past. A gong. We face the stage. Gasps from the audience. A fusty drawing-room; provincial ladies and gentlemen, frozen in attitudes of horror—among them ROZANOV (*the postmaster*) *agape, bent into a question-mark.* ZINAIDA *is at the centre-front of two semi-circular rows. The camera zooms in. Wax dummies. Cut to part of the audience. They too are waxen, agape. Cut back to the stage. The gong again. Darkness. The lights go up again at once, and men in black coats and hats march in from both sides. These are no actors. One pushes* ROZANOV, *who topples over lightly; his head breaks off. A modern phone rings. The head jerks, gasping for breath.*

Hallway. The phone rings. ROZANOV *stumbles down, pulling on his dressing-gown. He picks up the phone.*

SERGEI: (*Croaking and agitated.*) Rozanov . . . Who is it? Oh, hello . . . I was asleep. What time is it? Is that all? I went to bed early. (*Sits on the bottom step. His voice becomes clearer and calmer.*) How was the hospital? Good . . . Yes, it's colder. I saw some of it, but the TV's gone wrong, and anyway I couldn't keep my eyes open. Actually, I'll tell you a funny story. I'd arranged for a repair-man to call, this evening . . .

Fade his voice, as the scene changes to a dark road. An immensely tall, slim black youth, wearing boots, combat clothes, a back-pack

*and a rifle, is running with easy, giant strides. His head is
bandaged. Cut back to* ROZANOV. *He is agitated again.*

SERGEI: . . . can't Masha take him on? He must be Jewish.
And she likes Freud. But in Armenia we can talk it through.
Somewhere fresh and pure. With blue skies and the snowy
peaks. We can begin again, like Noah . . . What's upset you?
I've no *wish* to go with Nina. I want *you* . . .

SONIA's *living-room. In trousers and sweater, she squats on the
floor. She takes quick, jerky puffs at a cigarette, and stabs the ash off
angrily.*

SONIA: . . . why can't you be honest for once? Why are you
afraid of telling her about us? Tell me that! What are you
frightened of? Come on, I want an answer! I'm interested in
your explanation . . . No, why *should* I let you speak? I've let
you speak once too often . . . So am *I* tired! Tired of all your
fucking lies! All right, speak then. Tell me! Explain to me!
SERGEI: (*Sweating, swaying with exhaustion, his eyes almost shut.*)
It's because . . . It's partly because . . .
SONIA: (*Stubbing another butt, the ashtray noticeably fuller.*) What?
Speak up! What if you do wake him up? It's about time he
found out the truth about his precious daddy! It's no wonder
he gets ill in that house! It's rotten, from the basement
up. You make me sick . . . I'm not interested in your
partly-becauses; I want some straight answers. You weren't
exhausted when you screwed that empty-headed Canadian
cow! Five years you've kept me on a string, you bastard . . .

Back to: ROZANOV. *He holds the phone away, to rest; his head
slumps. War-documentary scenes of Barbarossa: surging German
tanks, gun-flashes, flying bodies, as her voice continues faintly
over. Cut to:*
   A city street; houses, lamplight; silence except for the padding

feet of the young black soldier. His boots are swung round his neck; he is breathing easily. Back to:

SERGEI: (*Puts the phone back to his ear, breaks into her monologue.*)   Look, I've got to have a piss. I'll be right back. (*Lays the phone on the table, stumbles upstairs.*)

SASHA's *bedroom. A nightlight. Disney shapes on the wall.* ROZANOV *picks up a fallen penguin, then pinches his son's arm, resting outside the blanket. The boy awakes with a cry.*

SERGEI: Ssh! It's all right, darling: you've been having a bad dream. (SASHA *howls and starts coughing, which increases his distress. He rubs his arm and howls louder.*) Come on, I'll make you a hot drink. (*Carries him out.*)

The hallway. ROZANOV *lowers the child gently.*

SERGEI: Sit there a moment—I'm on the phone. (*Picks up the phone.*) Sasha woke up; he's having a bad attack—can you hear him? I'll have to ring off and call you in the morning.

SONIA: You'd *better* ring me in the morning. I've something important to say to you. You won't like it, but it's your own fault. You won't like it one bit, but you'd better hear it! (*She slams down the phone, bursts into tears, and hurls the overflowing ashtray at the wall. A door-buzzer rings; she looks up, surprised; looks at her watch; gets up, wiping her eyes. She straightens her clothes and runs a comb through her hair. The buzzer rings again. She goes out.*)

SONIA: (*Voice off.*)   You! But I thought you were on manoeuvres!

ROZANOV's *bedroom.* SASHA *is huddled in bed with his father. He is coughing and shivering. Mugs of hot milk on the bedside-table.*

SERGEI: Dreams fade quickly, Sasha.

SASHA: (*Reflectively*.) I think I *might* have been dreaming about Sputnik.

SERGEI: Probably. It made you feel sad, I expect.

SASHA: I'm afraid she's lonely in heaven.

SERGEI: No, no. There are people to look after her. Drink your milk, darling.

SASHA: It's too hot . . . Like who?

SERGEI: Well, your grandpa, for instance. Not your grandpa in Rostov, but my father.

SASHA: Have I met him?

SERGEI: (*Smiling sadly*.) No, Sasha. He died when I wasn't much older than you. He was an officer in the cavalry; he loved animals. He's keeping an eye on Sputnik, I'm sure. Giving her a stroke.

SASHA: Is he the man in the photograph at Nana's?

SERGEI: That's right. (*Stretches past* SASHA *for his mug of milk*.)

SASHA: Did he have any medals?

SERGEI: Lots of them. I have some of them. I'll show you tomorrow. He won his first medal when he was only sixteen.

SASHA: I'd like to be in a war. When I'm a bit older.

SERGEI: (*Sighing*.) You are, Sasha.

SASHA: What do you mean?

SERGEI: Well, we're in a kind of cold war . . . You can stay home one more day if you like. Your cough's not gone yet.

SASHA: No, I'll go. Auntie Vera's calling for me.

SERGEI: Ah, yes—your chess tournament. Well, we must get some sleep. Don't you want your milk?

SASHA: No. (ROZANOV *stretches to put down his mug and switch off the lamp. They snuggle down. The window rattles*.)

SERGEI: It feels like snow.

SASHA: Can we have another kitten, Daddy?

SERGEI: (*Kissing him*.) We'll see. Goodnight, darling.

SASHA: 'Night.

The bedroom still. Pale moonlight shines in. Silence. MEYERHOLD *and* ZINAIDA *glide through the wall opposite* ROZANOV'*s bed.* ROZANOV *opens his eyes;* SASHA *sleeps on. The* MEYERHOLDS *are dressed in the style of the late 1930s.*

MEYERHOLD: One warm June night in '39 they came for me.

ZINAIDA: I was left weeping and tearing my hair.

MEYERHOLD: They accused me of spying.

ZINAIDA: Oy-vey! For the Japanese!

MEYERHOLD: One day I was dragged to Lavrenti Beria himself.

ZINAIDA: He wanted Vsevolod to produce *Hamlet* in the Kremlin. My husband was obsessed with *Hamlet*.

MEYERHOLD: It had to be ready in three weeks. I wanted Zina to play the prince.

ZINAIDA: A woman can easily play Hamlet. Bernhardt did it.

MEYERHOLD: But Beria wanted a male homosexual, to entertain an important English guest after. Lord Adam.

ZINAIDA: Eden.

MEYERHOLD: I could have the best actors, from anywhere. My grave-diggers were dug up in Kolyma. We were promised our freedom if all went well.

ZINAIDA: I knew nothing of all this, of course.

MEYERHOLD: Then Mirsky, the mobled quean, had food poisoning. (*He winks at* ROZANOV.) They had to fetch Zinaida in. She was wonderful!

ZINAIDA: (*Clutching his arm.*) Thanks to you, my darling! Vsevolod worked us like slaves. The great night came. It was Elsinore itself. Stalin, Lord Eden, and all the Kremlineers were spellbound.

MEYERHOLD: Then the mood darkened. " 'A poisoned him in

the garden for his estate"—that was the line when the trouble began.

ZINAIDA: Stalin, the Great Gardener, looked black. He scowled aside at Beria. Beria had just shot Yezhov, you see. Stalin gave a roar and stalked out. The English Lord scuttled after him, looking frightened.

MEYERHOLD: It was the day before the Ribbentrop Pact was signed.

ZINAIDA: We all thought it was curtains, as we were rushed in Black Marias back to the Lubyanka. We sat in our cells waiting for death.

MEYERHOLD: But instead, we were given hot baths, told to get dressed in our ordinary clothes, and were then driven in a bus to our apartment building in Nezhdanova Street!

ZINAIDA: The whole cast! We couldn't believe what was happening! We went on up to our flat, which was dark and silent—but the lights were turned on, and there was Beria, beaming us a welcome—

MEYERHOLD: Waiters in white coats . . . Champagne . . . Our table groaning with food we didn't think existed any more!

ZINAIDA: And western dance music started up on our gramophone!

MEYERHOLD: Beria said Stalin's exit was a joke—

ZINAIDA: To confuse the Englishman.

MEYERHOLD: He apologised on Stalin's behalf, and hoped we didn't mind the little surprise he'd fixed up for us.

ZINAIDA: God! We were free! We danced, and sang, and got tight . . .

MEYERHOLD: And the production had been quite good . . .

ZINAIDA: Good! It was the best. He knows it was.

MEYERHOLD: Well . . . Zina did a solo from *Camille*, at

Beria's request. He was very jolly. Then he clapped for silence.

ZINAIDA: He thanked us for our efforts.

MEYERHOLD: And said he would never forget Zina's stunning performance.

ZINAIDA: He called me forward, taking a slim box from his pocket . . .

MEYERHOLD: He took from it a pearl necklace . . .

ZINAIDA: I confess I always had a weakness for jewellery. He turned me, to clip the necklace on. I had my red silk scarf on, and went to remove it, but he said he could manage. Everyone was clapping and cheering me, I was flushed and a bit giggly . . .

MEYERHOLD: He was flirting with her!

ZINAIDA: Tickling my neck!

MEYERHOLD: Then I saw a surprised look in her eyes and an odd red line appear at her throat . . . (ZINAIDA, *in black dress, red scarf, falls on to a carpet; we see her from above, spreadeagled, her eyes bulging, blood gushing from her throat. Their voices continue, over.*) Gertrude was the first to scream. Guns appeared in the waiters' hands.

ZINAIDA: I could see a little silver-handled penknife soaked in blood.

MEYERHOLD: He ordered the cast to stab her. (*Her dress becomes slashed, and blood flowers.*)

ZINAIDA: Polonius was the first. He crawled away and was sick. Well, people had to think of their families.

MEYERHOLD: No one refused the knife.

ZINAIDA: Except Vsevolod.

MEYERHOLD: My fingers couldn't hold it.

ZINAIDA: Beria didn't like my eyes staring at him.

MEYERHOLD: So he took his knife and rooted them out. (*Her eyes become red holes.*)

ZINAIDA: My beautiful chestnut eyes . . .

MEYERHOLD: They shot the actors later that night. They kept me alive for another six months.

ZINAIDA: The rest is silence.

ROZANOV (*Weeping.*):   Thank you. They arrested my father in the same month. I never saw him again. You didn't catch sight of him in the Lubyanka, did you?

MEYERHOLD *shakes his head.*

ZINAIDA: (*Standing again, intact.*)   Beria was a psychopath.

MEYERHOLD: In Armenia, once, he asked the Party boss if he'd like a cigarette, took a gun from his pocket instead, and shot him.

SERGEI: I could do with a cigarette. You've reminded me, I have to ring my girlfriend. We're supposed to be going to Armenia on holiday, but suddenly she can't go. I think it's curtains for us.

MEYERHOLD: We'll leave you, then.

They withdraw through the wall. Morning-light seeps in. ROZANOV *wakes, looks at* SASHA, *remembers, groans. He removes* SASHA's *arm, and gets out. Putting on his dressing-gown, he looks at his haggard face in the mirror.*

A shot of First World War soldiers springing out of the trenches.

The hallway. ROZANOV *comes downstairs, croaking a rehearsal:*

SERGEI: Hi! I've been up all night with Sasha . . . (*Even more exhausted.*) Hi! I've been up all night with Sasha . . .

Sits on the bottom step; picks up the phone; and steels himself, and dials.

· 3 ·

SONIA's *living-room. The curtains closed; the ashtray and its contents lying where they fell the night before.* SONIA, *naked under her dressing-gown, speaks down the phone, quite pleasantly* . . .

SONIA: . . . but that doesn't mean you can simply forget it, Sergei.

SERGEI: (*Barely audible.*) No. We'll talk about it in Armenia.

SONIA: We'll leave it tomorrow night, shall we? I'll have to wash and iron—I'm all behind with everything this week thanks to your bright idea of bringing your guests around! (*A hint of amiability.*) I'll meet you at the airport—okay? Goodbye. (*She drops the phone, and falls to her knees, examining the vomit-stained rug.*)

ROZANOV's *hallway. Confused yet infinitely relieved, he takes a deep breath, and smiles. Light footsteps, off. He shouts up the stairs.*

SERGEI: Sasha, get dressed quickly: it's late! (*The door-bell rings.*) Auntie Vera's here already! Hurry up! (*Goes to the door and opens it. His welcoming smile freezes: a man in a general's uniform stands there.*) General Kolasky!

KOLASKY: Comrade Rozanov: may I speak to you for a moment?

SERGEI: Of course. Sonia told me you'd gone back to your regiment.

KOLASKY: Tomorrow.

SERGEI: (*Uneasily.*) I take it—it's about her?

KOLASKY: (*Impatiently.*) No, no. I've said goodbye to her.

SERGEI: Well, come in.

KOLASKY: I'd prefer to talk outside.

SERGEI: Ah . . . I'll get dressed, then. (KOLASKY *nods and turns away.*)

Outside the dacha. The general stands some way off, under a birch, facing away from the house. He moves into shadows as a buxom woman, holding a little boy by the hand, approaches the house. She rings, and goes straight in. Stray snowflakes fall from a dark sky. ROZANOV *leaves the house and strides across to the general.*

SERGEI: So—what's the mystery?

KOLASKY: Comrade—

SERGEI: We really should be less formal, Alexei! We have quite a lot in common . . .

KOLASKY: (*Stiffly.*) I'll come straight to the point. Next month, on the anniversary of the Decembrist revolt, General Jaruzelski will declare martial law in Poland, and Solidarity will be crushed.

SERGEI: I know.

KOLASKY: (*Taken aback.*) You do?

SERGEI: Sonia told me. But you can trust me.

KOLASKY: I believe that. It's why I'm here. (*They begin to stroll.*) Think of it! On the day our countrymen will eulogise our forefathers who strove for freedom under the Tsars, and suffered death or exile for doing so—the same thing will be happening, in Warsaw, Gdansk! No progress, in a hundred and fifty years! Only infinitely more hypocrisy.

SERGEI: You're right.

KOLASKY: Someone must make a stand. It's useless but essential. I did nothing at the time of Prague; nothing over Afghanistan. I could make the excuse to myself that I wasn't involved. But this time I shall be in the thick of things, in Gdansk, and I intend to stand by what I believe in. I've no illusions about my fate. But if others too—civilians—artists, writers, scientists—simultaneously take a stand, then there might be a little hope . . . You see what I'm leading up to?

SERGEI: I'll be with you. I've dynamite in that house. (*He nods towards the dacha.*)

KOLASKY: (*Startled.*) Really? But I don't think an act of violence . . .

SERGEI: You misunderstand. It's a poem. About Vsevolod Meyerhold. But it's also about Russia today. It's dynamite, Alexei. I'll release it in *samizdat* . . .

KOLASKY: (*Stopping in his tracks, confronting him.*) That's no good. I mean demonstrations—letters to the Press and Central Committee—maybe even a hunger strike . . .

SERGEI: That I can't do.

KOLASKY: Why not? Your father had courage. Don't tell me it died with him?

SERGEI: (*Bridling.*) I think not. Only last week, I signed a petition for the release of Kravchenko, the Ukrainian nationalist, from the *psikhushka* at Dnepropetrovsk . . . The poor guy's been drugged so much he thinks he's English . . .

KOLASKY: You think a petition will help Poland? and help *us* to freedom? No, it must be something open and dramatic.

At the very least, hold up a placard . . .
The buxom woman, with SASHA *and the other child, leaves the dacha; they give* ROZANOV *a wave, and walk off.)*

SERGEI: (*Waving.*) He's why I can't. (*The general stares at* ROZANOV, *then turns and starts to walk away.*) Will you have some tea? (KOLASKY *keeps walking.*) Tell me one thing . . . (KOLASKY *stops, turns round.*) Did you sleep with Sonia the other night? It must seem frivolous—but I have to know. (*The general gives him a contemptuous stare, turns and strides off.* ROZANOV *clutches his head. Fade.*)

SONIA's *living-room. She is kneeling, holding the phone. Her tone is pleasant, ingratiating. A notebook, open and turned over, rests by her knees. The curtains are open.*

SONIA: . . . really? She sounds an imp! Valentina wanted a little girl, didn't she? I remember her saying so the last time we met. You'd just moved there, I think . . . She gave me your number but I never got round to ringing—you know how these things are . . . One reason I rang, Gleb—I have to confess—was to ask her if she'd do me a favour . . . Someone mentioned she's working at a dry cleaner's . . . Of course—one takes anything one can get . . . Well, I have this rather nice rug which some drunken idiot threw up on. I wondered if—(*An immensely tall, slim black youth appears at the door; he wears only Army underpants and a head-bandage.* SONIA *mimes a cigarette-puff, and the youth vanishes.*) You think she would? Oh, that would be wonderful. Yes, I could get you a couple of tickets, no problem . . . We should! you're right . . . We'll arrange something. (*Suddenly on her guard.*) Oh yes, I see Sergei occasionally . . . Meyerhold, I think; but he doesn't discuss his work. (*The youth enters again; she gestures to him to give her a cigarette, and to light it with a match.*) So—I'll ring again this evening. Goodbye . . .

JOSHUA: *Him* again.

SONIA: It's none of your business.

JOSHUA: And again this evening! Last night, every time I stopped to ring you on the way from Zagorsk, you were engaged! You've been sleeping with him again, haven't you? (*When she doesn't answer, he snatches up the notebook from the floor.*)

SONIA: Give me that! It's private. I was ringing an old school friend who—

JOSHUA: Ah yes, it's him! I'll ring him up and tell him to keep his hands off.

SONIA: (*Calmly.*) You're really being very silly. I've not slept with him. Bring me the ashtray, Joshua, would you? (*She points. He strides to it.*) I'll clean up that mess later.

JOSHUA: (*Crouching before her.*) I'm sorry. I missed you so much, Sonia. I was almost glad when I got wounded. The road kept singing your name as I ran. Sonia, Sonia, Sonia . . . (*He kisses her.*) Please come back to bed.

SONIA: There isn't time. I have to take a party of Americans to the Lenin Museum. And you must go for your X-rays. (*She touches his bandaged head; her hand slides to his chest. She sighs.*) So young and beautiful . . . What a waste, training you for war . . .

JOSHUA: Then this evening! No—since I'm back, I must go to the political classes. Tomorrow! Are you working tomorrow? (*She shakes her head.*) Then I'll come in the afternoon, and we'll have all day together!

SONIA: I'm sorry, it won't be possible.

JOSHUA: Why not?

SONIA: (*A curt chuckle.*) If you must know, because in the morning I have an appointment at an abortion-clinic.

JOSHUA: (*Eyes bulging with shock.*) Abortion-clinic!

SONIA: Yes. Don't worry, it's very quick and easy. But (*an ironic smile*) I doubt if I'd be much fun for you in the afternoon!

JOSHUA *stands, paces around.*

JOSHUA: You're pregnant . . .

SONIA: Your deductions are very good.

JOSHUA: (*Smiling, crouching before her again.*) I see, I see! You thought I'd be angry—that's why you thought you should get rid of it! But I'm not angry, my darling! I'm very very happy! We'll get married straight away, and when I've finished my training you'll come back to Africa with me.

SONIA: Absurd. You must still have concussion.

JOSHUA: Then (*he sighs*) we make our home here. I'll return to you when the battle is won.

SONIA: Absurd. I'd really look good, with a black baby. Anyway, I'm much too old for you.

JOSHUA: You're not, Sonia, you're not! (*Tries to embrace her but she pushes him off.*)

SONIA: This is the only way.

JOSHUA: I won't let you murder my son! (*He grips her round the throat. She manages to tear herself away.*)

SONIA: How dare you! You can piss off! Put on your clothes and get out!

He bursts into tears, and buries his head in his arms. She goes to the window and stares out, shaking.

JOSHUA: Please, Sonia—don't send me away! I love you. I just can't bear it—my son . . . We're Christians. My Mama would never forgive me. Don't kill my son . . . (*His sobs continue. She goes to him, crouches, offers him a tissue.*)

SONIA: Here . . . (*He clutches her.*) You could do with a shave. You know where the razor is. Come—it's late.

JOSHUA: I couldn't bear it . . . My son . . .

SONIA: And if it's a girl? Anyway, it's neither. Just a few cells.

JOSHUA: I'd never forgive myself. God would never forgive me . . .

SONIA: (*Standing.*) There's nothing to forgive. It's not yours. (*His sobbing ceases; his head jerks up.*) It's Sergei's.

JOSHUA: But you said—

SONIA: The last time. Three months ago. I thought you'd be glad to cut-and-run if you believed I was pregnant by you—most of *our* boys would. Because—it really is pointless going on, you know. (*He starts to cry again.*) You'll be going home in a few months. I hoped you'd sigh with relief, and think, thank God, it was getting too serious; but you're not like that. (*He stands; stumbles blindly to the window.*) We can still see each other, now and then. As friends. (*He wipes his eyes with an arm.*) But not for a while. I'm going on a holiday, with Sergei. I shall need a rest.

JOSHUA: (*Not looking at her; his voice trembling.*) But last night . . . You were so tender . . .

SONIA: Last night was last night. I was upset—I'd just heard. And you're a wonderful lover. I shall never forget you. (*She goes to him, turns him to her, embraces him. She feels his body stiffen, sees his staring out of the window, where a few snowflakes twirl.*) Of course! You've never seen snow before! It scares you a little, doesn't it? You're a child still, really, aren't you? (*He stares at the snow. Fade.*)

A study. Desk and chest of Karelian birch; an ikon, and a nude, above the desk. ROZANOV *enters briskly, bringing a mug of lemon tea. He sits, bends over the portable typewriter, in which a sheet rests, already partly filled with verses. A notebook lies beside it. He whips out the sheet of paper and studies it. Simultaneously he presses the play-back button of a dictaphone. He makes an alteration while half-attending to what his wife is saying . . .*

NINA: Bliumkin rang to say he needs the proofs of your

Penkovsky essay by tomorrow . . . A car-factory in Gorky would like you to perform for them. A pity they didn't invite you earlier, then you could have combined it with screwing that crazy woman who thought you were dead. (ROZANOV *smiles*.) I told the man to write to you. That's all the messages, except for one from me, Sergei. It's high time you and I went our separate ways. (*He drops the sheet, the pen, and sits back*.) I'm tired of pretending I don't know about Sonia, for the sake of a quiet life. You must have made the same pathetic excuses to Valeriya, in our romantic period. The farce we've just been through is the last straw. Did your Ben Ikashagian, or whatever, tell you I was so upset I asked to speak to Sonia? When I get back, we must arrange a divorce. I'll live with friends till I can find something. I think Sasha should stay with you, until I'm settled, and then we can come to sensible arrangements about sharing him. You need a new wife to be unfaithful to, Sergei. Goodbye.

ROZANOV *gets to his feet; switches off the dictaphone. Walks round in a daze; but, slowly, shock is replaced by an expression of relief.*

SERGEI: Wonderful! She's going, and I can keep Sasha! (*Fade.*)

A music-room. Baby grand-piano; a harp; stereo unit and records. ROZANOV *sways by the harp, drunk, a vodka-bottle in his hand.*

SERGEI: Bitch! What woman could go off and leave her son? (*Tears spring to his eyes*.) I need her, in this sound-proof room . . . There has to be a balance of terror . . .

The hallway. SERGEI *comes lurching downstairs; crouches over the phone, fumbling through a notebook. His eyes glued to a phone-number, he dials.*

SERGEI: The stage-door, please.

Mix to ROZANOV *sitting on the stairs, clutching the phone tensely.*

SERGEI: We'll have a second honeymoon . . . I need you . . .
Yalta? I've got to go to Armenia for a few days, but then
we'll— Some readings. They've had terrible luck: Gsenin's
overdose last month, and now some Czech has let them
down, they were desperate . . . Saturday . . . Shit, I'd
forgotten they were coming. But Igor will understand . . .
Of course I'm not going with her. I tell you, it's over, Nina
. . . Well, you *could*; but I'll be busy, I'd rather there were
nothing to interfere. And by the sea, where it's fresh, and
pure. Okay, come with me to Armenia. So be it. (*Puts down
the phone slowly. Stares into space.*)

*The study. He slumps, sideways to the desk. Takes a key from a
drawer, and unlocks another. Inside are medals, a cap, a pistol.*

SERGEI: Poor father . . .

*He holds one of the medals in his hand; replaces it and grabs the
pistol; fumbles again in the drawer and takes out a bullet. He places
it in the chamber, which he spins. He rests the pistol on the desk,
rises, and walks around agitatedly. With sudden decision, he picks
up the gun, raises the barrel to his forehead. The phone rings; he
half-removes the gun then brings it back; pulls the trigger. A click.
The gun falls. He throws his head back in relief.*

SERGEI: Life!

*He stoops and picks the gun up; removes the bullet. Locks them
away. Strides out to answer the phone.*

A path through a birchwood. Light snow falls. ROZANOV *walks,
stroking the trunks, his head high, his breath frosted. Crackle of
leaves underfoot. He stops suddenly, under a broken branch. Cut
to a "reprise" of his* psikhushka-dream: KRAVCHENKO, *his head
twisting and jerking.*

SERGEI: (*Softly.*)   A breakdown! Yes . . .

He mimes KRAVCHENKO's *movements and expression; then walks on.*

He approaches a large wooden building, mounts the steps, and pushes open the door.

A corridor of many doors; behind each, the clatter of a typewriter —a symphony of typewriters. A round-shouldered man approaches, bearing a pile of folders. He greets ROZANOV *respectfully then, in response to a question, points him up a flight of stairs.*

Another corridor; the symphony continues. ROZANOV *knocks at a door; it is opened by a short, scruffy, owlish man holding a baby, its face milkily smeared.*

GLEB REZANOV: Ah, Sergei! Do come in. Excuse the mess.

SERGEI: Thanks, Gleb. (*He steps in.*)

A room, which serves as living-quarters, study and nursery. A crowded chaos. One side-door. On the walls, posters of Lenin, Brezhnev, and stern-jawed Soviet workers. The buzz of typewriters continues.

GLEB: Good of you to drop round.

SERGEI: It's no trouble. I have to collect Sasha from school.

GLEB: As you can see (*pinches the baby's nose*) I'm rather tied. Take off your coat, old fellow. And Valentina does the shopping tonight, so she doesn't get in until late. Throw those things off the chair.

ROZANOV *drops his coat on to a litter of foul papers, books, clothes, soft toys, etc. on the floor; and adds to the mess by lifting more books from an armchair. He sits.* REZANOV *sits down at a cluttered table, dandling the baby and picking up a spoon.*

GLEB: I'm just trying Dunya with some ice-cream. (*The baby pulls away.*) No, I think you prefer your milk, don't you, sweetie? (*He gives her the bottle. We see him through his guest's eyes: round, rimless glasses, thinning sandy hair, a bland youngish face, overlarge trousers and pullover, and slippers . . . Milk splashes on to a typewritten sheet.*)

SERGEI: You must find it tough-going, Gleb.

GLEB: It's bloody difficult. But we need Valentina's money.

SERGEI: I'm having to cope with Sasha for a couple of days, and I've done no work at all. Sometimes I think I'm too old to have a young child. (*Bells chime distantly.*) Ah, they're ringing for poor old Agafya. One of the village-women. She had a heart-attack right in our kitchen.

GLEB: How sad!

SERGEI: Well, she was pretty old. Full of years . . . and faith too. Russian salt of the earth. (REZANOV *puts down the bottle and starts to "wind" Dunya.*)

GLEB: This is the part I'm no good at—getting the wind up.

SERGEI: She followed the simple path of truth . . .

GLEB: I wish we saw more of the villagers; but I'm really stuck here during the week, and at weekends I have to go to libraries and so forth.

SERGEI: How do you find the House of Creativity? (*His eyes wander round the room; the hum of typewriters presses in from all sides.*)

GLEB: It's not so bad. We've made some nice friends. We all share a common purpose, so we get on well. (*Dunya cries.* REZANOV *bounces her.*) Hush, Dunya! Hush! (*The baby burps.*) Ah, that's better! That's a good girl! I don't seem to be getting on with my novel as well as I'd hoped, however. There's a terrible lot of research to do, and it holds me up. When did we last bump into each other? A couple of years ago?

SERGEI: It must be.

GLEB: Ah, well, I started it about eighteen months ago. *The Finland Station.* About Lenin's journey across Germany.

SERGEI: A heroic theme.

GLEB: Indeed. But it's so hard to get precise information

about the actual train: the disposition of the carriages, their
lay-out and furnishings and so on . . . Ah, you've got a dirty
bottom . . . The theme is historical necessity. Would you
mind just holding her for a moment, while I get a fresh
nappy. (ROZANOV *recoils in distaste as the baby is placed in his
lap.*) Mind your trousers. I won't be a minute. (*He goes out
through the side-door.* ROZANOV *holds the baby stiffly, giving it a
stern look. The father returns, lays the clean napkin on the floor,
and takes the baby back.*) But, indirectly, I'm also trying to
deal with present-day liberation struggles. Oh yes, rather
smelly, isn't it, little one? (*Adroitly removes the fouled nappy.*)
I'm sorry about this.

SERGEI: That's okay. It has to be done.

GLEB: It was pretty horrid while our toilet was blocked, I can
tell you. We were jolly glad to get the plumber.

SERGEI: It was quite a hilarious mix-up.

GLEB: There! That's more comfortable, isn't it? And now
we'll see if you'll have a sleep. (*Lifts her, and lays her in a
carry-cot; puts a rattle in her hand.*) I'll just remove this, and
then we can chat. (*Picks up the dirty bundle, and exits. The bells
stop ringing. Sound of running tapwater.* ROZANOV *gazes up at
Lenin.* REZANOV *returns and sits.*) Can I offer you some tea?
I'm afraid I've nothing stronger.

SERGEI: No, I'm fine, Gleb. (*Glances at his watch.*) I can't stay
long. What was it you wanted to tell me?

GLEB: What are you working on at the moment, Sergei?

SERGEI: (*Stiffening, scenting a trap.*) A history of the Trans-
Siberian Railway.

GLEB: (*Disconcerted.*) Oh . . . So we are both involved with
railways!

SERGEI: That's right.

GLEB: Well, it looks as though I may have dragged you here
under false pretences.

SERGEI: How come?

GLEB: I'd heard you were writing about Meyerhold.

SERGEI: (*Tensely*.)   Who told you that?

GLEB: A friend of yours and of Valentina's: Sonia Vinokur.

SERGEI: Ah . . . yes.

GLEB: She rang this morning, hoping to speak to Valentina, but she'd left. Someone had told her she's working at a dry-cleaning agency—Sonia has a rug, or something, that needs cleaning.

SERGEI: I mentioned it to her. I told her about the plumber, and his bag of clothes.

GLEB: Ah . . . Well, she sounded awfully nice. I happened to ask her what you were working on right now—and she said Meyerhold.

SERGEI: It's true I'm writing a poem about him.

GLEB: Ah, good! By the way, Valentina and I are the souls of discretion. We don't gossip.

SERGEI: I'm sure. Not that there's much to gossip about, in this case. But why should my writing about Meyerhold interest you?

GLEB: I happen to know how his wife was murdered.

SERGIE: (*Leaping to his feet*.)   Good God!

GLEB: (*Polishing his glasses*.)   I thought it might be helpful to you.

SERGEI: You're damned right, my friend! (*Sits down on the edge of his seat*.) But how do you know about it?

GLEB: (*Standing, padding around*.)   My grandfather was the criminal investigator in charge of the case. It's a dreadful story. He spoke to me about it just before he died, a couple of years ago. I've never told a soul, not even my wife, because it's too—delicate, even now, after forty years. But I admire your work immensely, and if it would help you . . . Only, of course, leave my name out of it.

SERGEI: (*Gripping the chair-arms.*)   Of course. So—what happened?

GLEB: Terrible, ghastly things happened in those times. I believe in some way they were inescapable, you know. Meyerhold himself would have understood that. By all accounts he drove his actors to despair, in order to realise his vision. Things happen as they must, don't you think?

SERGEI: Yes, yes, but how was she killed?

GLEB: People speak of eleven stab-wounds in her body, but in fact there were sixteen. I have, as a matter of fact, a scarf— (*There is a knock on the door.*)

SERGEI: A scarf?

GLEB: Excuse me. (*He pads towards the door. Over his shoulder:*) The scarf she was wearing . . .

ROZANOV, *trembling with excitement, leans back in his chair. From behind him:*

GLEB: (*Stammering.*)   Yes?

ROZANOV *turns his head casually, and is taken aback by an awesome sight: a slender, gigantic black youth, his cropped and scarred head lowered to avoid the lintel. He breathes heavily and is bathed in sweat. He wears only the ox-hide mantle and toothed necklace of a Zulu warrior. His eyes glitter.*

JOSHUA: Comrade Rozanov?

GLEB: Yes?

The youth brings a short spear from under his mantle, thrusts it right through REZANOV's *body. He falls.* ROZANOV *rises, with a stifled scream. The baby cries. The youth steps back, and vanishes.*

T·W·O

· LOVE-TRAIN ·

Like a fabled beast he is
For show, soon, in Petropolis . . .
PUSHKIN: *Count Nulin*

· I ·

Who can say what makes one snap? I guess that young black, in the play I showed you, was horrified later at what he'd done. Not that what I did was at all comparable. But isn't it a weird chain of coincidences? My date of birth; the fact that *Isadora's Scarf* was responsible for my visiting Russia; and that I find I was responsible for that fellow Rezanov's death? Masha would love it.

I wrote to her, of course, after the South Bank sensation, but she hasn't replied.

Lying in bed last night, I suddenly recalled something Shimon said. Something about Vrubel, the Russian surrealist painter. It may have lain in my unconscious and then—made me act so stupidly.

You say my dream about Meyerhold's wife, Zinaida Raikh, relates to my infancy, and was possibly a fantasy act of revenge against my mother. Yet I had a very happy, very secure childhood. Perhaps she fussed over me too much, but that's typical of mothers, and especially Welsh mothers.

I feel okay. It's just that I've had to have the window open because the central heating is turned on too high; and I can actually hear that bastard playing Wagner, very loud, on my stereo. I know it's three streets away, but I assure you it's true. I can even hear Alison playing the piano in the mornings. She's a bad pianist, but he's probably been on at her to practise more. In a way it's unfortunate it's so near; but I'm sure you're right that in the long run one has to confront one's ghosts.

It really didn't upset me that much to find out Anthony was gay. Except that, these days, with AIDS, one would prefer one's son not to be.

Excuse these ramblings. I'll concentrate my mind on the Russian visit. It will make a change to write in a more personal way—addressing myself, not to a million readers, but solely to you. I can't possibly write down everything, though; all records are selective. But I promise not to omit anything simply because it reflects badly on me.

You think Leningrad is the key? Merely because Peterson and Hermitage were at the wicket? All right. Let's begin in Moscow, though, at the station. A Friday night in November '82. I sat in the waiting-room with Shimon and Masha Barash; yet withdrawn from them, allowing them their tender farewells. One would have thought they were parting for months, not a few days. Yet only two nights before I'd seen Masha white with rage, abusing him for leaving all the housework to her! Now they canoodled like honeymooners, not like a ten-year-married couple.

My thoughts drifted back to the Savoy Hotel in London, some two years earlier. An interview with Remizova, the violinist who'd sensationally defected via Helsinki. With a sly smile she'd introduced me to her secret fiancé—Shimon's brother—one of the 50,000 Jews to emigrate from the Soviet

Union in '79. She'd allowed me to break their liaison to the world: news which stunned the Soviets and gave me my only "scoop".

Amid the confusion of travellers, mostly young couples, rushing to climb aboard the waiting train, I spared a thought also for Kravchenko. It was he, the *Izvestia* correspondent in London until a premature recall, who had urged me to take the love-train. That is, if I should ever be foolish enough to visit his country. His recall hadn't surprised me, nor Dick Johnson of the *Statesman*, his only other close friend. Johnson must have been even more shocked than I was, if he read *Isadora's Scarf*. I've no idea if he did. Since he joined the SDP, our paths haven't crossed.

To think of old Boris, big as a tank, drugged so high he believes he's that smoothie Johnson, in a London clinic! Ghastly! But it appears it's true.

Masha disentangled herself from her husband, seized my arm and walked me to the window facing the platform. Shimon ghosted to her other shoulder. "It was a wonderful idea to take this train, Lloyd!" she exclaimed. "So much more exciting than a flight. We have good memories of the love-train, don't we, Shimon?" Her lips brushed his cheek.

"And how!"

"But you'll be tired tomorrow. Make sure he gets a rest, Lloyd, so he'll be in a fit state for Sunday."

I promised to do so.

"At least the Leningrad is a comfortable hotel," she said. "You'll find it a great improvement on the Kosmos."

Brezhnev had died during my days in Moscow. With other unimportant tourists, I'd found myself turfed out from the Intourist Hotel, late at night, to a drab hotel on the outskirts, rushed up for the Olympics.

"If only I were coming with you! If only the old crocodile

had died some other time! I'm sure I could guide you *un*-officially round Leningrad much better than I've done here, rapping out their boring propaganda!"

"You've been a wonderful guide, Masha," I said sincerely. "Though," I added with a smile, "I don't think I'll ever get over the shock of finding our Cinderella of the Kremlin tour suddenly become the princess who opened the door of Shimon's flat to me!"

Shimon and Masha chuckled. They'd enjoyed my astonishment, on the evening after my arrival in the city.

"Look!" she urged me, nodding out at the hurrying figures, barely illuminated shadows. "This is Russia, my dear! Put this in your notebook! Everything confused, shapeless, turbulent, ghostly!"

"You've made Moscow live for me."

My compliment seemed to encourage her to poetic flights.

"Oh, did you see them?" she exclaimed, tugging my arm. "The two Annas . . . Karenina and Akhmatova. A tall proud bosomy woman, and a thin pale intense one!"

I stared at the vague backs of people, struggling to climb aboard. "No."

"They've just got on. You'll find everyone on this train: Blok, Dostoievsky, Chekhov . . . This is where all the connections are made. See the way all the spectres are brushing past each other! They're like charmed particles—totally unpredictable yet making a pattern, a meaning—flowing together . . ."

Masha was by training and rightful profession a physicist. It was hard to believe complicated mathematical thoughts could be going on under that fluffy blonde hair, so soft and fragrant against my cheek.

"This is where she'll start preaching her thesis at you," warned Shimon.

"I wish she'd talked like this before."

"I would have," she protested, "if I could have got a word in edgeways, Shimon!" She glowered good-naturedly at him. "I'm sure you bored poor Lloyd to death with all your practising."

"Probably . . ." He glanced round, distracted. They were expecting a friend, a Georgian singer who'd flown in that afternoon to give a memorial concert for the poet Gsenin. "I don't think she can be coming. Give her my fondest love, darling. It's a shame you couldn't have met her, Lloyd. Liuba's a fantastic woman—isn't she, darling? You'd have fallen for her."

"Yes, I'd like to have met her." I brought Masha back to her thesis.

"Well, it isn't really mine. There's a physicist working on it in London. Simply that everything in nature is implicated, involved, folded-in like a rose. A fish twisting in Lake Sevan affects a fan whirling in—in Madrid or New York."

"It sounds rather mystical."

"A Celt should appreciate that! But it also happens to be scientifically true. Science proves the mystics right. And the poets. What has time or causality to do with these living phantoms climbing aboard the love-train?"

"You're right," said Shimon.

"Of course I am! It's what makes Marxism so boringly dated. His beard like a great bee-hive . . . That grim, mechanistic determinism . . . It's so false!"

"But it helps people to eat," I observed. I had seen no beggars nor down-and-outs in Moscow.

"Oh, I know!" She gave a snort. "Man cannot live by bread alone. Tolstoy has more truth than Marx. All our great novelists—because they create a poetic emotion as well as—as well as exploring the texture of life fictionally. There can be no truth without poetry."

As she paused, I glanced at the clock and asked if we shouldn't be getting on. I've always been anxious about missing trains.

"You have great novelists too," she went on without answering. "Dickens, Galsworthy, Jack London . . . But I'm not sure if they get so close to the heart of things. Yes, you'd better get on."

We gathered up our bags and moved outside. Just as we were climbing aboard someone shouted "Shimon! Masha!" and I turned to see an extraordinary figure swooping towards us. Liubov Charents. My music colleague once described her as a lioness. He was right. Over six feet tall, dwarfing Masha on the platform, and overweight; yet handsome, with magnetic black eyes—and of course that golden voice. She rushed out apologies for being late, kissed Masha and Shimon in turn, and gave me a cursory handshake as I was introduced. The train started to move. Shimon leaned out. "Keep Masha out of mischief for me!" he shouted. Charents nodded, blew a kiss. Masha stretched up for a last embrace with her husband, then her hand fluttered a goodbye to me. I waved back. I saw her plump, tight-belted body—not unlike the *Matryoshka* doll I'd bought for my daughter—recede down the moving platform.

We fought our way along the crowded corridor. Shimon, glancing at his ticket, slid open a door. A young soldier and a girl were inside, locked in an embrace. They pulled apart, embarrassed. Shimon proved to them they were in the wrong compartment, theirs was next door. The lad stammered his apologies. Shimon, waving the apologies aside, asked him where he was serving. "Afghanistan." "Ah! Then enjoy yourself tonight . . ." The young soldier blushed; his girlfriend said cheerfully, "Thanks. We will!"

They picked up small, battered suitcases and left. We settled ourselves. Soldiers' belts and girls' blouse-buttons rasped against the glass. Hands squeezed waists. Curses and giggles rose above the engine's hum. My companion sighed. "Oh, to be ten years younger! Masha and I made this trip whenever we could afford the fare . . . How about you? Do you have romantic memories of trains?"

I remembered Cardiff Station; New Street, Birmingham. One or two mild adventures. But I said youth was too distant. He said I sounded like those old and dying men in Turgenev who turned out to be forty. I felt a bit like that, I replied.

"That's awful. I don't believe it. Look at our friend Liuba: you're—what was it you said? Forty-three? She's forty-five, but she has endless amorous adventures still. You should go to one of her parties in Georgia!"

"She obviously likes you, Shimon," I remarked. "Not many singers would rush from a big concert to wish a friend good luck."

"I guess she's our best friend. Not that we see her often. In the summer, when we stay at the Markovs' Georgian *dacha*. Though often, even then, she's away on tour. She's lucky; she travels the globe."

A morose look came into his face. I had seen it before. In its wake would come a flash of malice. Any excuse for it would do. This time, we happened to glimpse, in the seemingly endless jostling past, a groping hand. Evidently the man was a stranger to the victim, for the girl gave him an angry yet distant look. "I guess you think he shouldn't have done that?" Shimon asked challengingly.

"Of course."

"What's that committee you're on? Women Against Violence?"

"That's right."

"It's a load of shit. Life is violent, my friend. Life is tough.

You middle-class English radicals would have it otherwise, but you're fighting reality."

When I didn't rise to the bait, he continued even more goadingly: "You have squeamish, bleeding hearts, you people. You're so fucking worried some minority group or other may take offence you try to squeeze life dry. Okay, you'll say I don't know what I'm talking about, I've never been to the west. True. But I listen to plenty of Marxist idiots through Masha's Intourist work. Banning books, though, really takes the prize! I thought only we did that."

He should try, I said, putting himself in the position of a West Indian youth reading a sentence like *The sun cannot mate with the darkness nor the white with the black*—from a well-known children's book. Young blacks already had enough prejudice to cope with; besides every sort of disadvantage. Barash was unimpressed. "What's it called, this fucking censorship committee you're on?"

"It's not really called anything. It works for ILEA."

"Ilya who?"

I smiled. "No, the Inner London Education Authority."

"Ah, an acronym! Like GUM. . . Never trust an acronym."

I reminded him it was thanks to ILEA that, with luck, he would be visiting London next year. They were sponsors and organisers of the European Championships. This mollified him slightly. If Shimon managed to win the nationals, this coming week, he might be chosen to go to London. "This Ilya must be a decent guy, then. Are you involved in the planning?"

I was slightly taken aback. I'd spent an hour, on my first evening at the Barashes', explaining about the working-party and why I was here. Come to that, I'd mentioned it in my introductory letter to him. Shimon spread his hands apologetically.

He never read letters carefully, and on the night of our first encounter he'd been the worse for drink. That was true; and, in fairness, I'd been confused myself—struggling with my rusty Russian, and adjusting to the shock of seeing the dour, efficient Intourist guide of that day's Kremlin tour, transformed into the welcoming, warm, lively Mrs Barash, opening the door of their flat to me.

I repeated, with greater fluency, the reason I was here. The inexperienced working-party, already uneasy at promoting an élitist art. The magazine *Impromptu*, with that anonymous playscript, *Isadora's Scarf*. Presumed to be, like everything in that magazine, the work of a leading improviser, it was grossly sexist and racist. Even Shimon, I assured him, would have had to agree. But the aversion it had aroused on the working-party hadn't been on the left alone; two Tory councillors had been shocked by its bad language. All in all, if this was the kind of performance we could expect, on TV and in schools, better to pull out. That had been the strong feeling.

"Would I have to go into schools?" asked Barash.

"For a couple of mornings."

"Shit."

"Anyway, I persuaded them to hold back. If the Soviets allowed it, I argued, maybe our fears were groundless. That's when I offered to come as an observer, Shimon. And my paper was willing to pay for it. So—here I am!"

"I see . . . Well, whatever the reason, it's wonderful to have you here, my friend. Forgive my irritation. But how come you're involved in education?"

I'd been a teacher for a few years, I explained, before turning to journalism. And ILEA still tended to use me. Perhaps too much . . . I'd got entangled in too many causes. I'd thought my wife was happy enough, but . . . I sighed.

"Yes, it's a mistake. Masha and I were like that for a time."

"Anyway," I said, putting on a cheerful smile, "after hearing you, I'll definitely persuade them to go ahead. And here's hoping I'll be seeing you crowned in the Purcell Room!"

Shimon shook his head despondently. They'd be too scared he'd want to join his brother in Israel. His own application to leave, though later withdrawn, had damned him. Yet their fears, he lamented, were groundless. He knew it would be fatal to his art if he left his homeland. Look what had happened to Abram at Satakieli. (Picking out the theme of *St Teresa*, he had dried up completely.) It had never happened before, a complete "dry", in ten generations of Barash story-tellers. "If I were to emigrate, I'd foul up too; I'd become a tongueless nightingale."

"You believe that?" I asked, scribbling the vivid phrase in my notebook.

"I know it. But don't quote me. The bastards here would only think I was trying to ingratiate myself with them."

I drew a line through the phrase, and closed my notebook.

"I just wish I'd never applied for an exit-permit. Abram persuaded me." His glum face lit up suddenly. "You know what made me withdraw my application? A production of Chekhov!"

"Really?"

"Yes, really! It was full of laughter and tears, you know, and that sweet, sad, Russian spirit . . . I thought, no, you can't possibly leave!"

"I think you were wise."

"You're dead right, my friend. And then, of course, Liudmila vanished in Helsinki and turned up embracing my brother at Heathrow . . . All hell broke loose. They came on us like a ton of bricks. Masha lost her research post. I was banned from performance. It was just as well I'd made up my mind to stay. And ride out the storm . . . It's been bad . . ."

I asked him how Masha had felt about emigrating, and was astounded when he said she would have stayed behind.

"You would have split up?" I said, incredulous.

"Well, as a matter of fact, we were going through a bad period. Staleness, I guess; we married very young. We'd both started straying a little . . . But gradually we came out of our bad spell. We're okay now."

"That's easy to see."

"Well, we love and hate each other—just as I love and hate this fucking country. We row by day and fuck by night." His eyes sparkled. "Yes, our nights are good . . ."

Thinking of the chill atmosphere in my home, during the final stages, I remarked on how warm their home felt, even when they were arguing. I extolled his wife's virtues—not least her cooking. I would miss it.

"You must come back to see us soon," he said.

"I will! And she's full of surprises, your wife: that passionate outburst at the station! She might have been a poet."

He smiled. "She is! In secret. She doesn't make a song and dance about it, or care particularly about publication. But she's quite a talented writer."

"Really? Well, it doesn't surprise me—but how on earth does she find the time?"

"She gets up very early in the morning, five or six o'clock, and does an hour's writing.

His attention wandered, as a bosomy, trinketed girl strolled past, staring in. "A freelance," he remarked. "Should we invite her in? Maybe not. Where were we? Oh yes—Masha. But it won't get anywhere. She's almost too talented; she doesn't know which gift to concentrate on."

Also, he added with a sigh, she was right to blame him for

not pulling his weight in the house. He'd been brought up to believe it was the woman's place to do the housework. It was very Russian.

And very Jewish, I observed.

"I guess so. I bet you helped your wife a lot?"

"Yes." I glanced towards the window. The rushing darkness. Pain.

When I looked back at him, Shimon too looked pained. He was recalling their bad time, when Masha had actually asked him for a divorce. "But we both knew I was too reliant upon her, physically and psychologically, to survive unless there were some great iron curtain between us; an uncrossable barrier. So she encouraged me to apply for emigration. Ah, well"—his expression lightened—"thank God they turned me down! I wish she could have come with us . . . But, with the old croc dying, all the guides have their work cut out. We'd have had to find you a nice companion too." He winked. "I'm much too jealous to have indulged in the ancient custom of hospitality, in letting her entertain you too. Though I know she quite fancies you . . ."

Shimon leered. I blushed and glanced away. How tasteless he could be. Yet I couldn't but feel flattered that Masha had found me attractive.

In the riotous dining-car, two couples resentfully crowded up to allow us seats. Young men with shirts open to the waist, girls in bright, tarty dresses and jewellery, were drunk on wine and each other. At last, plates of fish soup and a bottle of cognac were shoved in front of us. Shimon, leaning across the table to be heard above the noise, gossiped about Liuba Charents. She lived, on the Black Sea coast, with a brother and sister. Rumour had it that she slept with both. I nodded and smiled in the right places, but my thoughts were far away, and sad. The conviviality of the dining-car, the crush of couples, re-emphasised my loneliness.

I thought of a phrase in *Whitsun Weddings*, by my favourite poet Larkin: "this frail travelling coincidence . . ."

Both Shimon and I were startled when a voice boomed in our ears and a hand grasped his shoulder. Shimon glanced up. "Ah, Lev! Lydia!"—a fat man, a greying woman—"So you too preferred the love-train."

He introduced Lev and Lydia Selvinsky. Selvinsky was one of his competitors. "And this is my English friend, Mr Lloyd George."

"Ah! A famous statesman, I think. Are you related?"

"I'm afraid not."

The Selvinskys chatted for a few minutes, standing, then left. Shimon told me Selvinsky had been the clear favourite for the Soviet title until his, Barash's, reinstatement in the Union; yet he wasn't in the least resentful. Improvisers were a close-knit, friendly bunch.

We stood up to let the four teenagers out. The dining-car was emptying rapidly. They were heading, observed Shimon, for the serious business of the night. We finished an anonymous meat-dish in peace, I settled the bill, and we walked unsteadily back down the train. All was quiet. Shimon stopped at the end of our corridor to have a smoke and breathe the stench of a toilet. One of the more attractive aspects of Soviet life, I had found, was that they didn't make life easy for smokers.

Alone in our compartment, I took out my *Progress* guide to Leningrad, but couldn't concentrate. I gazed at my ghostly reflection in the glass, where invisible forests rushed by. I stared out, stared in. Sorrow.

*   *   *

"*Hääyöaie!*"

Barash grinned as he pronounced the weird sound—interpreting and exaggerating the low moan which had reached us through the thin partition, behind him. "The soldier-boy and his girl are enjoying themselves . . ."

"Is that really the Finnish word for orgasm?"

He nodded. "Literally, *honeymoon-night-cry*. I haven't encountered it myself, alas . . . But I was told it in Karelia, which of course we stole from the Finns. Some friends of ours have a *dacha* up there. Karelia's a wonderful place; what one can see of it outside our militarised zone. Clean and fresh and open. I'd like to have taken you to see it, but there isn't time."

"I'll be happy with Leningrad."

"*Hääyöaie!*" he murmured wistfully, as another light moan reached us. "Love . . . It's the only thing worth living for; yet what pain it causes."

The faintest of male chuckles followed the female moan, behind him. Shimon leapt to his feet and took a few agitated paces up and down. "God! there's too much fucking going on. The train is awash with it."

He threw himself back in his seat, and closed his eyes. His breathing quietened. I thought he slept. It was the middle of the night. I closed my tired eyes too, and drowsed. An exclamation aroused me: "Look! Anna Karenina!"

I turned my head in time to see a flash of red; heard light footsteps receding. "Masha was right!" said Shimon. "A great beauty, looking distraught. She's trying to meet, and avoid meeting, Vronsky . . . And thinking with longing and remorse of her little boy . . . No, sorry—wrong direction!"

He sighed, and ran long slim fingers through unruly hair. "A kid would make our marriage perfect. But I can understand Masha wanting to wait a couple more years. Now that I'm back in the Union, she may get her old job back, which would

make it easier for her to get her doctorate. And then, perhaps
. . . It isn't that she's unmaternal . . ."

Stretching across, he picked up my *Progress* guidebook.
"The man who wrote this," he said, "is a pedophile from
Leningrad. A distinguished editor. We may bump into him.
Perhaps you should interview him, Lloyd . . ." A satirical
grin. "You seem to be interviewing all our weirdos . . .
You're probably on some committee trying to legalise
pedophilia. Are you?"

"No."

"Well, that's a relief." His face emerged from its malicious
phase. "Yes, this guy, Spassky, lures little kids to his *dacha* at
weekends. I know someone who goes beachcombing and
bird-watching on the Baltic coast. The bird-watching may be
of both kinds." He put his fingers to his eyes, miming binocu-
lars. "Anyway, two or three times, this summer, he caught
sight of Spassky in his bedroom, naked with different kids,
playing around with them. I hate that."

He picked his nose, wiped the snot on the upholstery. "It's
so silent," he observed. It was true: the noise of engine and
wheels had become a part of the silence. He rubbed his groin.
"Jesus, I want to fuck Masha! Or somebody!" He sought and
found another snot. "I'll have to sublimate! An improvisation.
Some more practice. Would you mind?"

I said sincerely it had been a great privilege to hear him
perform, just for me and his wife. Three times, in their tiny flat
high up in a Moscow tower-block, the late November dawn
had broken before Shimon had brought his improvisation to a
close—surrounded still by the débris of dinner.

"A quick sketch of Spassky, the pedophile editor. In the
style of *Egyptian Nights*, I think. You remember 'Charsky was
a native of Petersburg . . .'?"

I nodded. It was a fragment of Pushkin. Shimon had made

me read it as a way of approaching his art, about which I was still grossly ignorant. Pushkin's *improvisatore* had composed spontaneously in Italian; Barash, after only a few moments' thought, produced a stream of effortless, elegant Russian, a smile touching his lips . . .

Spassky was a native of Leningrad. He was not yet forty; he had a wife and various boys; his post with one of the literary journals was pleasantly onerous. He had a larger-than-average apartment, and a *dacha* on the coast. His life could have been very agreeable; only, unfortunately, though he published his own verses, he was not a poet.

Despite the great disadvantages suffered by poets (though admittedly, apart from their having been neutered, we know of no especial disadvantages laid upon Soviet poets), despite every possible disadvantage, these persons enjoy great benefits and privileges. The sweetest, most prized blessing of all is the title of poet bestowed on him by the Writers' Union, and which can be his till death, however mediocre his publications. He looks upon his public, and especially women readers, as his own property; in his opinion, they were born for his benefit and pleasure.

Should friends return from abroad they will say to him, "We smuggled in something we thought you'd like." If his mind is far away, because of a troublesome divorce or some imaginary illness, then at once a forgiving smile will accompany the forgiving exclamation: "Our friend's inspired!" Has he thrown a girl over? Then the young woman will nourish romantic thoughts of him for the rest of her life, while scorning her dull husband. Should he wish to get tickets for an opera or avant-garde play, the tickets will miraculously appear. And these are the more modest rewards for his art! Spassky confessed to his mirror that the compliments, the caresses, the flattery, were an irresistible temptation to him. Constantly he was forced to restrain himself from making rude remarks when he heard some other poet praised, without any mention of his, Spassky's, art.

He made every possible effort to acquire for himself the exquisite appellation. He avoided the society of his fellow bureaucrats, affecting to prefer the company of his creative brothers, even the most disreputable and dissolute. His conversation mimicked that of real poets, in being extremely frivolous and rarely touching on serious matters. In his dress he always observed the prevailing bohemian style, with the egotism and flamboyance of a young Soviet poet arriving in New York for the first time. In his office, which was furnished like a Parisian garret, there was nothing to recall the *apparatchik*: there were no papers in the out-tray; the sofa was stained with wine and vomit; there was none of that order which marks the absence of the Muse and the presence of an office cleaner. It upset Spassky if any of his hooligan acquaintances found him with a ledger in his hands. He was given to childish enthusiasms, hard to credit in a man otherwise unendowed with talent and strong emotion. At one time he pretended to be a passionate admirer of Jews, at another, a desperate gambler, and at another, a serious drinker; even though he could not distinguish between Jews of European and African breed, begrudged risking ten roubles on a cardgame, and secretly preferred a glass of tea to all the possible vintages of a French cellar. He led a life of great distraction; he was to be seen at all the dissident exhibitions, and his presence at secret porno film matinées was as inevitable as shoddy goods at GUM.

Nevertheless, he was a bureaucrat, and his passion was insuperable. When his "boring week" (so did he term his preparation of a journal) was on him, Spassky would shut himself up in his office and work from morning till late at night. He confessed to his genuine friends that it was only then that he knew real happiness. The rest of the time he propped up bars, scribbled doggerel, looked dreamy, dissembled, and waited in vain for someone to ask him the famous question: "Are you writing something at present?" ("If you do meet this guy," Barash interrupted himself at that point, "you must remember to ask him that, Lloyd. He'll be your friend for life. Well, on . . .")

One morning Spassky felt that happy state of soul when one's mediocrity is disguised by a mass of routine business waiting to be done. His mind was immersed in sweet oblivion . . . and poetry, and the inner world, did not exist for him. He was censoring someone's verses.

Suddenly the door of his office creaked and an unfamiliar head showed itself. Spassky gave a start and frowned.

"Who is it?" he asked irritably, inwardly cursing the office-girls who were never around when they should be.

The intruder entered.

He was short, squat, and seemed to be about eighty. The features of his pale face were nondescript: a low dirt-stained forehead, overhung by white hair, watery colourless eyes, a snub nose, and a thin beard surrounding puffy yellowish cheeks, showed him to be a Latvian. He was wearing a white coat, patched at the elbows; galoshes (although the season of spring was well advanced); a black insect was crawling towards his frayed shirt-collar; his ill-fitting hat of new and expensive fur had obviously been purloined. Meeting such a man anywhere but in a literary office, one would have taken him for a currency speculator or black marketeer.

"What do you want?" Spassky asked him.

"Comrade," replied the foreigner in Latvian, "excuse me for bursting in on you . . ."

Spassky did not offer him a chair; he himself stood up. The conversation continued in Latvian.

"I am an artist from the Baltic," the stranger said, "and circumstances have forced me to leave my homeland. I have come to Russia on the strength of my talent."

Spassky imagined that the Latvian was looking for work in a circus, and had come to the wrong building. He was on the point of giving him directions, to get rid of him as quickly as possible, when the stranger added, "I was hoping that as an important editor you could introduce me to some poets."

It would have been impossible to insult Spassky more painfully. He glared at this man who did not know he was addressing a poet.

"Who the hell are you and what do you take me for?" he demanded.

"Comrade," the Latvian stammered, "I believed . . . I thought . . . Please forgive me."

"What do you want?" Spassky asked curtly.

"I've heard that you organise public appearances for poets, and help them generally. That is why I came to you."

"You're mistaken, Comrade. I'm not an organiser; I'm just a struggling poet who happens to do a bit of editing in his spare time. It is true I have occasionally organised readings for myself and some friends, but that hardly makes me an organiser."

The poor Latvian was confused. He looked around him. The nude pin-ups, the erotic figurines, the empty wine-bottles, the books scattered on and under the desk, struck him. He realised that between the scruffy bohemian who stood before him in a forage-cap and denim-suit, and the bureaucrats with whom he dealt at home, there was nothing in common. He uttered some cursory apologies, bowed, and turned to leave. His show of bravado alarmed Spassky who, despite being a shit, was always on the look-out for fresh material.

"Wait a moment!" he said to the old man. "I felt obliged to set you right, but now let's talk about your affairs. I'll help you if I can. You have a manuscript you'd like to show me?"

"No, Comrade, I don't have manuscripts. I am a poor *improvisatore*."

"An *improvisatore*!" exclaimed Spassky, flinching and taking a step back. "If you'd told me that before, we needn't have wasted our time. The poet has no right to follow his inspiration, the Party must dictate what he writes."

"I agree, Comrade," said the Latvian; "and that's an excellent theme." He wiped rheum from his baggy eyes, lowered his gaze modestly, and listless verses, in tune with Party directives, spilled gracelessly from his lips . . .

"Why does the sun parch up the dusty
Ravine and wither its stunt trees,
Yet a proud ship spread out its thirsty
Canvas and drink the scudding breeze?
Why does an eagle, mounting, seek
The Red Star on the Kremlin's peak,
Not miserable church-spires? Why
Does Sonia, under a shy moon,
Caress a coloured youth and croon
An old Ukrainian lullaby?
Because the sea, and eagle's claws,
And a girl's heart, serve Marxist laws.
The sea is proud October blood,
The eagle, the Red Army's might,
The girl is Soviet womanhood
Helping the African to fight."

The Latvian fell silent . . . Spassky, bored but deeply envious, did not speak.

"Well?" asked the *improvisatore*.

Spassky clasped his hands together.

"Well?" repeated the *improvisatore*. "What do you think?"

"Astonishing!" the editor replied. "Why, you can produce acceptable verses without a moment's pause for thought. So, for you there is no toil, no subjectivity, nor the time-consuming research that is the prelude to respectable work-manship. Astonishing, astonishing!"

The *improvisatore* replied: "Every talent is beyond expla-nation. How does an architect see, in a sublime mountain, the hidden high-rise apartment building? I could not even explain it to myself."

"Well," said Spassky, "I think I might organise something after all. But you would have to perform in Russian."

"Naturally."

"We can use the Writers' Union theatre," said Spassky; "and then, we must think how much we should charge for admis-sion. We could split the proceeds—what do you say?"

It was distasteful to the *improvisatore* suddenly to fall from the heights of that genuine inspiration which had lurked behind his banal verses; but he understood the practical necessity of such matters, and he discussed the financial details with the editor. Spassky, in these dealings, demonstrated such savage greed, such an artless love of gain that he revolted the Latvian, who made haste to leave him before losing com-pletely that feeling of rapture aroused in him by artistic creation, above all when it was misunderstood. The preoccu-pied *apparatchik* did not observe this change of feeling, and he conducted the Latvian along the corridor and down the stairs, assuring him, with an arm around his shoulder, that they would both become rich.

When Spassky returned to his office, he busied himself with arrangements for the All-Soviet championships in oral story-telling due to take place in Leningrad the following week.

Against his strong disapproval, the young Moscow improviser, Shimon Barash, had been reinstated in the Union and
would take part. Fortunately, however, it had come to the
editor's notice that this Barash was going to be staying at the
Hotel Leningrad with a visiting western journalist. The bastard must have a death-wish! Grinning to himself, Spassky
launched into a memo for the KGB; and was so involved with
this that he did not notice his secretary's entrance. He gave a
start when a voice said, "Winter's here, Comrade Spassky—"

"—It's snowing."

Shimon, with that observation from Spassky's secretary,
glanced aside towards the window. I followed his glance.
Flakes were eddying, between the wet glass and the black,
invisible rush of forests. He threw himself back in his seat.

"Thanks, Shimon. Wonderfully witty!"

"Well . . . that's Spassky."

The latest of many soft cries came from behind him, a cry of
mixed pleasure and pain.

"Jesus!" he growled. "Don't they ever sleep?"

"That's youth! But the old couple are quiet." I nodded over
my shoulder.

"They're practising for death."

His dark, penetrating eyes, which during improvisations
always held my gaze, like some contemporary ancient mari-
ner, closed. They opened again as he was thrown forward by
the train's unexpected braking. We ground to a halt, in the
middle of nowhere. A silent minute passed; I was seized by
irrational anxiety. What if nuclear war had begun? But how
stupid . . . Tiredness was affecting me. I took out a notebook
and made a few observations on our journey.

Shimon suggested we go for a drink. I put my notebook

away and followed him out. We passed a couple entwined in the foul space for smokers, by the toilet at the end of the corridor; but generally the couples had melted away—the silence adding to the eerie atmosphere of a train halted amid dark forests. The dining-car was almost empty. The *babushka* who brought us cognacs didn't know why we'd stopped.

"To Leningrad, my friend!" exclaimed Shimon, and we clinked glasses. He recalled, with a wistful smile, his last train-ride north, all of four years ago, with his brother. "His application was in the pipeline, and they'd never have let him go if they suspected Remizova might want to follow. Or else, they'd have restricted her to the Soviet Union. So they'd meet by chance, like on overnight train-journeys. And even then they had to be very careful. Everyone recognised her; if a man was seen talking to her, *tête-à-tête*, he attracted attention."

He smiled down into his glass, which he warmed with his hands. "So I'd go with Abram, often." His eyes, glancing up, sparkled at the memory. "And Moscow–Leningrad was one of the trips. Summer of '78. We chose a mid-week night, of course, when it was much less crowded. Liudmila was sitting over there—" he pointed "—and we were just about here. We always put on a great show of being old friends meeting by chance; and a threesome at a table doesn't have the same connotation of intimacy, of course. Then, in the night, Abram would slip off to her compartment. And they'd talk and hug a little! Abram's too good a Jew to screw outside marriage!"

"When she defected," I asked, "did they get to know you'd helped them?"

"Oh, of course. And that—quite apart from the fact that I'd applied to get out too—made them come down on us hard."

"So you sacrificed a lot for your brother?"

He shrugged. What were brothers for? Then he nodded past

me, saying, "Here comes the passionate couple from next-door . . ."

I looked over my shoulder, expecting to see the young soldier and his girl, but it was the tottery couple from the other side. We had exchanged a few friendly words with them while stretching our legs in the corridor, and they'd confessed how out of place they felt. "This is no country for old men . . ." as Yeats had put it. I felt out-of-place myself. I was pleased, therefore, when Shimon greeted them pleasantly on their halting, careful walk down the dining-car, and asked them to join us. The old man, his face lined with Russia's sorrows, his teeth a Siberian gold-mine, showed his gratitude by ordering a bottle of cognac for us all. The faded cloth of his suit, pressed against me, smelt of mothballs. This journey was a rare adventure for them. Proudly the old lady told us they were on their way to spend a week with their son, a pediatrician, in Leningrad.

She reminded me a little of my mother: ruby-cheeked, spectacled, homely and friendly. I saw my mother in her rocker, and felt remorse that I went home so rarely. The desolation of a mining-village without a mine pained me too much, and I could stand only so many nights of *Coronation Street* and quiz-shows. This Russian *babushka* and her husband showed polite interest in my being British, but fascination that Barash was a story-teller. They begged him to give them a short sample.

Imagine my horror when—on his fourth cognac—he launched into an indecent improvisation. It concerned a search for a lost drawing. Courbet's *Creation of the World*. I have since found that it exists—or did, for it was looted in Budapest after the Second World War. The drawing, from life, was of a vulva; Shimon's hero travelled the world looking for the missing vulva—Shimon used the obscene Russian term. He searched, not in private vaults and safes, but under skirts. Wherever there was a skirt, he became suspicious; conscientiously and tirelessly he had to check. From Mrs Thatcher to the oldest Anatolian peasant-woman, anyone in skirts was forced to submit to being searched. In half an hour of impromptu pornography, Shimon swept the whole globe of sexuality, including all the perversions, from anilictus to zoophilia.

It was a brilliant performance, but so grossly insensitive to the feelings of a staid, rather simple and uneducated, old couple that I felt only an acute embarrassment. The lady, who was sitting across from me at Shimon's side, was bright pink; when her eyes met mine, she would bite her under-lip and try to smile, her expression a mixture of shame and bewilderment.

Her husband paid his bill and took his wife off as soon as Barash had come to a halt. I told him what I felt about his gross insensitivity, but he simply laughed and said he had "made" the old couple's journey. "They were feeling like ghosts, in this travelling brothel of fleshly fucking, my friend. Now they are stirred up with lust and disgust—a potent mixture. You should have seen the old man's face! By the time we go back, we shall be hearing *Hääyöaie!* from both sides . . ."

The train gave a jolt and started to move. Soon it was rushing again through the night.

"So tell me more about *your* sex-life," he said.

"There's nothing to tell. I can't summon up the interest."

"You're still in love with your wife?"

"I suppose so." I turned to the window, seeing my vague reflection in the snow-streaked glass. Bitterness. Anguish. *Angerth.*

"So who," he asked, as if following my thoughts, "is this guy who's moved in with her?"

"He's a philosophy lecturer."

"That figures . . . This philosopher has your comfortable house in Hampstead, while you have a bedsit in Bermondsey?"

"More or less. Two rooms actually, and I share bathroom and kitchen."

"And you support this bitch?"

"I support the children, and pay the mortgage. He hasn't actually moved in, you see; not formally."

"It's fucking awful. And I guess it's not cheap, a mortgage in lovely, charming Hampstead, close to the Michael Feet."

Ignoring his jibe—he seemed to require occasional thrusts of sarcasm, as he needed his nicotine-fix—I stared at my ghostly reflection. *Hiraeth* overcame me: that sad, sweet homesickness and longing, for which English has no word but which in Russian is *toská*. I saw the face of Philby, an unhappy traitor. I'd betrayed my class, my village, by moving away, moving up. I should have married a homely Welsh girl.

I heard Shimon say, "I'll find you a nice girl in Leningrad. I've got someone in mind: plump and swarthy and earthy! And you can do the same for me if I should get to London next summer."

I smiled, but made no comment on either possibility. Instead, I asked if his brother would be taking part in London. Israel . . . was it in Europe or outside it? Yes, he said, they would be rivals—in the unlikely event of his getting there. "But that's not important—it would just be so wonderful to see each other again. Though I suspect we would both feel secretly relieved when the week was over! We haven't all that much in common."

Recalling the black-bearded Abram, I nodded. I could not see that sternly Jewish man narrating a story about a missing vulva.

On our way back along the train, Shimon stopped off for a smoke, joining a notch of silent suicides breathing in smoke and urine. Twenty minutes later, when he slid open our door, he was scowling. "Bastards!" he growled, flinging himself on his seat.

"What's wrong?"

"I found out why we stopped. Some Lithuanian nationalist —they didn't know who—is being taken to the Leningrad *psikhushka*. You know what that entails. Shades of your friend Kravchenko . . . Apparently, he squirmed out of a toilet window. Of course, they caught him. Someone saw him with his face covered in blood."

"How awful!"

Poor Kravchenko . . . How he enjoyed that sunny day at the Oval . . .

"He knows they'll soon drive him crazy with drugs. No wonder he preferred a quick death in the freezing forests."

I had tried to get permission, I said, to visit one of the *psikhushkas* and interview inmates, but had been refused.

"Of course."

I said I'd been thinking a lot about Kravchenko, these past few days; wondering if there was anything at all I could do. His incarceration had been reported in the West, but Shimon and Masha had astounded me by their claim that he really *did* believe he was an English journalist, Dick Johnson, and was in an English clinic. A dream, ascribed to the main character of *Isadora's Scarf*, had said as much; but naturally I had assumed it to be a fantasy idea. I pressed Shimon as to its factual truth, yet again. He nodded. "Yes, it's true—according to very reliable information. Poor devil, it must be his way of easing his intolerable situation. An English clinic must be rather more comfortable than a Soviet *psikhushka* . . .

"They claimed he'd been plotting with subversive Ukrainian groups in the West," he continued. "Do you think he was doing that?"

I shrugged. It was not impossible.

"He was a damn good reporter. Most of the charges against dissidents are trumped up. Take Alaverdov, the former director of Egyptology at the Pushkin Museum of Fine Arts. They accused him of stealing three Vrubel masterpieces, including *Naked Madman at Lourdes*; but they couldn't risk letting it go to trial. So—he was crazy! Unfit to plead!" Shimon smiled sardonically. "I've heard the paintings turned up in Galina Brezhnev's *dacha* when she fell from grace. But poor Alaverdov is still in the Dnepropetrovsk."

"He's mentioned in the *Isadora* piece too," I said.

"Really? The guy who wrote it must have inside knowledge."

I asked him if he didn't think it was slightly immoral, mixing reality and fiction. Barash was emphatic in his rejection of my qualms. The trouble with most novels, he asserted, was precisely that they *were* fiction; in the final analysis, one knew they weren't true, and therefore they were boringly irrelevant.

In any case, he concluded, where could one find a more fictional reality, or a more all-too-real fiction, than in Russia? The common reality of every-day life was more surrealistic than Gogol—or Vrubel—could ever have imagined. We had just seen it demonstrated, in the halted train. "In coming here, my friend, you become fictional. Don't you feel it? *O tyen'*! O shade!"

He stared bitterly at the dark, snow-streaked window. "No hint of dawn . . . I wonder if dawn will ever break for us Russians."

"Someday, surely."

"Well, maybe with Andropov things will improve. I have

some hopes of the guy. From all accounts he's cleaned up the KGB a good deal, and he may do the same for Russia."

"Can I quote you on that?" I asked.

"Why not?"

I took out my notebook, already crowded with the observations of sundry *refuseniks*, Baptists, homosexuals and other dissidents. As I scribbled my personal form of shorthand, he asked me if it wasn't odd to be asked to report on so many things—drama, politics, cricket, books, etc. Not in the *Guardian*, I said. It was part of the English tradition of the cultivated amateur.

Shimon nodded, and said he admired us for it.

"The cricket-reporting is very occasional," I added. "Sunday matches. It lets me kill two birds with one stone: I can take my son to them. It's about the only time we meet, the only point of contact."

He nodded sympathetically. I looked at the window-reflections. Shimon was looking too. "Transparent profile through the carriage-glass," he murmured. "Akhmatova . . . She wrote that, in 1940, of a friend of hers, a Georgian beauty from pre-Bolshevik days. And now Akhmatova is a shade . . . Time, time . . . It comes over one in a train, don't you think, Lloyd?"

"Yes . . ." Grief. *Górye . . .* "I should read her, should I?"

"Oh, yes, she's wonderful! And we're coming to her city. I can already smell the Neva."

His eyes, when I straightened my head, looked wistful. "The Neva is woman," he said, as if guessing my query. "That's where the *Creation of the World* is."

We were silent. *Hääyöaie!* from behind Shimon's head. "Shit!" he exclaimed, jumping up. "I can't stand this! I want Masha! No disrespect!" he added hastily. With a heavy sigh, he sat again, and said, "I shouldn't begrudge the lad in there. He'll be back in Afghanistan next week, and could be killed. He's having the same feelings as Cleopatra's lovers. Well, since we can't make love shall we make a little art again? Shall I give you some more of the egregious Spassky? Or are you tired of my voice and want to sleep?"

Not in the least, I said sincerely.

"Would you like to tape this one, my friend?"

With effusive expressions of gratitude, I delved into my briefcase for my micro-recorder. At his home, I hadn't been permitted to tape his improvisations. It was too risky, he said; and of course I had understood, even though I was transcribing and erasing: there was a way of getting some notes back.

"It will be a keepsake of your visit."

"The best possible one! I'll translate it and print it in the *Guardian*, if you like. And assuming it's decent," I smiled.

Barash frowned. "No, I never publish. To publish is to compromise with falsehood, decorum, censorship."

"Well, it's a pity. You're a genius."

He tried to look modest.

As his eyes closed and his head swayed to the rhythm of the speeding train, I recalled earlier eloquence: fiery chapel-preachers full of *hwyl* and hell-fire. Passionate Union leaders. Aneuran Bevan on a stark, drizzled hill-slope, my exalted father clutching my hand. All of them had improvised out of familiar material; Barash could spin complex stories from thin air. His satire of a no doubt fictitious editor was a *bagatelle*; I would much rather have got his majestic *Ode to Justice* on tape; still, this was better than nothing. Sullen dawn glimmered by the time he ran out of inspiration: apologising for having given his Latvian a senseless theme. "I don't know why I did," he said. "Probably it will come to me when you're flying home."

Home . . . What a strange word, I thought. The damp, squalid flat in Bermondsey, my "home" for the past two years, since my wife's affair broke over me—that was not home. But neither was Abercwm, though my parents still lived in the damp old miner's cottage, with my sister Bron just down the road. In a strange way Moscow, with its queues of drably but neatly dressed people outside empty shop-windows, had seemed more like home, more like the Wales of my childhood. In present-day Moscow, as in post-war Wales, life had seemed hard yet purposeful.

Shimon dozed, and I gazed out at the grey rush of endless birches. Russia! The very word always brought a glow to my weary father's eyes. Workers of the world unite! How thrilled he'd been when, in my second term at Birmingham, I switched from French to Russian! I even taught him a few words. "Comrade!" the miners would call out to each other, passing in the coal-grimed village street. "*Tovarich!*" my father learned to say.

My heavy eyelids dropped; my mother was calling "*Cariad!*" Then Barash's voice was suggesting breakfast. I waited for him to have a smoke first—he'd been considerate in not smoking in my presence—then we walked through once more to the diner. It was rapidly filling up with quiet, sated couples. We joined the young lovers from the next compartment; and crammed up to allow their friends to sit. This second couple had heard of Barash; eagerly they asked him to sign the dirty menu-card. The young Muscovites plied me with questions about English rock-stars, which I couldn't answer. The soldier, boyish enough to be still at school, wrote his name and address down so that I could send him a record he wanted. Shimon ordered champagne, and flirted with the girls. I got tight, as much from exhaustion as drink; I called for a second bottle of champagne. The bill exceeded the amount of roubles I had in my pocket, and Shimon made up the difference. The forests thinned out and vanished, to be replaced by grimy factories and allotments, as if not Leningrad but Sheffield was approaching. The sky was leaden, though the snow had stopped, except for a stray wisp or two. I was told it was an exceptionally mild autumn.

The dining-car became noisy again. Shimon delightedly pointed to a table for four where the amorous arrangement seemed to have changed since dinner. "That's Russia!" he shouted above the babble. "Permanent Revolution in the heart! A few more nights and everyone would have screwed everyone!" He leered at the two tipsy girls, who giggled.

We said goodbye, staggered back to our compartment, and scrambled into our coats.

The train drew in. I lost touch with Shimon in the colossal rush to get off. I thought he was ahead of me, but when I reached the exit he was nowhere to be seen. I waited until the last of the travellers had gone through. No Barash. Baffled and insecure, I lugged my cases round an empty station, searching. The *improvisatore* had vanished. Hazy with champagne and sleeplessness, I pushed through the exit, to be blasted by an Arctic wind. I caught sight of a sign marked Taxis. The rank was deserted—which didn't seem hopeful—but I went to stand there. Remarkably, almost at once a taxi rounded a corner and drew up. "Hotel Leningrad," I told the driver, and scrambled in with my luggage. I brushed snow off my eyelashes and sank with relief into the upholstered warmth. My lids kept drooping. A glimpse of Lenin thrilled me briefly: his out-thrust arm. The Finland Station! My cold blood stirred. Then a humped bridge, and I saw between eyelid-falls the grey, swift, tumid waters of the Neva. The cab bumped along by the embankment.

We came to a halt outside a modern hotel. From its appearance it could easily have been a Hilton, and I felt grateful—too weary for anything with character. Fumbling for my wallet, I remembered I had no roubles left. Trying not to panic, I asked if sterling would do. Even as the driver shook his head, the passenger door in front was opened and a burly grey-suited woman threw herself in. Hastily I stammered my problem to her, and asked if I might go inside and change some money.

The burly figure, without turning, shook her head.

"*Nyet*."

· 2 ·

I might still be sitting in the cab, unable to pay without getting out, unable to get out without paying, if Shimon had not suddenly appeared on the hotel steps. I signalled frantically, he came bounding down, discovered what the problem was, and paid the driver. He seized my suitcase as I clambered out and —before I could ask him why the devil he'd left me in the lurch—he was asking, with a twinkle in his eye, if I'd paid the tart in sterling. "What tart?" I growled; and his face fell.

"You mean you didn't go off with that prostitute we saw roaming the train?"

"Of course not!"

"Well—I'm sorry! I could have sworn I saw you diving after her into a taxi. You must have a Russian double, my friend; he was short and sturdy, wore glasses and had red hair peeping out from under his hat. He was even wearing a black duffel-coat, like yours. Incredible!" We had reached the desk in the spacious lobby and he put down my case. "I confess it rather took me aback; it seemed out of character. But I don't know you very well, as yet. I was quite admiring your nerve."

"I'm sorry to disappoint you."

"Well, never mind, you're here now." He picked up a pen to sign us in. "I've asked for a room overlooking the Neva. Shall we have a drink first?" He nodded towards the busy bar-area, in a roped-off section of the lobby. "A couple of my rivals are over there. No? Okay . . ."

Our room turned out to be at the side of the hotel, overlooking watery waste ground. Incensed, Shimon charged off to complain; but came back with a shamefaced look. "They claim they're full. I've let you down, my friend."

I told him it was okay, it didn't matter. He was sure, he continued gloomily, that the Writers' Union had instructed the hotel staff not to give him the best service; though, in any case, *improvisatori* were treated as poor relations.

"Perhaps I'm the problem, Shimon," I said. "You implied as much in your improvisation. They don't like you being with a western journalist."

He shook his head, saying, "They won't object to you. Your paper has a decent reputation—as you can see by Jaruzelski granting your eastern correspondent an interview. You weren't wet about Solidarity the way one of our generals was—refusing to let his troops dress in Polish uniforms . . ." Barash smiled satirically. He stripped off his shirt, revealing the tanned torso of a beach-guard. He and his wife had spent most of the summer in Georgia, while I, the privileged western-er, had spent a depressing week in Abercwm followed by two rainy weeks with my bored children in a leaky Lake District cottage.

"You take a pretty good line on peace, too," he said, tapping lightly my CND lapel-badge. "And I happen to know they liked your sympathetic article on the Irish freedom fighters."

"Not exactly sympathetic," I pointed out. "I disapproved of

their methods, but tried to understand what drives them to violence."

"That's it—you're very balanced, very sensible, my friend. That's why they've turned a blind eye to your interviews in Moscow, and why we're sharing this room!" He smiled broadly. "I'm not a complete idiot; I weigh the risks."

"Good." I said I was grateful; his friendship had meant everything—especially since Markov, the Olympic finalist, had not even bothered to reply to my letter.

"Well—" Shimon shrugged "—you must try to understand Igor's position. He's under a cloud, after Finland, and he has a small baby to consider."

"Why is he under a cloud? I know you explained; but to be honest I didn't take it in. My Russian was still very hazy."

Stripped to red-striped underpants, he climbed between the sheets and stretched back luxuriously. "Ah! That feels good. Well, it was many things. For a start, he's very, very close to Riznich, the Italian. She toured with him here, last year about this time. And there was an extract from Riznich's final improvisation in Finland which was broadcast to us, and —caused some trouble. I don't think she meant it to. She gets so wrapped up in her performance she becomes a little crazy. I heard her, when she was here, improvise about your famous Florence Nightingale, and right after, to Igor and me, she said, 'Why did I call her Nightingale?' as if she'd created a fictional character! So, anyway, there was a little trouble and Igor suffered by association. But also his own piece was about Gsenin's suicide in Yerevan. They were close friends; it cut him up terribly. You don't know Gsenin's work?"

"No."

"Well, he was no great poet. Actually he was a good doctor, till he got struck off for dissidence. But it was a very sad, lonely death. He'd just divorced his wife to marry a young chick, then instantly regretted it. Markov's poem was a kind of tribute to him. Of course, he disguised it; he actually brought in elements from the suicide of Riznich's father—in the way we do, to create disguises. He himself became 'Charsky'—" Shimon grinned "—and a reprobate bachelor. Whereas he leads a blameless married life. But the poem couldn't have helped. Only someone as well-established as Charents could honour Gsenin without paying for it. Mind you, it was brave of her, too, to give a memorial concert."

He reached for his cigarettes, which he had laid on a shelf, then thought better of it.

"Was there *really* a rape in the next room, while this fellow was killing himself?"

He nodded. "It was all true, just as I told it. An American writer accused this Armenian of having Turkish blood; which made him so angry he raped her."

I flinched; said it was a horrific story. "But how," I asked, "do you know this?"

"Liuba told us. She knows the KGB operator at the Hotel Armenia in Yerevan. It's taped."

I shuddered.

"But from the next room, there were just some heavy snores, then silence."

He closed his eyes and relaxed his head. "So take care what you say, my friend," he murmured. "But you and I will have a good week: whatever happens in this fucking competition."

Weary as I was, I wanted to see Leningrad. Shimon excused himself: there was to be a reception at the theatre in the evening, so he would get some rest. By the time I'd bathed, he was lightly snoring.

After queueing to change some money, I hazarded the freezing wind, walking round to the rear of the hotel to a tram-stop. I had to wait a long time, in the bleak wind-tunnel of a street. At last a tram came, and with hunched, head-scarfed old women, I was rushed and bumped along. I got off at the end of the line, somewhere in the city centre. Having forgotten to bring my *Progress* guidebook, I wandered blind. Walking was unpleasant; the wind whipped through my corduroys and longjohns. Yet, at the Bronze Horseman statue, a bride stood in a flimsy white dress to be photographed. Her groom was in naval cadet uniform. A crowd of well-wishers stood around the couple under Peter's upreared steed. But elsewhere, there seemed few people about, considering it was a Saturday.

Lenin seemed everywhere. I gazed up at the statue outside the Finland Station, and a shiver of excitement passed through me. In spite of everything that had happened, it had been a great awakening. I recalled a line of Hugh MacDiarmid's: "The eternal lightning of Lenin's bones." I had stared down at that indomitable face in the Kremlin mausoleum, only a couple of days before Brezhnev's death.

I kept mostly within sight of the Neva. The greyness of water, low skyline, and sky, recalled to me Saturdays in Cardiff, in the austerity years of my childhood. Cardiff Arms Park, with my father and brother. A lump came up in my throat. I loved, in perhaps a puritan way, those desolate tiers of council-houses, a Labour Party poster in each one of them—a solidarity which Thatcher, of course, is striving to break up by loading the tenants with mortgages.

I pissed in a stinking urinal, behind St Isaac's.

Desperate for hot food, I looked in vain for a restaurant. There must surely be restaurants, I thought, in the Nevsky Prospekt—if only I could find it. Striding, hunched against the wind, down a lifeless and lightless street, I stepped in front of a tall, gaunt naval officer who bore down upon me. I asked him the way to the Nevsky Prospekt. Fixing me with a cold stare, he pointed a finger down towards his feet, and stalked past. So this was the glittering Nevsky . . . At last I found a restaurant. It was quite full but oddly silent. Diners raised their eyes to give me a stare, then bent to their food again.

The silent, cold atmosphere, and my encounter with the naval officer, gave me a feeling of unreality. I remembered Shimon's words about the blurring of fiction and reality in his country. Someone else had said almost the same thing to me, in Moscow—the famous poet Victor Surkov. It had been easy to arrange to visit him, since he had married, on a trip to America, a schoolfriend of my daughter's. A girl still in her teens, impeccably brought-up, marrying a foul-mouthed Russian poet almost three times her age—it had seemed a shocking mistake, and my evening with them in Moscow had only confirmed me in that view.

A plate of fish-soup was dumped before me.

As I ate, I reflected on that uncomfortable evening. Imogen Surkov had appeared miserable and—I plucked a fishbone from my teeth—like a fish out of water. I hadn't taken at all to Surkov: tall and gangling, his lean dark face, hectic eyes and long grey hair giving him the appearance of an old Red Indian chief. And indeed he had proposed to the girl in a desert-hotel in Arizona. Less than a year after his marriage, he treated her with contempt. He had taunted her, in my presence, with the women he had screwed . . . A Mexican servant at that hotel; quite recently, in Florence, the beautiful Italian *improvisatrice*, Signora Riznich, to whom Shimon had referred. An old acquaintance, she had "fictionalised" him and his courtship of Imogen at the Olympiad—and Surkov, far from feeling upset, seemed to take a childish pleasure in it. So, in recompense, he had screwed her, he said; and attacked his teenage English wife for getting angry! It was his right to screw anyone.

He mourned his ex-wife and little son, abandoned in a *dacha* at Peredelkino; sighed over an ex-mistress; then over his first wife, who he had recently discovered was now married to a KGB man in Gorky. He accused Imogen, hardly more than a child, of "fucking-up" his life. It was clear that he hated women. The only woman—incredibly—for whom he had a good word, other than sexually, was Thatcher. He saluted her Falklands courage! Said her action had given freedom to the islanders and also, probably, would restore democracy to Argentina! It was unbelievable. I saw red, and so did Imogen. That cold-hearted bitch, sacrificing our Welsh Guardsmen just to save her own skin! My evening with the Surkovs had been depressing and ghastly.

I ate my soup as quickly as possible, paid my bill, and left the silent restaurant. Frozen again, I searched for and found the Pushkin museum-flat on the Moika. I'd never read much Pushkin; at Brum we had concentrated on the language. I thought I should repair that omission. A janitor told me the museum was closed for *remont* and would not open for another six years. As I walked away, two young orientals accosted me, asking if I'd like to sell sterling. I declined.

The gloomy day gloomed further; the bitter wind grew still more embittered. Incapable of finding the right tram-stop, I searched for a taxi-rank. At last I found one, but a long and silent queue stretched away. I attached myself to it; waited and shivered. In half an hour, two taxis came. Night was falling swiftly in mid-afternoon. I spotted a figure darting along the patient line, pausing to speak and gesticulate. I wondered if he might be a freelance operator. As he drew near I stepped forward. "Taxi?" he said. I saw a Mercedes Benz badge on his lapel. "*Da*," I said, "how much to the Hotel Leningrad?" "*Fünf.*" He held up five fingers. It was only twice the official fare, according to Shimon's advice; and cheap by London standards. I nodded. He indicated that I should follow him. He made off at a crouching lope cross the street, his eyes darting left and right, and rounded a corner. I hurried after, and saw the Mercedes.

I felt, as we drove, a shade uneasy about having jumped the queue. Yet—I persuaded myself—I was not so used to bitter cold as the Leningraders in the queue, many of whom must have been survivors of the Siege. After I'd warmed myself with a cognac at the bar, I took the lift. Barash was in bed still, reading.

He felt rested, he said. How had I liked Leningrad? When I told him about the currency dealers he put his finger to his lips and nodded towards the phone. I felt annoyed at my carelessness. After all the warnings, both in England and from Shimon himself, I blurted out the first thing that came into my head.

He got dressed and we went down for dinner. I was hungry, and would like to have eaten straight away, but he insisted we have a drink at the bar. And a second, and a third. He kept glancing round, looking at his watch. Then a dumpling of a girl in an off-the-shoulder dress slid on to the bar-stool next to me. Shimon greeted her with effusive surprise, and the tart, equally astonished, almost fell off her stool in the effort to lean across me and kiss him. I caught a reek of cheap perfume.

"Shura, this is my very good English friend, Lloyd George. Lloyd, Shura's one of my dearest friends in Leningrad!"

We shook hands. She simpered. Sweaty pores, green eye-shadow, lush scarlet lips. Simon ordered her a vodka. He offered her a cigarette but she said she'd given up. They exchanged gossip—her left, overflowing breast pressed against me—then she engaged me in clumsy small-talk. What did I do? How did I like Leningrad? Shimon ordered more drinks, over my protests. Though her breast had moved away, her knee now pressed against mine. She'd managed to get tickets for the Circus, she said: an amazing scoop. But her escort had fallen sick. Would we like to use them?

That was kind of her, said Shimon; unfortunately he had to go to a fucking boring reception. But perhaps I would like to go with Shura? "Oh, would you?" she asked, with a flutter of glued-on lashes. I apologised, saying I was desperately tired.

They tried to persuade me. Eventually I had to say I didn't approve of circuses. Shura soon took herself off, waddling away on absurdly high heels and turning to give Shimon a final pout.

I said to him, smiling, "It was a kind thought!"

He spread his arms in a wry admission of defeat. "I'm sorry, my friend. That was the girl I mentioned on the train. I thought you'd take to her."

"Not my type, I'm afraid."

"Too coarse? Maybe so. Well, if I can't arrange an erotic experience for you, let me try with a religious one. You still want to go to the Nikolski in the morning?"

I said yes. An *émigré* I'd interviewed in London had talked so eloquently and sorrowfully of the Nikolski Cathedral that I wanted to experience it. Shimon had agreed eagerly, having sampled it himself on one of his infrequent trips to Leningrad.

"You won't regret it," he said, as at long last we walked towards the dining-room. "It's an unforgettable atmosphere. Something to tell your cousin, the bishop."

"My brother."

"Are you religious?"

"Not in the least, I'm afraid." Nor, I might have added, was my brother, particularly.

"Nor am I. We're very alike, you and I. And we both have religious brothers! But it's the singing and the crowd . . . Unless you'd rather we went to the Hermitage?"

No, I said, there were plenty of days for the Hermitage. He could take me to church.

After a forgettable but filling meal, he ordered a taxi to the Ostrovsky Theatre and I went to our room. I read a biography of Pushkin for a while, then took a hot, luxurious bath. I looked forward to an early night, a long sleep. I lay in bed, watching through half-closed eyes a ballet involving kolkhoz workers in *Tashkent*. It pleased me that my Russian had come back so well, after twenty years. The curtain fell; the studio announcer introduced an interval talk, *Heroic Kitezh*, to be given by the literary editor N. I. Spassky. "Good grief!" I thought. "So he exists!" I pulled myself up in bed and attended with interest. A rather handsome, even noble, face appeared, set off informally by a blue cravat. "Kitezh," he began, "was a city of ancient Kiev Rus." When the Mongol hordes attacked it, sweeping across the dusty plain, it preserved its freedom by sinking into its lake. Every Midsummer Eve, so the legend tells us, one can still see the lights of heroic Kitezh shining in the water's depths.

"Isn't that the way with us Russians? Death rather than enslavement! Did not our Leningrad become Kitezh, when the Mongol hordes surrounded us in the great Patriotic War . . . ?"

I heard Spassky out; then, leaving the ballet on to cover Barash's voice, began playing through the short tape he had allowed me to make in the train. I began to transcribe it, but soon decided I was too tired. I listened drowsily; then, as Shimon's inspiration wilted under an impossible theme, fell instantly asleep.

★   ★   ★

The public arrived at the Writers' Union building. The audience was large. All awaited the beginning of the performance with every appearance of boredom; at last, at eight o'clock, the sounds of a recording of folk-music died away, there was a settling into seats, and silence. And the *improvisatore*, greeted by perfunctory applause, walked forward to the edge of the stage and made a curt bow.

Spassky waited uneasily to see what sort of impression the first minute would produce. The old Latvian, expressing himself in poor Russian, asked for volunteers to write down some themes for him on pieces of paper. At his unexpected invitation, all looked at one another in silence. Pausing awhile, the Latvian repeated his request in an abrasive voice. Spassky was sitting immediately in front of the stage; he was seized by anxiety; he began to sweat, foreseeing that the performance would not get under way without his help, and that he would be forced to write down some theme, which would undoubtedly be scrutinised by certain parties, both left-wing and right.

The heads of several people turned towards him, and they began to appeal for his assistance, at first in whispers, then louder and louder. Hearing Spassky's name, the *improvisatore* sought him out with his eyes and discovered him to be sitting straight in front of him; with an unpleasant smile he crouched and handed him a biro and a piece of paper. Spassky, who was wearing a loud open-neck check shirt and orange trousers, stood up and, ostentatiously turning towards the audience, scribbled a few words. The Latvian, holding out his fur hat, stooped again to allow Spassky to drop his theme into it. His example had the required effect: two assistant editors from Spassky's journal likewise wrote down a theme; the cultural attaché from the Czech embassy and a young man recently returned from a visit to Cuba placed their folded papers in the hat; finally, a stern-faced Komsomol leader wrote down a few words and handed her slip of paper to the *improvisatore*. He placed his hat on a table near the microphone and began to pick out the slips one by one, reading each theme aloud to the audience:

' "*The family of Engels* . . . *The Wall Street Crash* . . . *Turgenev and the Foot* . . . *Spring, seen from a South African gaol* . . . *Castro's Triumph* . . . Okay, how do you want to choose?" demanded the Latvian. "Pick one out of the hat, or appoint a committee?"

"Appoint a committee!" shouted most of the audience.

"Pick it out of a hat," suggested a well-known personage in the front row.

"Agreed," everyone shouted. The Latvian placed the slips in his hat again and asked for a volunteer to draw his theme. No one responded. Accustomed to such Russian inertia, the *improvisatore* asked again, more urgently. Suddenly he noticed, to one side, a red, robust arm raised; he turned quickly and went towards the sturdy and severe middle-aged woman who was seated at the end of the first row. She stood up, quite unembarrassed to be seen wearing greasy overalls, and plunged her proletarian hand into the hat. She brought out a crumpled slip and read in a loud voice:

"*Turgenev and the Foot.*"

The *improvisatore* bowed low to her, with a look of profound distaste, and returned to the microphone.

"Comrades," he said, "I am required to improvise on the theme of *Turgenev and the Foot*. I respectfully request the person who wrote this subject down to explain to me which of his feet he had in mind, for the great novelist had two . . ."

At these words many in the audience tittered. The *improvisatore* grinned back at them.

"I should like to know," he continued, "to which biographical event the person who chose this theme alludes . . . I should be most grateful if he or she would be good enough to explain."

Some of the Party members turned their gaze towards the Komsomol leader, aware that she worked in a factory making sports-shoes; but the young woman stared back at them expressionlessly. Spassky could not bear the thought that she might be credited with the cautiously suggestive theme he had written down, so hastily he got to his feet and, turning towards the audience, said:

"The theme was proposed by me. I had in mind a footnote by Boris Dolgorukov, in his *History of Chiropody*, which suggests that on several occasions Turgenev kissed a young woman's foot instead of her hand." He smiled, but suddenly paled: recalling too late that the anecdote had referred to Pushkin not Turgenev. He croaked, "But it seems to me that the subject is a trifle facetious . . . Why not choose one of the others?"

But already the *improvisatore* felt the approach of the god . . . He signalled to the sound-engineer. The first bars of Mosolov's *Factory* blared out. The Latvian's face became red, he pushed back his white hair, and with a handkerchief wiped his forehead, which a gross fly had been tickling. He stepped forward, folded his arms . . . The music stopped. The *improvisatore* began . . .

"Spassky gave a talk on *Kitezh*? That's incredible. *No one* talks about Kitezh. No one's heard of it any more."

We were dressing by lamplight. The late dawns disturbed my body-rhythms.

"Why is that?"

"Who knows? It's sure to be some secret military

installation. The name's vanished from the *Soviet Encyclopaedia*. In its place is a long article on *kitaika*, nankeen cloth. Spassky's crazy. If he's not careful they'll start taking an interest in his taste for fondling small boys."

Shimon was hungover, and tense, at the start of his important week. I assured him I would be greeting him in London next July; and possibly, if there was a summer election, we'd both have something to celebrate. We gulped our permitted small cup of coffee, and ordered a taxi. As we jolted towards my "religious experience", Shimon groaned and clutched his head. He wasn't sure he could stand the loud chants and the singing. Couldn't we give it a miss and look at some quiet pictures? But he saw my look of disappointment, and said a few breaths of fresh air would revive him.

Blue and white domes towered, against another grey morning. The flash of a canal. I saw why it was known as the Marine Cathedral. Inside the iron gates and railings, black crones shuffled about, muttering to themselves; their paths seemed to crisscross, as if together they were weaving a spell to protect some obscene rite going on inside. A legless cripple on a trolley propelled himself around. I threw a few kopecks into his hat, thinking it was better to be safe. I knew about Holy Fools.

Inside, a bizarre, even bazaar, atmosphere: a mêlée, confusion, with queues for candles as if we'd entered a GUM. I'd heard that if we pushed further in, we'd see funerals taking place, as well as baptisms and blessings for the sick. But a couple of crones had grabbed Shimon's arm—perhaps his black leather coat made him look foreign—and hissed, "*Navyérkh! Navyérkh!*" pointing through an archway and up. We climbed winding stone steps. Male and female voices singing the Church Slavonic liturgy floated down to us. At last we stepped into the domed cathedral itself. I gasped. There was scarcely room for us to push our way in.

A sea of faith. I felt it, was battered by it. Not even at CND rallies in Trafalgar Square or Hyde Park had I seen so many thousands possessed by such fervour.

Bent crones. Candles being passed from hand to hand; or kopecks to buy candles. Whispers, nudges, rustles. Nobody standing still, yet somehow stillness. The choir sang from somewhere I could not see, and went on singing continuously. I could hear the theatrical chanting of priests but, being fairly short, I saw only the golden glittering iconostasis. Shimon and I were perhaps twenty yards from the back; it was impossible to move further forward.

All around us were the poor, the humble and despised; shabby people—like, I reflected, the early Christians. I hadn't seen these old and beggarly people on the streets, here or in Moscow. They had crawled out of the cracks, like the cockroaches in Moscow's Kosmos. In front of me, blocking my view, was a workman, a haversack at his feet. His head was shaven, and his body tilted awkwardly to the left. His arms were at attention, except when he made the sign of the cross. He reminded me of my father, coming black and exhausted from the pit.

I felt my eyes moisten embarrassingly. Glancing left, I saw that Shimon's eyes were fixed on the priestly drama in front. From time to time I stood on tiptoe to see, but generally I was happy to feel myself a part of this crowd. I caught, in the Orthodox harmonies—I decided they were coming from a gallery above our heads—the sweet sound of a Welsh chapel choir.

Was this, I began to wonder, a religious experience? I didn't think so. It was the emotion of belonging to a mass, a community, which I had known in my youth at miners' rallies but not since, except vaguely at peace-demonstrations. I felt myself almost wishing that I too could weep unashamedly, as many of the worshippers were doing; could cross myself, prostrate myself, and light a candle for the dead.

My legs felt cramped. Looking at my watch, I was amazed to see that over an hour had gone by. I moved my weight from one foot to the other. The shaven, awkward workman at whose back I stared never moved.

Others were moving; behind us, there was a constant stream of people in and out. And suddenly, as I glanced over my right shoulder, I saw a woman who had appeared from nowhere. She stood head-and-shoulders above the crones who surrounded her, and was distinguished also by beauty and comparative youthfulness. I found myself unable to draw my eyes back to the dirty raincoat of the Gogolesque workman. What struck me first about the woman was her proud, militant straightness; she stood perfectly erect, her shoulders thrust back, her eyes unflinchingly gazing ahead. Her stern face might have been made of granite. She wore a black coat, and had short black hair, almost hidden by a grey fur hat.

I dragged my eyes back to the front too—but a few moments later looked over my shoulder again. I tried to photograph with my eyes the turned-up black collar, the arms rigid to her sides. She crossed herself with infinitely graceful and precise movements of her arm and black-gloved hand. I became almost hypnotised by that ritual movement.

I found myself turning to look at her more and more shamelessly. And, almost inevitably, she became aware of my glance, and turned her head in my direction. My face burning, I jerked my head to the front. Shimon, sensing some disturbance in me, had followed my glance and he now furrowed his brows at me questioningly. I stared at the workman's back long enough to let my face cool, then irresistibly my head was drawn round again. I saw a tiny speck of white peeping from her clenched glove, when she touched her brow; and she flicked her eyes. She was crying. But with such simplicity, and without melodrama. I wondered why she wept. Was there some deep suffering? Did she think she saw or heard God? She seemed at once above, and at one with, the shabby crones around her. At once majestic and humble. Incense, and the unknown figure, made my head spin, my heart thunder.

Barash nudged me, and started to inch back towards the door. I followed, with a last glance at the woman. The sung liturgy, as an expression of her, lingered in my mind as we left the building. My throat was shocked by the rasping wind. Shimon hunched behind his coat-collar to light a cigarette, then muttered that he was dying for a piss.

I was too. We walked quickly, in silence, leaning into the gale. As we stood side by side in the urinal of the Bronze Horseman, I broke the silence by saying, "That was beautiful."

"Good."

We walked, then, to a restaurant and ordered some lunch. He was in an uncommunicative mood, for which I felt grateful. I could try to keep the woman's face from fading too quickly.

"Normally, at home, I'd be frying fish fingers for one of my children," I said, after an unusually long silence. He came out of a trance. "I'm sorry, Lloyd—what was that?"

"Nothing important. How's your hangover?"

"Oh, it's fine. I guess I'm getting a little nervous about this afternoon." The first round of the Championships was due to start. "Forgive me . . . So you enjoyed the Nikolski, h'mm? I'm glad. We could have stayed a little longer, only you seemed restless."

I confessed my vision of the Marine Cathedral. Shimon hadn't noticed her, but it sounded like Nadia Sakulin. A very fine actress. He knew her to speak to. "Yes, it must be Nadia. I

remember seeing her the last time I went. She's a regular
worshipper. A kind of stiff-upper-lip bearing? That's her . . .
You're right: she's very striking. If she wasn't a bit antique, I
might have tried my luck with her!" He gave an unpleasant
leer.

But he'd heard, anyway, she was pretty cold.

I said that hadn't been my impression at all. She had moved
me deeply with her secret tears.

"Well," he said, "she's had a hard time. Her husband was a
naval commander, but he drowned in the Baltic about three
years ago. She threw herself into the feminist movement—I
guess that might interest you—and as a result she's got into
trouble. She doesn't get many roles any more."

"Could I meet her?" I asked, my heart starting to quicken
once more. "I should interview a Leningrad feminist."

"It might be possible. I've a friend who should have her
phone-number." He leered again. "Of course, your interest is
purely professional!"

I smiled. "Of course!"

"What would you say this is—mutton?" He prodded the
vague meat.

"It's hard to tell."

"Not your English spring lamb, huh?"

The foyer of the Ostrovsky Theatre was crowded and buzz-
ing. As we entered, several people clapped Barash, and his
pen was out straight away, autographing programmes. I saw
him write a longer message on the programme of a rather
pretty girl, and she blushed on reading it. He had the looks and
confidence of a Wimbledon tennis star; in that foyer, the
tremor of young female hearts was palpable. He greeted some
of his rivals and introduced me to them. Half a dozen times I
was forced to explain that Lloyd was my first name and I

wasn't related to the famous Prime Minister. Selvinsky and his wife came up and chatted to me affably.

A warning bell rang. The glittering theatre enfolded us. We found our seats near the front. "Amazing!" I said, turning to wonder at the crowded auditorium, the tier on tier of lights. "We'll be happy to get seventy in the Purcell Room next summer."

"Well, you Londoners have so many alternatives. Here, we don't. Also, they come hoping for the unexpected. But of course, even Apollo would be circumspect, seeing the *Pravda* critic in the front row."

He asked what I'd be doing if I were at home; would I be taking my kids to the zoo? At seventeen and fifteen, I replied, they were a bit old for that. Maybe, in winter, a film or exhibition. They were visiting me more and more infrequently. Soon they would come no more.

The buzz of conversation stilled. Applause rang out for a dark-suited master of ceremonies. He announced the special guest: Settembrini, winner of the 1950 Olympic laurels in Alexandria and vice-president of the Italian Communist Party. The Russian strode off and returned, guiding gently by the elbow a tall, blind, stooping, white-haired man. Applause rang out. Brought face to face with the microphone, Settembrini bowed and, in so doing, struck his head. The bump rolled like thunder through the theatre. I heard Barash suppress a chortle. The old laurel-winner's hand was guided into a large bowl resting on a table. The master of ceremonies took from him the slip of paper and read aloud: "*Che Guevara!*" More applause rang out. The old blind bard took a step back, bowed his head, pondered, stepped cautiously forward, groping for the microphone. He began to speak in a hoarse, rapid, highly rhythmic voice.

I whispered: "How many know Italian here?"

"Even fewer than in Pushkin's day."

Histrionic in gesture, continually shuffling his feet, the old man gradually turned away from the audience, until he was facing the back of the stage, his voice inaudible. The master of ceremonies had to jump off his seat, take the blind bard gently by the shoulders and turn him round. He went on composing and declaiming as if unaware of the interruption.

The audience was springing to its feet, clapping and hurrahing. Settembrini clapped them back, then was led off.

"Wonderful!" said Barash as we sat down. "Didn't you think he was terrific?"

"I've no idea."

"My God, he can still do it! Impassioned, revolutionary stuff! At eighty-eight, he's still totally naïve! He still thinks he can change the world! Well, not exactly. He pretends. He's an actor, like all good *improvisatori*. His turn-round was calculated for effect . . . He knew he was talking through the back of his head . . ."

The dark-suited man strode on again, and announced the first round of the Soviet Championships. He introduced by name the twelve judges, from all parts of the Union; each name was greeted with polite applause. Shimon excused himself, and slipped out through a side-door. Respectful claps greeted the first contestant, whose name I did not catch. I was seeing again the vision of the Nikolski. That proud, erect head. Tepid clapping followed him into the wings; a roar greeted Barash, his black mane flowing, his leather jacket gleaming under the stage-lights. He bowed, and tossed back a stray lock. A woman behind me sighed. He dipped his hand in the bowl; unrolled the slip of paper.

"*Night!*" he announced, before taking a pace back and closing his eyes in thought. After a few moments he opened his eyes and stepped forward to the microphone. Sweat trickled

from his brow; his tanned skin appeared to have turned
pale.

A plain, middle-aged lady in the front row leapt up, with a cry
of "*Chudno!*" Wonderful! and she clapped her hands above her
head. I jerked myself out of a momentary lapse of attention,
expecting *Night* to begin; but apparently it was all over. The
whole audience except myself was following the example of
the lady in front by leaping up and applauding wildly. All
around me were shouts of "*Chudno! Prekrásno!*" Shimon had
already left the stage; he returned to a crescendo of clapping
and stamping, in which I now joined. I stood up. He had to
come back six times. As the acclamation faded at last, and we
resumed our seats, I caught whispers from all sides: "Wasn't
that wonderful!" "An extraordinary poem!" "He's even better
than before . . ." and so on.

Before the next competitor could be announced, I slipped
out, and made my way to the foyer. A few minutes later,
Shimon joined me. He was flushed with triumph. "What did
you think?" he asked.

"It was beautiful."

"Did you see that woman jump up? She's a niece of Andropov, and a great fan of mine . . . Almost maximum marks!"
He gave a crow of delight. I said he deserved it. The audience
had inspired him, he said. From now on, it would not be nearly
so atmospheric, since the competition would take place during
the day, when everyone was at work. "They could quite easily
stop showing plays for one week; but the bastards make sure
we don't get too much public attention. Still—" he punched a
fist into his palm—"that's not a bad start! Listen! Selvinsky's
beginning . . . Let's creep in at the back."

Selvinsky, whom Shimon regarded as his most dangerous

rival, was clearly thrown by the young Jewish *revenant's* success. He stuttered and stumbled; quite soon, he bowed and strode off, to modest applause. "He's fucking lucky to get that," whispered my companion, as the marks flashed up on a scoreboard. "Let's go."

A teenage couple rushed after us as we left the auditorium, holding out programme and biro. They gazed at Shimon with worshipful eyes.

We were fortunate in flagging down a taxi, and we sped back to the hotel in the darkness. He slumped back in the upholstery, evidently drained. The lights of the cruiser *Aurora* passed: the flagship of the October Revolution. We drew up.

He revived after his second glass of champagne; bubbled with triumph once more. A percentage of the first-round marks would be carried forward, rather as in ice-skating. Selvinsky would find it hard to make up such a huge gap in the semis and finals; and no one else had a serious chance of winning. Maybe, after all, he would get to the European Championships next summer, and I could show him Bermondsey.

"The image just came to me!" he chortled, knocking back his third glass. "And the metre and rhymes followed instantly. I think it was my greatest poem!"

"It was wonderful, Shimon."

He looked thoughtful. "*Night* was a strange theme to occur . . ." He explained that Adam Mickiewicz, the great romantic Polish poet, had won the laurel crown in 1824 with a poem called *Night*. It was his most famous improvisation, and had been interpreted as a secret cry for Poland's freedom. "The judges are responsible for the themes," said Shimon. "One of them, I'm sure, is using Aesopian methods to protest about the destruction of Solidarity. That's interesting . . . And the audience picked it up, believe me. They're experts in Aesop.

Maybe your English censor, Ilya, will have the effect of making your people more literate." He smiled sardonically.

We would celebrate tonight at the best Georgian restaurant outside Helsinki. We took the lift. The normally sullen *dezhurnaya* at the end of our corridor gave us an almost-friendly smile with our room-key. On entering, he went straight to the phone, saying he must tell his wife the good news. "Give her my love," I said, "And tell her I miss her cooking!" "I will. That will please her." I retired to the bathroom for my first Leningrad bowel movement. I heard faintly the mingled tones of triumph shared and husbandly affection.

By the time I emerged he had ended his call and was stretched on his bed. "What do you know about this guy Jones?" he asked.

For a Welshman especially, this was an unanswerable question, and I said so. "Your Socialist MP," he added a little more helpfully.

"Emrys Jones?"

"That's the guy."

"He's a good man," I said. "Intelligent. Eloquent. Bags of charisma."

"Is he likely to be important one of these days?"

Within a year, I replied, he would be in Michael Foot's cabinet; and there was even a chance he might eventually take over.

"That explains why we got given this fucking room," he growled. "His wife's in Moscow; she came over for the funeral. Now she's told them she'd like to see Leningrad. She's coming here tomorrow."

"Good Lord! I know her quite well. She's on the Women Against Violence committee, and I also meet her occasionally at CND meetings."

"Really? What's she like?"

"Nice-looking. Intelligent. Caring," I said, recalling auburn hair and freckles. "She does fine work with underprivileged teenagers in Hackney."

He gave an uneasy, slightly malicious, chuckle. "Maybe you won't need a Leningrad woman to screw," he suggested. "Maybe you can make out with your Mrs Jones."

Coldly I told him I didn't go round getting involved with married women. "I'm sorry; forgive me," he said, springing up, whirling into life and good humour. "Actually, this could be rather a pleasant coincidence. Her interpreter's a friend of Masha's. You might find her interesting. She's unattached at present and—who knows!" He danced around me, leering merrily. "She's kind of a dour woman on first acquaintance, like most of them. Not so outgoing as Masha. But there's more to this one than meets the eye. Yes, she could be your Russian fuck, my friend!"

I disguised with difficulty my revulsion. I had other things on my mind. "Well, let's go and eat," he said. "I could eat a horse. I always feel ravenous after a performance. Whether on stage or in bed."

He took a brush and gave his leather jacket a polish; slicked a comb through his hair; gazed at his handsome face in the mirror. I glimpsed behind him my own nondescript features.

"Could you do me a favour before we go?" I asked.

"Anything!"

"Try to call that woman—Nadia."

"Ah, yes—of course. Volodya may know." He riffled through a notebook, dialled a number, and spoke to his friend Volodya. With relief I saw him jot down a number. After some friendly chat, he rang off and re-dialled. My chest tight with anxiety, I heard him speak: identifying himself as an acquaintance, commiserating with her—she would have made a great Irena; telling her he had an English friend with him, called

Lloyd George, a famous journalist, who would like to talk to her about the feminists. "Till Saturday," he said. He grunted, and my heart fell. Covering the mouthpiece he turned to me: "She says she's very busy this week, except for tomorrow night. But we've got tickets for the Kirov. What shall I say?"

Plunging into misery I said: "I guess you'll have to say I can't make tomorrow."

Smiling, he took his hand from the phone and said into it: "Tomorrow night would be fine. Why don't you meet here in the bar, say eight o'clock? The Leningrad . . . We must get together sometime . . . *Do svidániya.*"

He put down the phone. "Thank you!" I said.

"It's my pleasure."

"You went to a lot of trouble getting those tickets."

"No problem. I have about fifty friends in this city who would lick my backside to have a ticket."

At least ten of those friends were at the Georgian restaurant. He hugged; was hugged. "This is my good friend Lloyd George . . . He writes about cricket, drama, workers' rights, sexism, racism, lesbians, and works for Ilya the censor . . ." But it was all good-humoured. A lively band played. He tried to get me off with a warm girl from the Institute for Arctic Studies. Empty bottles littered the table. I sang Welsh hymns, soft arms were thrown round my neck. I recall drunkenly begging Shimon to recite *Night* to us; recall him launching instead into an equally drunken panegyric to Mickiewicz, his idol, his god next to Pushkin; recall endless toasts, to Mickiewicz, freedom, friendship, love, women . . . Barash at last consenting to recite *Night* . . . Then I recall no more.

I sat waiting for Nadia Sakulin. Around me, German and Finnish businessmen were babbling raucously. My brain still felt a touch sensitive to noise.

All day—once the worst of my hangover had gone—I had felt a tender, adolescent excitement at the thought of meeting Nadia. Not for twenty years, since those Friday nights in Brum when I had waited for Alison, my fiancée, to arrive on the London train, had I felt such a trembling anticipation.

But she was late. It was eight-twenty. My heart was heavy; I was sure she had changed her mind.

Then I saw her, striding through the foyer. At least, I was fairly confident it was she. Away from the ritual splendour and emotional atmosphere of the Nikolski, and without the poor, bent crones to stand out against, she looked less striking. She was carrying a black coat. Her skirt and sweater were non-descript. If I had passed her in Oxford Street I would probably not have given her a second glance.

Yet, as she entered the bar-area and glanced uncertainly around, I realised that my impression of her had not been false. She *was* beautiful, in that strong and austere way which epitomised her city. I stood up, waved; she saw me and came up. "Mr George?"

"That's right." We shook hands. Her grip was firm. I pulled back a chair for her to sit. "I'm sorry I'm a little late," she said in English; "my cat has just had kittens. A neighbour's child came up to see them, and delayed me."

"That's quite all right. What will you drink?"

"Just a mineral water. I have to drive."

When I came back from the bar she was smoking. "Would you like one?" she asked, pushing the packet across.

"No. Thank you."

She may have noticed me flinch as a waft of smoke blew into my eyes, because she said anxiously, "You don't mind my smoking?"

"Of course not!"

"Some people have very strong objections."

I didn't smoke myself, I said, but didn't mind being with smokers—luckily, since I was sharing a room with Barash! She smiled slightly, and asked if I had known him long. My reply, that we had met for the first time a week ago, seemed to make her more wary. She enquired about my journalistic work, observing my face with care as I talked, then said: "So are you interviewing me? Are you going to get me into even deeper trouble than I'm in at present?"

I assured her I wasn't interviewing her, and would never write anything about her without getting her agreement. She seemed to make up her mind to trust me; her tensed shoulders relaxed. She stubbed her cigarette and lit another.

We moved from my life to hers. I sympathised with her bereavement and the tough time she was having in pursuing her acting career. Conversation began to run more easily. We talked of English and Russian drama; London and Leningrad; childhood and youth. Her father had been a dock-worker, killed in the war. When she learned that mine had been a coal-miner, a chord of sympathy and recognition was struck. She understood, when I spoke of the painful alienation which education can cause. It was a paradox, I said: my parents had made sacrifices to give their sons a good education; they had been immensely proud when we both got scholarships to University, yet there was also a loss. I recalled the walnut radiogram they'd bought in Cardiff; their bewilderment when I played on it my first LPs, brought home from a trip to London: the Modern Jazz Quartet and Schoenberg's *Verklärte Nacht*. My father had quietly left the room.

Nadia said she did not remember her father. That was even more painful. Gloom for a few moments filled her large, beautiful grey eyes. Gradually it cleared, as I explained that the Welsh weren't English and she told me a Russian political joke. Dangerously we tried to guess each other's age. I thought she might be about forty, but tactfully offered "Thirty-seven?" which proved correct. Most people think I'm a good deal older than I am, so I was rather flattered when she guessed forty-five. "Ageing is not a problem for a man," she said. "They can look more attractive as they get older."

I was nerving myself to mention Sunday morning, and to ask her if she remembered seeing me there, a rudely staring stranger, when I heard someone call my name. I jerked my eyes away from Nadia's, to see Angharad Jones standing a few feet away. My compatriot's fresh, freckled face wore an amused smile which said, probably, "I wonder if I should intrude . . ." I jumped up. She took a step forward. "I heard you were here," she said. "What a coincidence!"

She and her interpreter had just flown in from Moscow. They'd been invited for drinks by some city officials, and she'd just been changing some money.

"Have you time for a quick drink with us?" I asked her.

"A *very* quick one." She came inside the red rope.

"Angharad," I said, "this is Nadia Sakulin. Nadia's a feminist."

"Oh, that's wonderful!" Angharad exclaimed.

"Angharad is—" I was on the point of mentioning her famous husband but corrected myself in time "—very active in the Peace Movement; and Welsh too!"

They shook hands. Angharad asked for red wine, and I persuaded Nadia to drink one glass with us. I went to the bar. When I returned, Angharad was briskly questioning Nadia about the organisational set-up of the feminist movement in Leningrad, their numerical strength, etc. She wondered if it would be possible for her to sit in on one of their meetings, during her short visit. Nadia answered non-committally. Her shoulders had stiffened again. I tried to help the situation by asking her what was the main thrust of the movement in

Leningrad. She sipped her wine reflectively, then said—looking now at Angharad, now at me:

"I suppose our main thrust is against one-dimensional *homo sovieticus*, whether male or female. We believe our society is enslaved by secular values, and we must return to a religious conscience, a transcendental view of reality. Women, though they should of course be able to work outside their home if they have a strong vocation, are esssentially the bearers and bringers-up of children, the keepers of the hearth-fire . . . We seek an end to the horrors of casual abortion, communal *crêches*, easy divorce. We in the Club Maria do not believe strict logic can be applied to the relationship of the sexes. Men and women are equal but complementary. We think women should try to be pleasing to men, and in return we hope they will provide for us and our children. It pleases us when they are courteous—as, for instance, when Lloyd helped you into your chair. We don't wish to be dock-workers or coal-miners. In other words, we are totally opposed to the prevailing *ethos* of our society, in which women are the slaves of slaves . . ."

She drank. There was silence. Even the Germans and Finns seemed to have quietened, listening to Nadia's excellent English. A flame had risen to Angharad Jones's cheeks.

When Nadia wrote an address down on the back of an envelope, and said she would be very welcome on Wednesday evening, the Welshwoman put the envelope in her handbag but mumbled that it mightn't be possible—she thought her guide had arranged for her to go to the ballet that night.

She soon departed—an evident Westerner in her smart green trouser-suit, hurrying across the foyer towards the lifts.

"I think I offended her," said Nadia.

"She was shocked by your views."

She smiled. "Maybe you were too."

"A little, I admit. Though I heard in Moscow you Leningrad women took a slightly different line."

That was true, she said; and some of her exiled sisters had found themselves totally at odds with western feminists like Mrs Jones. "But—" her eyes twinkled "—I exaggerated the differences! I found her too bossy; too sure of what *I* believe. I hate people who *assume*. Anyway, what are *your* views?"

I argued—less strongly than I would have done had she been less beautiful—on behalf of women in my country who got bored to death huddling by electric-fires they couldn't afford to keep on; unable to get the most menial job; perhaps abusing children they hadn't wanted.

"Well, I can't argue with you about the situation in England. But the essential, whether there or here, is to believe in something beyond logic. How did you like the mass on Sunday? It *was* you I saw there, wasn't it?"

I nodded; asked her forgiveness for staring; confessed how strongly she had moved me. She reddened. It was the liturgy that moved me, she suggested; and the impact of faith: "You felt God there, perhaps."

I shook my head; confessed I was a non-believer, like the bishop my brother. She did not smile at my joke. Not wishing to create a division between us, I added that of course one had occasional pantheistic apprehensions; they came over me very often when I returned home to Wales and went hiking in the hills. I had felt them too while listening to the Nikolski choir. "—Don't they sing wonderfully?" Nadia exclaimed enthusiastically.

"They were magnificent!"

She lit her fifth or sixth cigarette. "You smoke too much," I said. She shrugged. "I know. You don't need to point it out."

"I was trying to understand what was in your mind at the cathedral," I resumed; "what seemed to give you joy and anguish at the same time. And I could *almost* understand. But don't you find it difficult, knowing that around you are people who believe very literally and simple-mindedly in a body of myths?"

"How do you mean?" she asked sharply.

"I mean, you are there worshipping on one level, and the poorer people are presumably believing very literally in the Virgin Birth and the resurrection and so on . . . I should have thought you'd find that disturbing: no?"

"*Verúyu.*"

"Yes, but in something intangible, something deeper, whereas—"

"I believe." She turned away her head, and looked upset.

"I'm sorry; I'm afraid I assumed—"

"You shouldn't."

Smoking her cigarette agitatedly, she stared into the distance. Then she said if one didn't believe in God there were no restraints on human action; anything was possible. That it was time for her to return and see to her family of kittens. I apologised if I had been crass. She suddenly turned to me, touched my hand, and said it was she who should apologise. "It's these people," she said, nodding towards the table of declaiming, guffawing Germans. Their noise had reached such a drunken pitch it was difficult to make ourselves heard. "I know I should forgive," she said, "but they killed my father and drove my mother to an early grave. I don't find it easy, especially when they come here and behave like that . . ." At a crescendo of braying laughter, she flinched. I begged her to stay a little longer. I placed my hand over hers, and she did not withdraw straight away. I suggested we could take a bottle to my room. She hesitated; another Teutonic bray and a thumping of fists on the table decided her. She would come up for a little while.

The surly *dezhurnaya* looked suspiciously at Nadia as she handed me the key.

Nadia stood by the window, gazing out at the darkness. "What a shame you're not on the river-front."

"Yes."

She stayed looking out as I put a bathroom-glass of wine into her hand. She sat in a chair, I on my bed, and we stared into our glasses. "It's the room," she said, and I saw her shiver. "It bothers me. It's bound to be bugged." She glanced from the phone to the radio, which I had found worked only fitfully. Sometimes, when least expected, it would crackle into life.

The room filled with smoke. Shimon had actually been very decent about not smoking often in our room; but I didn't mind Nadia's smoke. "What's this?" she said, stretching, touching my CND badge.

"The Peace Movement."

"Ah! Good . . . And this one?"

I thought quickly. "It's Aid State Health," I said. I explained about the savage cuts in the health service being carried out by the Thatcher government.

She smiled. "The iron lady!"

"That's a good description." I spoke about the weakest going to the wall, and Nadia said curtly, "We can't get near our wall."

She began to talk about her dead husband; of her loneliness. He had been away most of the time, as a submarine-commander, but the loneliness after death was different. So was the loneliness after divorce, I said. Thoughts of our partners, dead to us in different ways, brought the flow of sympathy between us once more. From her eyes, I began to feel that she liked me. I told her I felt happy, for the first time since my wife left me. "I'm glad," she said. "I feel very at ease with you too. It's strange, isn't it?"

Our hands met, and our eyes. She broke free—jumped up, saying, "Before I leave, let me try to prove God's existence for you!" She went to the radio and switched on. She turned the knob. Orchestral music came through the crackle. "Ah, Mozart!" she exclaimed. "Do you know this symphony? The *Linz*, I think."

I confessed I had always been rather deaf to Mozart. He seemed lacking in seriousness.

"But that's just it! Divine play! We are never more human than when we're at play. Who said that? Was it Schopenhauer?"

"I don't know."

She pirouetted to the music before sitting again and crossing shapely legs. "What music do you like, then?" She lit another cigarette.

"Well, I like jazz."

"Ah, so you can be playful too. I'm glad. I'm very fond of Armstrong and Fitzgerald."

"And I like—" I was going to say Stockhausen, but changed it to Beethoven.

"Oh—well! There I agree too. Of course! But there's something special about Mozart. If I awake from death to the sound of Mozart, I shall know everything is okay."

I blinked a sting of smoke, but kept my eyes on her. The vision of the Marine Cathedral blazed before me. Sorrow and animation, intelligence and playfulness, as we went on talking, joking, drinking. I had no idea what time it was, but dreaded Shimon's return from the concert. Passing behind her, after a trip to the bathroom, I took my courage in my hands, bent over, and kissed her. Startled, she moved her lips away . . . moved them close to mine, accepted the next kiss with the most delicate turning-away as she did so: my lips, scarcely touching hers, tingled. She sighed; said, "You're very nice. It's disturbing. I didn't expect this. I've not been attracted to anyone since my husband drowned." Our faces close, I touched her breast, gently. She let my hand rest there for a few moments, before lifting it to her mouth and kissing my palm. A thrill ran up my arm and along my spine. "There are eyes and ears everywhere," she said. "I have to go."

She stood. I took her hand and persuaded her to sit.

"I must see you again."

She shook her head. "This week is impossible: we're getting the *Almanac* out . . . I'd love to have been able to invite you for a meal. It would have been very modest, I'm afraid . . . Well, I suppose I could skip the Club Maria for once. That's the only possible time. Are you free on Wednesday evening?"

"Of course."

"Then . . . good!"

She wrote down her address for me, and—when I produced my *Progress* map—pointed out where she lived. I enquired about streets where there were people I had arranged to interview, and asked her advice on what I should see in Leningrad—the less obvious places, really just to keep her from leaving. She accepted a glass of mineral water and settled back. I did not hear her list of interesting buildings to visit; joyfully I kept all my attention on that strong, simply carved face. "I've fallen in love with you," I murmured, breaking into her travelogue. She flushed. "That's nonsense! You don't know me. I expect you've loved many women."

"No. Only my wife."

"Why did she leave you? Did you try to stop her?"

"Strictly speaking, I left her," I said. "She wanted me to stay, but for us to lead separate lives. I couldn't do that."

"Why not?" She looked at me severely. "Marriage is till death. You should have tried to see it through. You were wrong to go."

I stared at my clasped hands. She said gently, "No, it's none of my business. I'm sorry, Lloyd. I think your wife must be crazy to want anyone else!" I looked up into warm, smiling eyes.

"Now I must go! I'll use your bathroom, if I may." Returning, she drank the last of the mineral water, and picked up her coat. I helped her on with it. "It's been—wonderful but disturbing," she said, standing irresolutely. We embraced. A brush of fur. We kissed. The kiss endured. A shudder of joy passed through me as she leaned her head on my shoulder, whispering, "I like you too much."

After she had gone, I paced up and down; and stared at the faint sheen of puddles, far below the window.

I threw myself on my bed and was soon asleep, in my clothes. Barash, in the morning, made stupid remarks about a wild night, while I cherished the remnants of a dream. Nadia and I were in Petrograd; we wore the caps of the Red Guards. The *Aurora*'s gun boomed. We leapt for joy.

· 3 ·

Against a stage-set for *Three Sisters*, and before a small but enthusiastic audience, Barash performed his semi-final improvisation. Again he had been fortunate in his theme; spared the *Komsomol Heroes* that his rival Selvinsky would draw, he was able to employ his love of woman and beauty to good effect in *Nefertiti*. I saw in his portrait of the Egyptian queen the face of Nadia. Yet clearly Barash was seeing before him the more demotic features of his wife.

His marks were almost as high as in the first round. He was out of sight of his competitors.

I congratulated him, and we arranged to meet at the hotel. I set off walking. It was very cold, but I did not feel it. My steps took me along the Neva. The grey, turbulent, swollen waters fitted my unrest. Nadia was never out of sight. I recalled her "Marriage is till death," her chin lifted sternly. She was right. A recent article of mine, advocating a liberalising of the divorce laws, came back to haunt me; but there was no real contradiction, I felt. I sought—and for several years thought I had found—a sacred marriage, an absolute commitment.

The thought of not seeing Nadia for another thirty-six hours was dreadful. And after that—solitude again. "Stupid" my instant love might seem, but I was sure that I loved her, and would go on loving her.

I arrived at the *Aurora*. It encouraged revolutionary thoughts. I turned and strolled back the way I had come. I ought to have been interviewing dissidents, but it would have been pointless, I would not have been able to concentrate.

Suddenly I stopped dead in my tracks, a thrill of joy and horror running through me. It was as if the *Aurora*'s gun had gone off in my heart. I swayed, staring into water.

Defect!

Impossible!

Really? But why? Who would miss you?

I stumbled on: the impossible swiftly becoming the inevitable. True, I would miss my children; but they could come on a holiday sometime. Secretly they would be relieved they could have their Sundays to themselves. My parents, too, could come to see me. What else did I have to lose? Liberal values that seemed every day more threadbare, though every day I had to pretend as much enthusiasm for them. Girlfriends, of a sort, who, fed from childhood on those very values, maintained a listless existence only through increasing doses of pot, alcohol, cigarettes, valium or ideology.

My comrades of the CND movement, whom I had thought I liked, I pictured with sudden distaste.

If a taxi had been passing I would have thrown myself into it and headed for the University Embankment where Nadia lived. Instead, I rehearsed what I would say when the tedious hours had at last passed and I stood in her presence. Marriage, defection. She would tell me what to do, who to see. I would say I had loved my wife very much, yet never with this

intensity and purity. And, since love was the most precious
—perhaps the only—thing in life, I would be even crazier to let
this go. "So my fate is in your hands . . ."

Yet what right had I to assume I was important to her, on the
basis of one evening? She would surely laugh at the idea. I felt
this even more strongly as, returning to the Leningrad, I stared
at myself in a mirror. A "short, stocky" man—as Shimon had
by implication described me; with unattractive dandruff-
ridden red hair that stood up, glasses, and a slightly receding
chin. And Nadia, so beautiful!

I sought forgetfulness of my dream by running through
some of my notes from Moscow. A poor harried homosexual
who—ignorant of the rising threat of AIDS—was desperate to
get to San Francisco . . . While I . . .

I felt claustrophobic, choked; couldn't stay indoors. A thin
layer of snow had fallen, silencing my steps. I passed few
walkers; those few kept their faces shut and impassive. It was
not snowing; it was not *not* snowing: stray tiny pellets whirled
around me, against that background of grey river, grey palaces
beyond, grey sky. From the West's Kodacolour, if Nadia by
miracle said yes, I would be stepping back into black-and-
white photography. Well, that would be fine. I preferred
black-and-white.

I could even see a tranquillity in being told what to believe,
just as Christians must have felt in the Middle Ages.

The Soviets, I presumed, would make me welcome. I would
be a minor triumph; hardly to be compared with Nureyev or
Stalin's daughter, but I was a reasonably well-known journalist, and *any* defector from the West would surely be treated
well, if only for propaganda reasons. They would weigh my
publicity value against Nadia's modest dissidence, and the
scales would fall in our favour, I thought. They would want
me to obscure the romantic reasons for my staying. I was

perfectly willing to do that. We mightn't be able to meet openly at first; but in time I would naturally meet a Soviet woman and settle down. I would be given a job with a Soviet newspaper or journal; and—who knows?—the pressures I would start to feel might drive me to write, in secret, something worthwhile.

Nadia's flat, which as a naval officer's widow she had been allowed to keep, was apparently very comfortable by Soviet standards. Three rooms, she had said. Living there with her eventually, I would become—I confess to this thought reluctantly—privileged again, in relative terms; whereas, at home, I would never rise far beyond my squalid Bermondsey flat. My ex-wife would see to that. Relatively, I would be restored to the large detached house in Hampstead, not far from the Foots. Everything was relative.

These mercenary thoughts came and went, quickly—like the craving for a cup of coffee I had felt at the Nikolski, between my stares at Nadia. Nadia . . . Nadezhda. Hope against hope. The aurora, the dawn. Was it possible she might respond, or were these idle dreams?

I was striding along the bank of a narrow, murky canal, the Fontanka. Tall, imposingly baroque buildings soared on my left: palaces once, according to the *Progress* guidebook, and now housing official departments. My eyes drawn by one of the brass plates, I halted. Was it destiny which had led me to the offices of Spassky's journal, *Cement*? Despite Shimon's satire and moral slurs, I had liked what I'd seen and heard of Spassky on TV. On impulse I rang the bell. I presented my *Guardian* card to the dark-suited functionary who opened the door to me. He asked me to wait while he made a phone-call.

Yes, Comrade Spassky would be happy to see me for a few minutes. Would I come with him? I followed him into a lift.

None of that stuffy bureaucracy one finds at the BBC, say!

When I was ushered by a friendly secretary into Spassky's presence, I found the handsome, informally dressed editor dandling a little boy on his knees. The editor greeted me and shook my hand without standing, and introduced me to Vanya, his little nephew. It was the lad's birthday, and Spassky had treated him to lunch and later would take him to the Circus. The affection between uncle and nephew was clear to see; I recalled with distaste Shimon's slander about Spassky's liking for children.

Spassky's office showed none of the disorder predicated by Barash's improvisation. It was pleasantly informal yet with an air of purpose and efficiency. On the wall were portraits of Lenin, Andropov and Gorky, the journal's founder, and two landscapes in oils. I sank, at Spassky's invitation, into a comfortable leather sofa. His secretary took the child from him, and came back a few moments later with a tray containing a bottle of cognac and two glasses.

I apologised for breaking in on him; thanked him for seeing me. He said he was delighted I'd called; he warmly admired my newspaper for its support of progressive causes and its high stylistic standards. Spassky spoke in fluent English. He poured two generous measures of cognac, and proposed the toast of peace and friendship. We clinked glasses. I told him I'd heard his talk on Kitezh and enjoyed it very much. He blushed with pleasure; explained he had begun to write a libretto on the Kitezh legend. He and the composer with whom he was working hoped their opera would make a contribution to the Victory Anniversary celebrations. He lamented the small amount of time for his own writing that his editorial labours permitted him.

He wrote, he said, mainly at weekends, at his little *dacha* by the sea. It was a shame I was leaving Leningrad at the weekend;

otherwise he'd have been pleased to invite me out to his *dacha* for a meal.

I was thinking, "But perhaps I won't be flying out . . . Could it be possible I might one day find myself working for this man?" I could imagine worse editors, worse fates. We had, I discovered, much in common; not least that we were both children of the working-classes. His father had been a simple factory-worker. I began to see why, for all Shimon's generosity and friendliness, there was a certain gulf between us: he was the son of intellectuals. Such a person can never understand the emotional life of someone raised in the humble, warm atmosphere of a working-class home.

I found a second large cognac pressed on me. "One for the road." My head was spinning. The cover of the latest issue of *Cement*, presented to me, split in two. I expressed my unfeigned astonishment at the circulation-figures. One million! I contrasted it with the few thousands who read a similar literary journal in England—the *London Magazine*, for instance. I nodded and murmured in genuine agreement as Spassky ascribed the popularity of his magazine, and others, to the policy of treating literature as belonging to the people rather than to a small privileged class.

He stood. I stood, dizzy. We shook hands. His secretary appeared, to escort me to the lift. Spassky came running after me with my copy of *Cement*. I took the lift, and staggered out into the bracing Leningrad air. My heart felt light; but soon tightened with despair as I considered the impossibility of a miracle happening. Nadia would laugh at my proposal.

The evening and night that followed were sheer horror. I had to endure an evening out with Shimon, Mrs Jones and her tight-lipped bespectacled interpreter pretending sociability, while I could think only of Nadia, the next night, the fateful encounter. The Moscow guide dragged me into a dance between the crowded tables; Mrs Jones, I could see, was charmed by Shimon; and Shimon seemed not unattracted to the important, goodlooking guest.

Then, after we'd driven back in a taxi and I thought the torture was over, I found myself dragged to the women's room, which was along the corridor from ours, for a "night-cap". Angharad had brought some malt whisky. Also we must see the spectacular view from their window. I pleaded exhaustion, but they would have none of it—my arms were taken firmly by Shimon and Sonia. "Ten minutes," insisted Mrs Jones. "Don't be a kill-joy, *cariad!*"

I looked out at the light-streaked river. *Bol'sháya Nevá.* It could be "my" river for the rest of my life. If . . . The guide kicked off her shoes, took off her jacket. I saw the ugly outline of a black bra under her white blouse. She sprawled on her bed, sipping whisky. Angharad Jones vanished to get mineral water from the *dezhurnaya*; Shimon vanished also, to bring glasses from our room. I was left alone with a chain-smoking, square-faced, unappealing Intourist guide.

Time passed. "Where on earth can they have got to?" I asked.

She shrugged. "Maybe they're having a walk to clear the fumes."

That made sense, as far as Mrs Jones was concerned. It had been she who, at the first meeting of our Women Against Violence committee, had proposed a no-smoking rule; devoted to healthy living, she had met her husband, she'd told us while ordering dinner, on a vegetarian cycling holiday in Pembrokeshire. I wished I could have joined her in the cold night air; her interpreter out-smoked Barash; foul smoke forever curled up from green-painted fingernails—it did so now.

The green nails were an incongruity, since she wore no facial make-up. Her pale, impassive face stared at me from the pillow.

"I think if you don't mind," I said, "I'll go to bed. I'm really dreadfully tired; I hardly got any sleep last night."

"I think you should wait a while."

"Why?"

"They may be there."

"Really? Good heavens! I see what you mean."

"Can I not entertain you for half an hour?"

A thin-lipped smile.

"Well, of course, but . . ."

"Have a whisky."

"No, thank you."

"It's very warm. Why don't you take your jacket off—make yourself comfortable."

I took my jacket off. Turning on her side to flick ash, she coiled her legs up and I couldn't avoid seeing a glimpse of blue panties before she smoothed down her navy skirt. I realised I was in a classic situation, and that Shimon had engineered it.

The guide from Moscow told me some fairly amusing anecdotes about the people she'd interpreted for, and I smiled politely, stifling yawns. An hour, two hours, went by. Cigarette after cigarette was consumed to ash; I could scarcely see her through the smoke. It had been the same with Nadia —but then I hadn't noticed it. I was desperate for sleep, so that I would be fresh the next evening. But still Angharad Jones did not return. My eyelids drooped; my mouth tasted like the inside of a rugby-player's proverbial jock-strap. My companion had almost got through the bottle of malt whisky; her voice had become slurred and morose.

When the phone rang, I jumped in my chair. I'd dozed off.

The guide mumbled down the phone, frowning, then replaced the receiver. "Who was it?" I asked.

"Mrs Jones. She sounds angry."

"Where is she?"

"Oh, in your room. She seemed to think you've been here long enough. I simply don't understand."

I leapt from my seat, grabbed coat and tie; bidding her a hasty goodnight I rushed along the corridor. Our door was opened before I had time to knock. My compatriot hissed, "*O'r diwedd chi wedi dod!*" and pushed past me angrily. Shimon was sprawled in an armchair.

"Hello!" he greeted me. "What was that she said?"

"Something about coming. Coming at last."

"She got tired. I persuaded her to give you some time . . . Don't tell me nothing happened? Shit, I'm sorry; I thought you liked her and were getting on well, the way you were dancing with her. And I've had to put up with three fucking hours of socialism and feminism . . ."

Pages of Cyrillic script, as I fumbled blindly for my breakfast coffee-cup . . .

PROSECUTOR: Your name is Sonia Vinokur?

VINOKUR: That's correct.

PROSECUTOR: You know the accused?

VINOKUR: Yes. Slightly.

PROSECUTOR: Would you tell us how you met?

VINOKUR: I work for Intourist as a guide and interpreter. Last summer I was taking a party of English-speaking tourists around the Kremlin, and among them was the accused, N'dosi. He seemed very shy and rather lost. I felt a little sorry for him, and so I talked to him. He told me he'd just arrived to study at the Lumumba University. His Russian was almost non-existent. As a kindness, I offered to give him some extra coaching. I think we should be hospitable to visitors, especially when they are from countries involved in liberation struggles. N'dosi came to my apartment a couple of times a week for Russian lessons.

PROSECUTOR: (*Warmly.*) I wish more of our Soviet peoples were as generous to strangers, Comrade!

VINOKUR: Thank you.

PROSECUTOR: What sort of impression did you get of the accused?

VINOKUR: A favourable one. I thought he was a nice young man. He worked hard at his Russian, and quickly improved. He was sincere and idealistic. He obviously felt passionately about his people, the victims of *apartheid* and fascism. Yes, I liked him.

PROSECUTOR: You liked him. And did he like you?

VINOKUR: Yes, I think so.

PROSECUTOR: No more than that?

VINOKUR: (*Hesitantly.*) Well, I did begin to feel a shade uneasy. He would turn up at other times than when he was supposed to. I began to suspect that he was developing too strong an attachment to me. I think, in a way, I took the place of his mother. He's seventeen or eighteen, I'm thirty; he was in a strange land. It's not surprising he started to rely on me too much.

PROSECUTOR: Yes, it's understandable. But did you feel, perhaps, he began to see you not only as a kind of mother-substitute?

VINOKUR: Yes. He would become jealous if I said I was going out for the evening with a friend. He wanted to know who I was seeing. That kind of thing. I became alarmed; I tried to—keep him more at a distance, while trying not to hurt him.

PROSECUTOR: Would you please tell the court what happened on the morning of November 18 of last year?

VINOKUR: I was just getting up to go to work, when my door-bell rang. It was N'dosi. His head was bandaged; he told me he'd been injured in an ice-hockey match and had concussion. He just wanted to see me. I was really too busy to see him, but I made him a cup of tea. He seemed very disturbed, and I put it down to his injury. I made a phone-call to a friend—Valentina Rezanov.

PROSECUTOR: That's the widow of the deceased?

VINOKUR: Yes. Well, she'd already gone to work . . .

PROSECUTOR: Excuse me, why did you ring her? Did you have any special reason?

VINOKUR: Yes, I had a bad stain on a rug, and I was going to ask her if she could arrange for it to be cleaned. She worked at a cleaner's. Well, since she was out I spoke to her husband. We'd never actually met, but we chatted pleasantly for a while. N'dosi, who wasn't in on the beginning of our conversation, became violently jealous, convinced I was speaking to a lover. I imagine it was because of his injury. He was completely irrational. He snatched up my address-book, noted Rezanov's address, and rushed off. The next thing I heard was the news of Rezanov's murder at the hands of a black youth. I was absolutely horrified.

PROSECUTOR: You *must* have been. You must have been horrified that your kindness to a stranger had led to this tragedy.

VINOKUR: Yes.

PROSECUTOR: Were you told that a poet by the name of Rozanov was with the deceased when he was killed?

VINOKUR: (*Uncertainly.*)   I honestly don't remember. Perhaps.

PROSECUTOR: You know Rozanov, of course?

VINOKUR: A little. I've read some of his work.

PROSECUTOR: You haven't met him?

VINOKUR: Once or twice.

PROSECUTOR: Come now, Comrade—you've been sleeping with him for the past five years! (*A babble of voices.*)

VINOKUR: (*Faintly.*)   I—

PROSECUTOR: Well, isn't that so? (*Genially.*) It's not a crime, Comrade, to be a married man's mistress! Isn't that what you were?

VINOKUR: (*Distressed and agitated.*)   Yes.

PROSECUTOR: I can't hear you.

VINOKUR: Yes. I—I was.

PROSECUTOR: Didn't it occur to you that the accused was perhaps confusing the names Rozanov and Rezanov? It's easy enough to do.

VINOKUR: Possibly.

PROSECUTOR: Possibly? Well, I would have thought it very likely!

VINOKUR: My relationship with Comrade Rozanov had been over for several months.

PROSECUTOR: Really? Then please explain why you slept with him, and also with an American businessman and his mistress only two nights before the day of the murder? (*Public clamour.*)

VINOKUR: (*Almost collapsing.*)   I—How—?

PROSECUTOR: How do we know? It's our business to know, when a trusted employee gets mixed up in an obscene, unhealthy, decadent entanglement with enemies of our state! Do you keep a bordello, by any chance? (*Laughter.*)

VINOKUR: I . . . That situation was without precedent. I had too much to drink, and was taken advantage of. I didn't invite the Americans to my flat. Rozanov brought them unexpectedly.

PROSECUTOR: I see. Well, these orgies can crop up! (*Laughter*.) But let's get back to the point. I can understand your embarrassment, and your morals aren't on trial, Comrade. *You're* not on trial! You were teaching this young student, this stranger, our language: right?

VINOKUR: (*With some relief*.) That's right. He was doing very well. We were more than half-way through *Hot Snow*, a war-novel. I thought, if he could enjoy reading a story while he was learning, it—

PROSECUTOR: Oh yes, I agree, enjoyment is very important! Is that also why you were sleeping with him regularly? (*Hubbub*.)

VINOKUR: (*Choking*.) That's not true.

PROSECUTOR: We have witnesses from your apartment-building who saw him arrive, several times a week, usually around midnight.

VINOKUR: That was when—

PROSECUTOR: (*Genially*.) That was when you gave him hot snow! (*Roars of laughter*.) In point of fact, he didn't turn up that morning, did he? He arrived the night before. Well? Please answer. Or you needn't bother. We have many witnesses, and N'dosi himself will tell us so. You battened on this youth, didn't you? This stranger? You're something of a sexual harpy, wouldn't you say? Perhaps even a nymphomaniac? A black student that night; a middle-aged poet of dubious reputation, not to mention a foreign couple, the previous night—all at once! And the night before that, didn't you entertain someone else?

VINOKUR: (*Crying*.) Yes.

PROSECUTOR: A certain General Alexei Kolasky, who not

long after betrayed his high calling when our army helped to support our Polish Comrades? No?

VINOKUR: We were—we were friends. It had never happened before. (*Laughter.*)

PROSECUTOR: I'm sure it hadn't! They were all without precedent, isn't that so? You're not really a whore, Comrade! Not really a pole-cat! Not really a nymphomaniac! It was all completely accidental . . . (*More laughter.*)

"Morning, Lloyd!"

I looked up into the sparkling Celtic eyes of Angharad Jones. Beside her, her guide's square, unsmiling, Slavonic face.

"Oh, good morning! Good morning, Sonia."

"Good morning."

Around us, in the cavernous dining room the chomp of breakfasters. I'd long finished eating, but had sat on, immersed in *Cement*. The magazine had even taken my mind off Nadia.

"Please . . ." I indicated the untouched place-settings. "Do join me."

"No, we've had ours," said Angharad. "Sonia's taking me to the Hermitage. I'm very excited. What are you reading?"

I showed them the cover of *Cement*. "A magazine given me by an editor."

"How lucky you are to know Russian."

I said I was reading a most fascinating transcript of a murder trial in Moscow. I expected Sonia knew of it. She glanced over my shoulder and gave a slight nod. I was launching into an enthusiastic description of the prosecutor's pantherine stalkings—ironically, in pursuit of his own witnesses—when I found myself talking to the air: they were in a hurry; they must go. Picking at some remains of cheese, I finished reading the transcript. As soon as I had started reading it, the ground underfoot had shaken. It was *Isadora's Scarf!* So it was real! I was sure my colleagues on the ILEA committee hadn't heard of Rozanov either, and believed the play to be fiction, as I did. But why hadn't the Barashes told me? But perhaps they'd tried to. There was much I had missed, during my first few days, while my Russian slowly came back. I've since realised I ought to have known of Rozanov. His work is much less familiar to us than Yevtushenko's or Voznesensky's; but he's toured the West in his time, and his work is well thought-of.

Having begged the waiter in vain for a second cup of coffee, I returned to my room. I'd woken late: happily so, since it meant fewer hours to kill before my fateful meeting with Nadia. Shimon had already dressed and gone, leaving a note that he would see me back at the hotel for a drink after the finals. He was walking into the city, to clear his head.

I enjoyed an hour's solitude in my room, rehearsing over and over my speech. Not being an *improvisatore*, I needed to be word-perfect.

Still perfecting that speech, I stood alone in the crowded bar of the Ostrovsky.

I felt my arm gripped; turning, I looked into the warmly smiling eyes of Nikolai Spassky.

"Oh! Hello!"

"Didn't you think Selvinsky was splendid? And the old Latvian lady wasn't bad."

"Yes."

I had heard nothing of Selvinsky or the old Latvian lady.

"Come and sit down! We can squeeze up."

He persuaded sullen drinkers to make room on a long plush seat, and I perched at the end. "Of course, your friend will sew it up after the break. Everyone's talking of his *Night*—the greatest poem since Pushkin, it would seem: though no one can remember it. Was it good?"

"Extremely good."

"I wish I'd heard it. But I've had to put our December number to bed; this week has been sheer hell. And maddening, because all I've really wanted to do is work on my libretto. I'm on the final chorus—I always believe in getting the end right first—and have this wonderful vision of it: you can hear the faceless, slant-eyed Mongols thundering nearer to Kitezh; and the hero, a kind of Komsomol youth, gives the order for the city to sink below the lake-surface. All the citizens are massed on stage, with the golden towers behind them, and they go down under the water, singing 'Glory to Freedom and Rus!' Well, that's what I can see and hear in my mind. I have to find the right words."

His eyes glowed with excitement. "But I never have enough fucking time. I should give the journal up, but somebody has to do the damned job. Did you read the latest issue?"

I'd read some of it, I said. And I'd been fascinated by the trial-extracts.

"I'm so glad." He chuckled. "What a prosecutor that Glob-kin is! It's something new—a series of excerpted transcripts from actual trials, to show Soviet justice in action. I believe one of your compatriots—" he spoke the name of an English writer who had struck it lucky with a shrewd mixture of sex and violence "—wrote a completely twisted account of the murder. Have you come across it?"

"Yes. But actually I didn't know it was based on fact. I didn't read about the murder or the trial."

"Well," said Spassky, "we don't like to wash our dirty linen in public. But we thought the time was ripe to show that a poor young immigrant student can receive justice here. Two years for murder, followed by repatriation—and quite right too!

The lad was grossly mis-used. Whereas in Brixton, I read, a poor unemployed black kid got five years recently just for snatching a purse. Actually I'm hoping to persuade N'dosi to write his story for us. We'd ghost it, of course. But what a fantastic story it could be! Two months on the run, in the depths of a Soviet winter! The poor chap's been through hell. Far from home, in a foreign gaol. But with luck he'll soon be paroled and sent back to South Africa."

I couldn't, I said, quite work out why Vinokur had sounded so cool at the beginning, when she must have known her part in the affair would come out. Ah, said Spassky, that was where I was wrong: he was sure Rozanov and his mistress thought they had it all fixed. "Her father's physician to Chernenko, who was Brezhnev's favourite. I shouldn't speak ill of the dead, but there was a lot of corruption and fixing·towards the end of Brezhnev's reign. The prosecutor asked for a short sentence, a remarkably short sentence. Clearly there'd been a trade-off—N'dosi would keep quiet, and get off lightly because of extenuating circumstances.

"Unfortunately," continued Spassky with a chortle, "by May, when the trial took place, Brezhnev's star was waning. Comrade Andropov is a man of old-fashioned Communist morality. Someone from his camp must have seen an opportunity to strike a blow for justice in the N'dosi trial.

"By great good fortune I happened to be in Moscow, attending a board-meeting of *Progress*, and was tipped off that the trial might be interesting. Well, it was more than interesting, it was hilarious! Rozanov's an unspeakable character. His wife's been playing round for years with an oboist, but no one blamed her or tipped off Rozanov, knowing what a hell of a life she lived. They were here together, in Leningrad, when Rezanov was killed. Well. Globkin had two tapes played in court. One was a flagrant piece of fascist propaganda, which Rozanov had tried to smuggle out through the American couple he and his girlfriend had 'entertained'. The other, equally revolting, contained some nocturnal ramblings from a hotel in Gorky. Ah, the bar's clear: you'll have another?"

Spassky returned with two vodkas. We clinked glasses and toasted friendship and peace. Then he resumed: "Where was I? Oh yes: they'd also found some filthy stuff at Rozanov's *dacha*. Some lies about one of our finest mental hospitals, the Dnepropetrovsk, and a so-called poem slandering one of our greatest theatrical directors, Meyerhold. These also were produced in court. Collapse of the main prosecution witness!" Spassky chuckled involuntarily, spraying vodka. "He hadn't heard his mistress's evidence, you see; he started as coolly as Vinokur. Well, to cut a long story short, it was easy for the defence, supported by the prosecution, to show that poor N'dosi knew all about his rival's fascistic beliefs and—having suffered dreadfully under *apartheid*—burned with righteous anger. And jealousy too, of course, being in the hands of that whore. So, while concussed and mentally disturbed, he'd set off to execute Rozanov. Only, unfortunately, he got the wrong man—a decent writer."

Reflectively he sipped his vodka. The room was beginning to empty, and we were able to spread ourselves on the plush seat. "I wonder how all these students," he observed, "have managed to get an afternoon off to hear their hero, Barash? In my day, we had to work."

"And in mine," I said. "And felt I had a duty to—I knew how much my parents were sacrificing."

"True." He examined the palms of his hands. "Callouses! I've been doing a spot of digging at my *dacha*. I look at my father's hands, as tough as leather, and I feel guilty."

Our eyes met. A glance of sympathy, of fellow-feeling.

"Still," said Spassky, sighing, "we too work. For Communism. It will come."

Should I tell him I was not a Communist? But he must have assumed that. There was no point. I asked what had happened to Rozanov.

"Ah! Well, in the immediate aftermath of the trial, there was a certain amount of misplaced sympathy for him and his girlfriend. And people were a little shocked that the black had got off so lightly. But then a curious event turned the tide. You've heard of—or perhaps met—Signora Riznich, the Italian *improvisatrice*?"

"Yes—heard of her, naturally."

"Well, she was over here not long after the murder—performing with Markov. Take that how you wish." He smiled. "They had dinner with the Rozanovs. It was just before Rozanov's wife finally left him. Anyway, she must have got interested in Rozanov, because she brought him quite openly into one of her stories at the Olympiad. I don't approve of that. But these people have no literary morals."

I recalled my tape of "Spassky was a native of Leningrad", and blenched. I said, "Barash hinted as much to me. At least, he told me there was a broadcast which caused some trouble."

"That's right. Trouble for Rozanov! Our TV reporter from Finland was a pretty unsavoury customer called Troshin. He presented extracts each day. For some reason best known to him—probably to embarrass the government—he broadcast a large slice of Riznich's Rozanov scenes. They showed him in such a corrupt light that opinion turned right against him."

"So what happened?"

"He was arrested for offences against the State, but found unfit to plead. He's being treated in the Serbsky. It was clear he was completely schizoid. But the Serbsky has the finest psychiatrists; they'll help him, if it's possible."

The Serbsky . . . It had a terrible reputation. But it would have been pointless to have brought up the question of dissidents sentenced to *psikhushkas*. The love-train . . . The time would come, perhaps, when I could contribute to the struggle for civil rights.

"What happened to his mistress?"

"I've no idea," Spassky said. "I think she's still in Moscow. She hasn't committed any crime. She's just a whore and a pervert. It's a little odd for a white woman to want to be screwed by a black, wouldn't you say? It's not a question of prejudice, simply of—" he shrugged "—nature. I think we'd better go in. That's the second bell."

As we stood up, he gave me a quizzical look. "Are you thinking," he said, "I've been taking a pretty hard line—especially with a fellow poet?"

My expression evidently confirmed that this was so. He smiled, and put his arm round my shoulder. "I can see I must have sounded that way." His hand resting on my shoulder, we moved slowly towards the swing doors. "It comes back to our working-class origins," he said. "A hatred of privilege. What got at me was that they thought they could fix a trial, because of who they knew. I'm no hard-liner. Ask any of my writers. There's an awful lot I don't like—and corruption is the worst, Mr George."

"Let's hope Andropov will get rid of it," I said.

"He will, I'm sure. We need a cleansing fire." His eyes were grave. "I have to go right, here; and you?"

"Left."

We shook hands. I hesitated, then said, "I might need some advice. If I do, could I come and see you?"

He looked me shrewdly in the eyes. "Of course! Any time."

"Thank you."

As we were turning aside, he called, "Wait! Let me give you my home number."

Spassky fumbled in his breast-pocket and came out with a Polaroid snap and a biro. He scribbled on the back of the photo, then gave it to me, face-up. "That's my little *dacha*," he said. I looked at the bright Polaroid colours and felt instantly drawn to the cheerful white house, nestling amid trees. Blue sea sparkled through the birches.

"It looks lovely."

"It's very peaceful. It's a shame you won't have time to see it. But listen, should you ever be in need of a quiet, peaceful retreat—it's yours. During the week, it's empty. Thanks to this fucking journal I can only get there at weekends; my wife, who's a very busy doctor, doesn't even manage it that often. So remember . . ."

"That's very generous. I will."

His warm eyes seemed to see right into me. I felt sure he sensed what I had in mind. He slapped me on the shoulder and turned away. I followed two other stragglers through the door into the stalls, made my way to the front rows and slipped into my seat. A buzz of expectancy.

Barash strode on to the stage, rapturous applause greeted him from the half-full auditorium. He smiled, his eyes flashed; he dipped his hand in the waiting bowl; unwrapped his slip. His eyes bulged, his voice cracked as he announced, "*Mickiewicz.*" He stepped back; stepped forward. He opened his mouth but no words came. The audience started to murmur in consternation. Shimon bowed, and strode from the stage. Andropov's niece, to my left, buried her face in her hands.

Mid-afternoon dusk. I took a taxi back to the hotel. The windscreen-wipers flailed a snow-shower.

Entering, I caught sight of Shimon in the bar. He was

slumped over a bottle. I walked across. His suitcase and fur coat rested by his chair. I touched him on the shoulder and he jumped.

"I'm very sorry, Shimon."

"For what? Oh, because I died." He re-filled his glass and tossed the drink back. He stared, red-eyed, at the glass.

"Does it put you out of the running?"

"Of course it fucking does! I'm flying back to Moscow in an hour. I left you a farewell note."

A desk-clerk shouted out a number; he glanced at a taxi-docket in his palm, then re-filled his glass. "Get yourself a glass," he muttered.

I shook my head, but sat down.

"So you won't be showing me Bermondsey next year!"

"I'm sorry."

"I know too fucking much about Mickiewicz."

I was sorry to have to say goodbye to him, I said: though wondering if it would, indeed, be goodbye. I asked to be remembered to Masha; they'd both been very kind.

"Well . . . I'm glad you think so."

He pulled himself up straight on the chair. Gazing somewhere over my shoulder, he said, "Lloyd, my friend, I should tell you something. I've been struggling with my conscience. Maybe this afternoon's fiasco was a visitation on me. I was going to chicken out, leave without telling you. But I'm glad you've caught me."

He grabbed the bottle, tipped it up and drained it into his glass. He gulped. He fumbled for his cigarettes.

"It's not easy being a Soviet artist. You know that. I've been under a cloud. You're expected to give a little, take a little. Since I blotted my copy-book, I've had to give a little. I've had to appear patriotic—helpful. But I've never caused harm to anyone." He gulped from an empty glass.

"The fact is, I set you up to meet Nadia Sakulin. I called her and told her to turn up at the Nikolski. I don't think she's ever been to church before. She's Jewish, as a matter of fact. A Jewish non-believer. I knew you'd see her and fall head over heels for her. How could you help it? She's very beautiful. She's the finest swallow in Leningrad—possibly the whole of Russia. Are you okay? I know this must be a great shock. I'm sorry. She's a terrific actress. If I hadn't known, I'd have been taken in completely too in the cathedral. Astonishing. And she's also, of course, immensely intelligent and cultured. You must have found that out, the other evening. It's the swallow system of pedagogy, like I said. She went to the Leningrad school—the finest. It probably offers the best, most liberal, education in the world. Languages, poetry, music, drama, gymnastics, as well as the erotic arts which are neglected everywhere else, east and west. That's why a lot of bright girls, including Nadia, choose to go to them. It's about the only way of escaping the one-dimensional Soviet educational system."

I found from somewhere a weak voice to say, "I don't believe it."

"I'm sorry."

"She was even worried about our room being bugged!" I croaked.

"Of course! You're being set-up for this evening. Where's that fucking taxi? That's six numbers she's called while I've been sitting here."

"You know I'm seeing her tonight?"

"I know. I admired your English reserve in not telling me. She has a very nice apartment. The bedroom is very well provided with modern gadgets, many of which you won't see. Audio-visual equipment. You look ill. Shall I get you a drink?"

"No."

"Then some water."

"Yes."

His fresh, normally pleasant face seemed touched with the demonic as he came back with mineral water and glass. There was a haze before my eyes. I could barely hold the glass as I drank.

"I hate myself for betraying your trust," he went on. "Believe me. But I know Nadia. I know she's a decent woman, who does her job but never pulls any dirty tricks. She has her own moral standards, and the KGB respects that in her. Her orders, so far as you're concerned, are a straight fuck, that's all."

I shivered at the crudity. "Why me?" I stammered, seeing a glimmer of hope in the absurdity of their making such an effort with a nonentity.

"It's your name, my friend. Oh, I know Lloyd's your first name, but they're pretty stupid, these people, they just saw 'Lloyd George' and jumped to conclusions. And you've got a brother in the House of Lords."

"But only because he's a bishop."

"A bishop—exactly! Very important. The church can be a centre of dissidence. You saw that for yourself, on Sunday. A secret underground. Who was the first Decembrist, almost two thousand years ago? And look at Poland. They thought, if they could get at you, they'd have a toe-hold in your House of Lords. Besides, you're a famous journalist in your own right. But then, they almost don't need a good reason. They like to keep Nadia in practice."

"What about her feminism?"

"A blind."

"What about Sonia?"

"Sonia's straight. And so is Shura—Shura's a tart, of course, but honest and warm-hearted. I was trying to make it up to you. You should have had Shura, then maybe you wouldn't have fallen for Nadia. I wasn't surprised, though, when you turned Shura down. Me, I like fishnet stockings and French perfume; but I was sure you'd go for Nadia. Or rather, her type—because I don't know her, we've never met. I told my contact the kind of woman you'd like, and they came up with the perfect fit. You see, I don't only *tell* stories, I watch my audience. I sum them up. Do you really think I'd have expended all that energy on just one person, however pleasant? I observe . . . Your journalism, what you've shown me of it, reveals nothing of your inner life, which is to say your sexual life . . . I shall miss the plane if my taxi doesn't arrive soon . . . Your face, as I spun stories, revealed your inner life. You weren't turned on by fat women or skinny girls, orgies or troilism, fellatio or cunnilingus, sadism or masochism, big tits or small tits. You showed no particular interest in boots or shoes, suspenders and black stockings, silk or satin panties —you're dead straight. Well, we could expect that from an anti-smoking peace-loving left-winger. The only time I caught a flicker of excitement was when I brought in some lantern-jawed idealistic heroine. You go for the spirit, for a kind of Joan of Arc purity. You have a hunger for absolutes; you'd have fallen like a sucker for the Revolution. You like women with cleancut faces and short mannish hair. Am I right? Like Nadia . . ."

He gulped down the full glass of Ararat cognac he'd brought from the bar. He glanced at his watch, then stared despairingly at the desk-clerk.

"Of course," he said more calmly, "the bastards wouldn't trust my judgement. They had to check. That old couple in the train—they're psychologists from the Serbsky Institute. That's why I made up that pornographic tale."

"My God, my God," I mourned, staring at the broad, high windows filling with night.

Shimon nodded. "Our country is one massive theatrical illusion, a theatre of Meyerhold. They checked on me too, of course. Since we came back from holiday this summer our flat has been bugged. Well, Masha and I could keep our noses clean, making sure we said one or two nice things about Andropov—that cunt. So they tried me out with you. If it had worked, they might well have rewarded me with the trip to London, in spite of Selvinsky's victory. I take it he did win?" I nodded. "But now I've blown it by warning you."

Muttering "Shit!" he rose unsteadily to his feet and walked across to the clerk. He lurched back and sat down heavily. He laid his hand on mine. "You'll never forgive me. But I thought I was actually doing you a good turn. You really shouldn't leave our country without sampling a Russian woman. How can some blue film damage you? You're divorced; it's not as if you have a jealous wife. This is where they're so fucking stupid! If they tried to blackmail you, you could make a big story out of it. MY NIGHT WITH A SWALLOW. You'd bump up your newspaper's circulation, and your reputation with women would soar. All your friends will envy you like crazy!

"Well, that's the way I saw it. You've no reason to want to do me a favour but why not, for your own sake, go and have a good time? Nadia loves sex, she won't be faking that. And, believe me, you can trust her, she won't start asking you about your secret fantasies in the middle of a screw. Not that I imagine you've got any. Actually she likes you very much, she told me so this morning when she called me."

I blinked through the mist. My wife telling me she'd enjoyed the Italian class . . . yet somehow never learning a word.

The weekend "re-union" at Cheltenham Ladies' College . . . How long, I asked dully, had this been planned?

"Ever since you wrote saying you were coming."

A number was shouted; Shimon looked at his docket and said, "At last." He stood up, wrestling into his coat. "Don't get up," he said. "I hope we meet again some day, I really do." He slapped a gloved hand on my shoulder, and strode away.

I walked past the *dezhurnaya* without seeing her, and was summoned back. In the bedroom, intending to empty the ash-tray, I took the *Matroyoshka*-doll to the waste-bin instead.

I leaned against the window; saw in the pale sheen of puddles, far below, the drizzled coal-dirt where the lorry dumped our free coal every month.

Turning to face the room, the chair where Nadia had sat, I saw only a mist. I took off my glasses and wiped them, but the mist remained.

I threw myself on my bed. Shocked, as I had only once been in my life before, when Alison told me of her affair, I willed unconsciousness. It would not come.

For a moment, hope surged back: perhaps Barash had been lying. Disappointed by his failure, he had compensated for it by making up a cruel fiction. But no: he knew I was going to Nadia's. I'd kept it from him, not wishing to have my pure emotions besmirched by his filthy innuendoes; had excused myself from attending the last-night dinner on the grounds of a suddenly arranged and important interview.

And Nadia's appearance in the cathedral, at just that spot, seemed in retrospect entirely "arranged", stage-managed. There was no escape from the truth.

Even the elderly couple in the train. Of course! My soft Celtic expression always did give me away. How shrewdly the old lady, so reminiscent of my mother, had examined me.

I wanted to be undressed and bathed in the tin-tub in the kitchen, with Mam screaming at Bron to get ready to come in next: those warm, innocent days before Gareth and I paid for a bathroom-extension. Failing all that, I ran a bath and undressed. As I lay up to my neck in hot water, anguish began to give way to a curious relief. The turbulence of the past three days had vanished. I would not have to commit myself to a new woman, a Russian dissident; I would not have to defect. How absurd the idea seemed, suddenly. My life would go on much as it had done. I would continue writing my moderately radical pieces about drama, culture, disarmament, the class struggle, sexism, racism, the health service, civil rights, cricket, etc.

There were—after all—no big solutions. It was actually a relief to have that confirmed. And also to realise how shallow had been my eternal love for Nadia. The effect, largely, of Russian singing, a goodlooking face, booze, and my own emptiness.

I would go to Nadia's, because otherwise I would spend a boring, lonely evening; and besides, it would be fun to sleep with her. It would be interesting to see how she went about it. She wouldn't know that I knew, so I would have the upper hand. Shimon was right: it was laughable to think sex with a beautiful Russian woman would make me open to blackmail. It would, on the contrary, bring me credit.

I was not particularly bothered at the thought of being filmed. I wished I'd told Shimon I did have a mild fantasy: to be watched while making love. But maybe he knew that already.

Pulling myself up in the bath, I took the soap and flannel and began to wash myself purposefully. I would abandon my long-johns in favour of the maroon Y-fronts. Suddenly the silence was broken by a boom from somewhere outside. The bathroom-floor shook. Then another. Definitely an explosion. It was so inexplicable, I truly thought war had begun; the Americans were sending over some sighting shots. A third explosion boomed; I was already out of the bath, running to the bedroom window. Blackness. Nothing unusual. Yet another explosion, clearly from outside the hotel, but no light flamed in the darkness; nor were there shouts of panic. But *I* was in a panic, shaking uncontrollably. Were there Latvian or Ukrainian terrorists at work? My articles on IRA terrorism came back to haunt me; if I were killed by some nationalist explosion I would most definitely not understand. I rushed back, rubbed myself with the towel, and scrambled into my bathrobe.

No one in the corridor. Not even the *dezhurnaya* at the end of it—an ominous sign. I saw a light at the other end under Mrs Jones's door, raced to it and knocked.

"Come in."

They were at the window, wearing blue silk dressing-gown, Marks & Spencer housecoat: turned to me, surprised but calm. "What the hell's happening?"

"Come and look," said the Intourist guide.

I came and gazed out. Another boom; a Kalashnikov gun-shot; the Neva's sky flowered with a cascade of fireworks.

"We're thanking the Red Army for defending us during the Great Patriotic War. The turning-point of the Siege of Leningrad, forty years ago."

"Ah! Of course."

"Join us in a toast to peace," said Angharad Jones.

"Thank you."

"Would Shimon like to join us?"

"He's left for Moscow."

Angharad looked distressed.

"He fluffed his performance, I'm afraid."

Sonia looked distressed.

Clutching my taxi-docket, I perched on a bar-stool, feeling calm and numb. Since most guests were at dinner, the foyer and bar-area were almost empty. The barman and I desultorily watched a programme about art-education for blind children flicker on a small black-and-white screen.

My thoughts reverted to Spassky—who would not now become my boss—and the revelations about Rozanov and the trial. Later revelations had blotted them out; but the TV programme recalled to mind the report to our ILEA working-party on the Finnish Olympiad. Our "man" there, who represented handicapped groups on our panel, was a blind councillor; reporting unfavourably, he had specified the distress caused to him by a scene involving a Russian poet and a blind woman. I'm not sure if he didn't actually mention "Rozanov". At any rate, if I'd been on my toes I'd have seen the resemblance to the plot of *Isadora's Scarf*.

In retrospect, of course, as the only member with literary and Russian interests, I ought to have known that Rozanov was real. As I've said, he is not without a reputation. A blind-spot, on my part. There were even, I discover, a few voices of protest when it was learned that he'd been sentenced to a *psikhushka*. I can only assume I was too involved in my own problems—the divorce, and in wider issues— Cruise, the *Belgrano*—to notice. Well, it was of no particular moment; but my professional mistake added to my general sense of failure, of wasted life, as I sipped cognac, stared at brave little blind kids, and waited for the clerk to shout my number.

★　　★　　★

The taxi stopped in a street of substantial apartment-buildings, just off the University embankment. I buzzed Flat 5; Nadia's voice told me she'd be right down. In spite of everything, the sight of her clean-cut, smiling face, caught in a shaft of light from the entrance-hall, took me back to the cathedral.

I followed her up three flights of stairs. Shapely buttocks swayed before my eyes. Black trousers, white sweater, sandals, was hardly the attire of Olga, the traditional spy. Joan of Arc . . . Yes, I liked the way she looked.

She led me through her small hallway to a large living-room. It aroused an instant envy. My mind flashed, in fact, to our lounge in Hampstead: the Bechstein, a wedding-present from Alison's parents. A grand piano was the focus of this room, as of ours. Tasteful pictures, packed bookshelves. A rich-piled carpet, elegant modern three-piece suite, three or four large, well-chosen lamps, a discreet stereo-unit. I thought of the philosophy lecturer listening to Wagner on my expensive stereo. Curse my wife to hell.

"What a lovely room."

"*I* like it. Let me hang up your coat. Oh, what a nice jacket!" She fingered the lapel of my London-Welsh blazer. "There's wine—help yourself. I must see to the meal; I'm afraid something's boiling over. Make yourself comfortable, Lloyd."

"Thanks."

I sank into velvet cushions. I poured red wine into a blue glass. From the stereo, softly, the "Moonlight" sonata.

She returned and perched on the arm of the sofa. It was difficult to associate those large, beautiful, clear-grey eyes with monumental deception. I said I'd seen the sphinxes on my way.

"I've stopped seeing them," she said.

"Even when you look in a mirror?"

Smiling, I stared into her eyes, but she did not flinch. She simply smiled, as at a feeble joke, and asked how Barash had got on.

"He fluffed. He flew home."

She struck a match to light a candle; then lit a cigarette from the candle-flame. "Really? That's too bad. I spoke to him this morning on the phone, and he sounded very confident. Why do you think he fluffed?"

"You phoned him?"

"Yes, didn't he tell you?" She cocked an ear towards the speakers. "Oh, isn't that wonderful? I haven't played it for ages. That change of key . . ." She brought her attention back to me. "Yes, I was intending to ask him if he could take some copies of *Almanac* to Moscow for us, and to suggest I could give them to you this evening. But as soon as he picked up the phone I realised how stupid it was to involve you. Your taxi-driver will have reported where you are, and you could easily be stopped and searched on your way back. And then I thought, I don't really know Barash well enough either, so I dropped the whole idea. I had to find a quick excuse for having rung, so I asked if I could speak to you. He said you were dead to the world still. Why do you ask? You seem a little bothered about it."

"No, it's just that he knew I was coming here tonight, and I wondered how. You've solved the mystery."

"Didn't you want him to know? I'm sorry. I did mention it, I saw no reason not to. Was there?"

"Of course not . . . He told me you've never actually met each other."

Nadia frowned. "Well, we've *met*. We've shaken hands at a party, if you call that meeting. The summer before last, when the Taganka directors very bravely asked me to play Liubov Ranyevskaya in *The Cherry Orchard*." She nodded towards a large framed photograph of herself in Edwardian dress. "My last good role." She looked sad and distant, and brought her thoughts with difficulty back to the subject. "He has a reputation for decency. But I decided to hold back, just in case." She excused herself once more to go to the kitchen. "A few minutes longer," she said on returning. "It's nothing very grand, I'm afraid." She stooped to turn the record over. "Are you hungry?"

I nodded. "Is that your husband?" I asked, pointing to a photo on one of the shelves.

Without glancing at it, she answered, "Yes. Taken just before—before he drowned."

"How did that happen?"

She kneeled on the carpet, her face turned from me. "He was on the deck of his submarine at night; a freak wave swept him overboard. That's all they told me."

"He's a fine-looking man."

"He *was* fine-looking. And a fine man." She stretched towards the table to pick up her cigarettes again.

"How do you manage to live? Is there a pension?"

She frowned. "I think you're interrogating me. You want to write a feature, *Conversations with a Leningrad Dissident*."

Hastily I apologised. Her frown lifted. Yes, she lived on her husband's pension. It was not much, but she got by. At least, she did not have the curse—though it ought to be a blessing —of having a child to support. She told me the horrifying story of an abortion she had endured, in the first year of her marriage.

She had had German measles early in the pregnancy, so an abortion had been unavoidable. She queued up at the clinic for hours, then was dragged in with three other women; shown what position to lie in; told irritably to hurry up. The Novocain they injected didn't work till long after. The doors were open; those waiting their turn outside could see her rolling in agony, and the bloody mess coming away. Then she was pushed out and half-carried by two of the waiting women to another room, where she was alone, writhing, vomiting.

"This is the country which is supposed to care!" she said, taking agitated puffs at her cigarette, her eyes blazing. "They get through two or three hundred women a day in that clinic. My friends say it's not much better in the maternity wards. No decent treatment, no compassion, unless you can pay for it. The infant mortality rate is rising! Rising! And do you know why there's such brutality?" I shook my head. "It's because there was a total rejection of the female principle in 1917. That's why they could maul me about in that clinic!"

"It seems terrible," I said, "that something obviously intended to be enlightened—a woman's right to abortion—should lead to such horror."

She exclaimed fiercely, "Enlightened?" startling me. "How do you mean?"

"Well, it's obviously enlightened to allow women the right to choose—"

"But what choice does the baby have—tell me that!" Her eyes blazed. I flinched from her unexpected anger. "A foetus isn't a part of a woman's body, it's a soul!" She grasped her arm. "If it was growing here, on the outside, would you stand by while I burned it to death in this flame?" She held her arm to the candle. She was flushed, and panting.

"I'm sorry."

She relaxed. "No, *I'm* sorry. I lose control. Our meal should be ready."

"Can I do anything to help?"

"He would have been fifteen next month."

"This herring is delicious, Nadia!"

"Good. There's almost never any meat."

"We always used to have fish on a Wednesday, in my childhood."

"I knew that, of course."

The candle flickered, the wine slid down my throat. Like a Count in a Pushkin poem Shimon had shown me, "in half an hour I was half in love" again. The golden voice of Liubov Charents poured out melancholy, passionate Rachmaninov songs, and Nadia's eyes glistened with unshed tears. "Ah, Lloyd!" she lamented. "You have three rights we'd give up everything for—to believe in God or not, to read what you like, and go where you like . . . My poor country!" Then, rapturously: "Listen to those words! 'Ne poi, krasávitsa, pri mne,/ty pésen Grúzii pechál'noi . . .' How would you translate that into English?"

I pondered; said, "Do not sing, Beauty, in front of me/your songs of Georgia so sad." After a moment's silence we burst into laughter together, at the hopelessness of translation.

Touching my arm gently she said, "But I don't feel any distance between us. I'm glad you didn't tell Shimon you were coming here. He spoke suggestively even on the phone this morning."

Yet I had warmed afresh to Shimon, for having set this meeting up. Even for setting *me* up. I still wasn't completely sure. I kept recalling that, by his account, she was a superb actress. Yet as I remembered his fearless attacks on Communism, it struck me as exceedingly unlikely that he knew or believed we were bugged. His tale was beginning to look —like the debris on the table—decidedly fishy.

My knee kept brushing Nadia's; I stroked her hand. "You're a remarkable woman, Nadia," I said, a little tipsily; "and I love you."

She glanced away; traced an invisible hieroglyph on the table. "Are you sure you know what love means?" she asked, turning on me the full power of her deep grey eyes. "I think you're just searching for it. Wouldn't you say? Shimon, this morning, said he thought you were on some sort of a quest. I said—I should hope so! We should all be on a quest. But you mustn't think you've found what you're looking for in me, my dear."

"But I have, I'm sure."

"Really?"

Her eyes, moving close, seemed to become larger and larger; her index finger brushed my cheek. A thrill ran through me. I moved to kiss her; she turned her face aside. I stroked her hair, so trimly cut at the back that I could feel bone through it. I touched her cheek, guiding her mouth to mine. It was a very gentle kiss. The next moment we were clinging tight.

She tore her mouth away, pushed back her chair. "This is idiotic, pointless!" she exclaimed. She gazed at me mournfully; then her lips curled up at one corner and her eyes softened. "Come with me to the bedroom."

I swallowed hard. "Yes." I could hardly say the word.

She seized my hand, and I followed her from the room. She pushed open a door and switched a lamp on. Its glow fell on the pink cover of a double-bed.

Trembling I turned her into my embrace. She accepted it, but only for a moment before sliding away. She crouched down by the bed, motioning me to crouch too. I didn't know what was happening. I got down on my knees. She was holding up the pink coverlet. "Take a look."

At first I could see nothing. Then a humped shape, two small round green flames. At last, three or four tinier forms exploring the hump. "Aren't they gorgeous? She had them there. I didn't know where she'd got to, till I heard little mewing sounds under me one night. I must get her some more milk. Now, *that's* love!" She pulled out an empty saucer, sprang to her feet and left.

Feeling—not for the first time that evening—foolish, I got to my feet and loked around. A plain room. On the white wall opposite the bed was a wedding-portrait: Nadia, young and beautiful in bridal gown and veil; a handsome young naval officer; behind them, the eternal flame of—I presumed—the War Cemetery.

Books, a transistor-radio; on the dresser, a few items of make-up, and a bottle of Chanel. I could see no obvious hiding-place for a camera.

She came in with a brimming saucer, crouched, and pushed it under. As she stood up, she palmed from the bedside-cabinet a phial of pills and put it in a drawer. "My sleeping-pills," she explained. "I try not to take them very often. They make me dream too much, too vividly; but I've had terrible trouble getting to sleep since I've been alone." She switched off the lamp and we returned to the living-room. "When Ivan was away—which was most of the time—I didn't feel I was sleeping alone. Now I do."

Often in the night she got up and played the piano, she said. For a couple of hours or more. Softly, so as not to disturb the neighbours. She was standing by the keyboard, and she struck a chord. I asked her to play something, but she declined, saying her poor playing would sound even worse after Ashkenazy. I begged her, and she sat down. A Debussy score was open in front of her, but to my surprise she played a plangent melody from *Cats*, the Broadway musical; and sang the lyrics in a soft and husky mezzo.

Glancing at my watch I saw with astonishment it was indeed midnight, as her song proclaimed. I wondered if it was a hint I should leave. The mood of the feast had been broken; the atmosphere had become elegiac. Desperate to keep the evening going, I lightened the mood by re-telling a rather amusing anecdote related by Angharad Jones's guide: entertaining an Indian politician, she had nodded at the gypsy band and asked him if he would like anything. "Debussy," he had said. She'd said it wouldn't be possible, but he kept insisting. She'd kept saying no. At last he'd scribbled on a napkin, "W.C." I laughed delightedly—the anecdote seemed much funnier, now, than last night; but Nadia's smile was merely polite. "I've heard it before," she confessed. "That must be Sonia Vinokur?"

"Well, certainly Sonia. I don't know her surname. Vinokur!" Realisation dawned. I groaned and buried my face in my hands.

"What's wrong, my dear?"

"Please tell me I'm wrong! Tell me she wasn't involved in a murder trial."

"Yes, that's the one. We meet occasionally. She's told me that Debussy story."

"Oh, God!" I explained how I'd been reading her trial-evidence that morning, when she came by, and actually joked with her about the prosecutor's skill.

Nadia looked upset. "How cruel, to print that! Can't they let it rest?"

"Sonia Vinokur! Jesus! I didn't think! Every second Russian woman's called Sonia. But she kept her poise wonderfully."

"She's trained not to show emotion."

I said I found it incredible. She seemed so dull and nondescript. Nadia shrugged. "She must have something."

"But how come she's still trusted to interpret, Nadia?"

She smiled. "Guess."

"You mean—? Good heavens, I suppose so! It did cross my mind last night. She tried to seduce me."

"And failed?" She raised a mocking eyebrow.

"Yes."

"That's sad. You might have had some fun. 'Cleopatra', some people call her, very unkindly. Because she had a general, a poet and a youth, on three successive nights—as Cleopatra did in a story by Pushkin."

"Ah—yes! How odd . . ."

Nadia shuddered. "I can't understand a woman doing that. I can't even begin to imagine it, such promiscuity. And a boy of seventeen! God!"

"Rozanov," I said, "is how old? I can't remember."

"Early fifties? From his photographs he's quite a handsome man. Or rather, he was handsome. I guess he probably isn't any more. He's in a *psikhushka*."

"The Serbsky."

She shook her head. "He *was* there, for diagnosis. He was transferred to the Dnepropetrovsk *psikhushka* a couple of months ago."

So he was with old Boris . . . I told Nadia about *Isadora's Scarf*, and Rozanov's dream. It was obviously a prophetic dream, she said: by the author as much as by Rozanov. Or rather, nightmare. Now he was living it.

"And in a certain sense," she said quietly, "I was responsible for what's happened to him. And for Rezanov's death. Oh, without realising it, of course! I didn't know either of them, though I love Rozanov's work, don't you?"

"I don't know it well. But what do you mean, you caused it?"

Clasping her hands in front of her, she started to glide round the room. Despite her bell-bottomed black trousers, she took on the motion and appearance of a tight-waisted, wide-skirted lady of the Edwardian period. The transformation was clear to me even before she indicated her portrait on the wall. "Apparently Rozanov saw me in *The Cherry Orchard* at the

Taganka, and liked my performance. Enough to wish to see me again on TV, when a recording of it was broadcast, last November. It was because of me that he badgered his wife into finding a repairer for their TV, which had gone wrong. So, at any rate, he told a feminist friend of mine, who knows him quite well."

She stared at her Chekhovian face, then resumed her gliding.

"Otherwise, he said, he wouldn't have bothered about the TV set. They didn't watch very often, since they were trying to discourage their son from becoming an addict. But, because of me—although I didn't think my performance was particularly good—he'd got Nina, his wife, to ring round, using her influence; and he knew a repair-man was coming that evening. He didn't come—he was involved in a road-accident on the way; but a plumber came—a plumber who'd been sent for by Rezanov . . ."

"Ah, yes! I remember that . . ."

She continued in a cool, logical manner, but with a tremble to her voice: "Because of me, he expected a tradesman to call. Because he expected a tradesman, he let the plumber in. Because he let the plumber in, he had a funny story to tell Sonia when she happened to ring him. If he hadn't told her the funny story, she'd never have found out that her old school friend, Valentina, had a job at a dry-cleaning agency. Sonia had a coat she needed cleaning."

"A rug."

She shrugged. "They'd lost touch since her marriage. If Sonia hadn't rung the Rezanovs' number, her crazy black wouldn't have jumped to the wrong conclusion and dashed back to his hostel to change into Zulu war-gear . . ."

I smiled. "It seems very intricate!"

"Not really," she said, still gliding agitatedly like Madame

Ranyevsky. "Rezanov was murdered, and Rozanov is enduring a living death, because I performed in a play by Chekhov!"

She stood at her window, and twitched the curtain aside, gazing out.

"You're hardly to blame."

"No, but it's curious, isn't it?"

"Yes."

"But then—" she turned from the window, smiling "—you could say it was caused by a hare who died a hundred and fifty years ago."

"How is that?"

"Well, it was a little play by Pushkin that first made me want to be an actress. *The Stone Guest.* Have you read it? No? It's wonderful! But if Pushkin had been involved in the Decembrist uprising of 1825, he'd never have written that play. And he was only saved from being in Petersburg—and right in the midst of it, with all his friends—because a hare jumped out in front of him as he set out for Petersburg, a couple of days before. He was superstitious, and turned back home. It saved his life! And killed Rezanov!"

She gave a rich laugh, then covered her mouth with her hand penitently. "I shouldn't joke. It's not funny."

"It is! It is!" I laughed too. "I've just read about that in the biography I'm reading. He went back home and dashed off *Count Nulin*."

"That's right! His funniest, most carefree poem."

Shimon's wife, Masha—I remarked—would enjoy her train of coincidences. I explained Masha's theory of everything being implicated and involved.

"What's his wife like?" She had again twitched the curtain aside and was gazing out and down. "She's a physicist, you say? I thought she was a guide, too."

"She is. She lost her research post because of Shimon."

"Ah . . ." Her face was pressed against the glass. "And are they happy?"

"Oh, they fight like cat and dog, but they're very happy."

"I see," she said in the same vague, preoccupied voice, clearly not the least interested in Masha Barash. Letting go the curtain, she turned towards me, lighting a cigarette and taking quick, nervous puffs. "I thought we were being watched. A car stopped outside. But it's gone again. I think it's okay. What were you saying about Barash's wife? I'm sorry; I wasn't with you. You should go soon, my dear. I'll drive you back. I'm rather tired." And she yawned.

"I don't want to go."

"Well, I don't mean at once. Finish your drink."

She twitched the curtain again. "I don't want you to go either," she murmured to the glass. "It's been a lovely evening. But this crazy, terrible country! One can't even pass a pleasant evening with a visitor from abroad without being afraid—for him and for oneself. They'll question me about you. Shimon's wife will write a report on you. As for Sonia —God knows what they expected from her. I'm sure she's a decent woman, but the KGB must really have got their hooks into her, to allow her to keep her job. It's awful, awful!"

Silence fell. She rested her head against the frame of the window. Her arm hanging lifelessly, a long ash gathered on her cigarette, and fell.

"I'll go if you wish," I said. "I don't want to put you at risk."

"Oh, to hell with them!" she said bitterly. "Stay . . . for a while. I'd like you to. I'm not really tired. That was—how do you say—a white lie? I wake up at night."

She left the window and walked in an aimless, disturbed way around the room, crossing her arms and clasping her elbows. "It's all so complicated!" she exclaimed. "We make plans for happiness, but they go adrift. Something beyond us decides our fate." She glanced sadly at her husband's portrait.

I ached to rush to her, take her in my arms and comfort her, but dared not.

"We can't be trusted to know what's good for us," she continued. "And men most of all—" her eyes, finding me, seemed to accuse—"don't know what they want, who they want. Rozanov, for instance: he confessed to my friend that, when the Zulu struck, he felt—after the first shock, and along with sympathy for the widow and orphaned child—a relief. You know why? Because he'd got himself into a great mess, promising to take both his wife and Sonia to Armenia, his ancestral home. He knew the police investigations would save him from that problem. Well, he also felt annoyance, because Rezanov was about to give him some important information —I don't know what. God, what poor sinful creatures we are, Lloyd!"

Her footsteps brought her to the curtains again, and again she twitched them aside and stared out. She said over her shoulder: "Of course Rozanov's relief was short-lived. His wife left him anyway, taking their son with her, and Sonia wouldn't have anything to do with him, she was so stunned by what had happened."

"Did she have an abortion?" I asked.

"What? I've no idea. Was she pregnant, then?"

"I believe so."

"Then I'm sorry for her if she had to go through that too."

Silence fell. She stared out. I saw her through a haze, the room shimmering like a desert.

Wandering to the piano, I struck a few chords of *Smoke Gets in Your Eyes*. She turned from the window, surprised. "Oh, you play! That's wonderful!"

The Pump Rooms at Bath. Alison's Mum and Dad. "Do you row for your College, old chap?" "Isn't this Keble?" "Yes, Gareth's graduation . . ." "And is this your sister?" "Bronwen, yes." "Your parents look awfully sweet, don't they, Arthur?" "Frightfully nice . . ."

"Please don't stop." But I threw myself on the sofa and began to cry. I took off my glasses and sobbed. A release of tension and dammed-up emotions; a gathering conviction that Shimon had played a cruel joke on me, that she was no swallow and that my first feelings for her had been true. That she was my fate, my destination. She came quickly and sat by me, taking my hand, gazing puzzled into my face. "It's stupid!" I said, sobbing unconstrainedly. She laid my head on her shoulder and stroked my hair. My sobs eased at last; I snuffled like a child. She kissed my wet cheek. She let me embrace her and we kissed. As the kiss became prolonged, hysteria gave way to desire once more. She appeared to share my hunger; but wrenched her lips away, pushed my arm from her, and sat up straight.

"This is wrong," she panted. "We mustn't."

"Why?"

"Because I can't go to bed with you. Forgive me, it may be far from your thoughts. But I know how easily roused men can be, and this isn't fair on you. I'm not a teaser."

Stroking her arm, I asked why she couldn't go to bed with me. She was free, and so was I.

No, she wasn't free. It was too soon after her husband's death. Only three years . . . Yes, it was perhaps time to make another relationship, but she couldn't leap into bed with me after just two evenings. It wasn't her nature. And it was pointless. In a few more days I would go home, returning to my life and leaving her with hers.

I confessed, then, my thoughts of the past forty-eight hours.

Of marriage. Of staying in the Soviet Union. Nadia looked astonished, flattered, gratified, disbelieving. "You really thought of doing that?"

"Yes."

"What can I say? I feel immensely honoured. And astounded, But it wouldn't work, my dear."

"Why not?"

"I couldn't let you make such a sacrifice. I'm a dissident, a hooligan, in constant danger of arrest. It would be out of the question." She fumbled for a cigarette, lit up, put a barrier of smoke between us.

"Besides that," she went on, "there's a personal reason why marriage would be out of the question between us. I couldn't marry someone who didn't believe in God."

This was such an absurd statement that I smiled. "Why on earth not? Surely one can be tolerant of one another's beliefs or lack of them?"

"No, it's something fundamental. I couldn't go on living—" she pressed a hand to her bosom "—if I didn't believe that one day I would see my husband again, my parents, and others whom I loved. Whom I love. Living with an atheist—well, an agnostic, then—would be a constant drip of water on my head, wearing my faith down. I can put up with an atheist state because I have to; but I couldn't put up with an atheist husband."

"Shimon," I murmured, "said you don't often go to church."

She reddened. That was nonsense. Shimon didn't know her. Why should he say such a stupid thing?

"I don't know. But you could teach me to believe, Nadia."

"Faith can't be taught, only experienced."

In the stillness that followed those words, I tried to kiss her again, but she drew back. I buried my head in her bosom. She stroked my hair, saying, "When you were small, did your mother tell you what beautiful red hair you've got?"

"No."

"I think you need tenderness, don't you?" she murmured. I nodded against the soft sweater. Kisses would be enough, I pleaded; just that warmth would be enough. I lifted my eyes to hers. She said, "I've heard that before . . . It's not that I think you don't mean it, but . . ."

"They would be enough. Please . . ."

She brought our lips together. Then she was lightly kissing my nape, my ear, my throat, making me shiver all over. I felt something warm and soft and wet penetrate my ear, but so briefly I wondered if I'd only imagined it. I lost all control, fumbling for her breast but she pushed my hand away. Her tongue brushed my ear again, however, and I simply had to reach her breast, her naked breast. I tried to tug the sweater out of her waistband; she gripped my wrist, bit my neck. The bite inflamed me still further—I managed to claw her sweater up over her bra, which I yanked at, exposing a nipple. My mouth plunged, but a fist struck my skull and I had to let go. I felt rage that she wasn't a swallow. And—don't ask me to explain this—I saw in her for a moment that power-crazy bitch at Number 10. That schoolmarmish bitch who'll probably blow us all up. Her fingers were tearing at my hair, she was fighting me off but—so it seemed—drawing me in. Some nerve of pure pleasure, never touched nor threatened, jangled at my ear-drum. I pulled down at her loose trousers; found myself toppling with her on to the floor. The fall, and my weight, weakened her; her groin was hard against my erect penis. I tugged, touched stubbly hairs. She panted, "*Nyet.*"

Her trousers and briefs were off, my knee jammed between

her thighs. My penis was out and prodded the stubble, but the fierce effort had weakened my erection. Her nails scratched my cheek, I tasted blood on my lip. But her strength was ebbing; her nails, scraping my scrotum, was more like a caress. Her legs yielded, parted, I was gliding into her, with a feeling of wild triumph. She found new strength, thrust me off, and rammed a knee into my groin. I bellowed with pain.

Nausea flooding me, I staggered to my feet, clasping myself between the legs. I lurched, gagging, to the bathroom, where I vomited into the washbasin and over my shirt. I washed out my mouth, gulped tepid Neva water. I rested my head against the bathroom cabinet. The pain eased gradually. I zipped myself up and sat on the rim of the bath, my head in my hands.

I couldn't believe what I'd done. To have raped a Soviet citizen! I knew who was to blame—Barash. His "warning", from whatever sadistic motive, had created the frenzy which swept all control away.

It wasn't any longer a question of blackmail. I'd have been overjoyed to see the KGB walk in. I had to pray Nadia wasn't ringing the militia at that moment. Rape, in any language, was an ugly word. They might even shoot rapists in the Soviet Union—I had no idea; either that, or one of those twenty-fivers Solzhenitsyn wrote about. The hairs on my nape erected with terror.

I heard, with unspeakable relief, tranquil sounds. The "Moonlight" sonata again. When I entered the living-room, Nadia was sitting peacefully in an armchair, smoking. She waved the cigarette towards the sofa. I sat.

I murmured, "What can I say?"

She said tartly, yet with a blessed lack of real anger, "Did you say you were a co-opted member of Women Against Violence in your country?"

I hung my head.

"Or perhaps you don't consider that violent?"

"Of course. Inexcusable."

"Then why?"

"I can't explain it." My voice sounded remote and hollow. "It was when you put your tongue to my ear . . ."

"Oh, so if a woman puts her tongue in your ear that's an invitation to make love to them, is it?"

"No! No! It just made me lose control."

"I was taking you at your word," she snapped. "And trying to be kind, giving you a little pleasure, as I thought."

I groaned, "I know. Forgive me!"

Her voice became gentler. "It was partly my fault. I should have known better." Silence. The calming piano-chords. "I can't pretend I haven't thought it might happen. Not in that way, I mean. Probably that's why I put on trousers. I don't usually wear them. A protection!" A brief smile. "Shimon told me he thought there was a certain violence in you. Unknown to you, I suspect. He was right. It must come from the void in you, your lack of transcendental value, the vacuum, the West."

I raised my eyes. "Shimon warned me you were a swallow."

She frowned. "A swallow. What is that?"

"That you were ordered to sleep with me."

She gaped, laughed. "What! So you'd have a good time in our city? So you'd take back warm memories and write nice things about us? Shimon said that? How funny! You didn't believe him?"

"I wasn't sure at first."

Her smile faded. "Well," she said drily, "so this was your love! All the same, it was an extraordinary and unpleasant thing for Shimon to say."

"I know. And I've no idea why he said it."

"Because you are free," she suggested. "You can come here, but we can't go to you. We all feel dreadfully bitchy when we meet a free man." She heaved a sigh. "When did he say this? Before or after he'd spoiled his chances of going to London next summer?"

"After."

"Well, that's your answer."

We fell silent, listening to the last movement of the Beethoven. I had closed my eyes, and was picturing my ex-wife poised over the keys, when Nadia chuckled. Surprised, I looked at her. "A swallow!" she murmured, the corners of her eyes crinkling in amusement. "How rich! I must tell my friends in the Club Maria—they'll find it hilarious! Of course, these things do happen. If Barash hadn't been looking after you, you'd probably have had a friend of mine, Natasha, as your guide. She's given the American and English writers. I remember last year, around this time—just before Rezanov was killed, actually—she was ordered to sleep with her 'charge'. So that he'd write nice things about us. What was his name? I forget . . . I met him, briefly; she brought him to tea. He kept . . . how do you say it?—giving me the eye? Most uncomfortable."

"Did your friend enjoy her task?"

"No. But she obeyed orders. She was very glad when he left for Moscow. I believe Sonia was meant to look after him there, but she got out of it. I don't know who had him. So, it happens, Lloyd. But I'm afraid I don't do it!" She smiled. I winced.

I looked at my watch as the music stopped. It was two o'clock. "I'd better go," I said. "Can one get a taxi?"

"Difficult. I would drive you back but it might be tricky getting you into your hotel. You'd better sleep here."

I said it might make difficulties for her; but she replied that she was already a marked woman for entertaining me. She could sleep on the sofa.

I insisted, of course, that I take the sofa. She brought a quilt and a pillow. When she'd said goodnight, with a forgiving peck on the cheek, I undressed. I stretched out on the sofa and switched off the table-lamp; but sleep would not come.

I tossed for about an hour, then got up to go to the bathroom. On my way I saw that her door was ajar and a light was on. Something compelled me to glide up to the door and push it open an inch or two, just enough to glance in. She was lying on the bed naked, stroking herself between the thighs. Her eyes were closed. I tiptoed to the bathroom. My heart pounded. I gulped a glass of water. I sat on the toilet-seat, trying to make myself stop trembling. In the silence I heard the click of a lamp.

I waited a few minutes, then crept to her dark room. I pushed the door open and slid in; stood by the bed. A sheet covered her. In pale moonlight through the curtains I saw her eyes open. "Please, *cariad*," I whispered.

A hesitation; then she murmured, "*Khoroshó*." She pulled back the sheet. I saw her gently-curved, snowy breasts.

She put her arms around me, we kissed, she drew away, her head tilted, her lips parted, her teeth shining faintly in the dark. "*Listen!*" I listened. A mewing from beneath us. She let out her breath; smiled again. We embraced.

I flowed into her. It was like the ebb and flow of the Neva. I wept, for the second time that night. Whether she had learned to make love like that in her husband's arms, out of the depths of her Russian soul, or even in a school for swallows, did not matter.

She brought glasses of water; smoked a cigarette beside me.

Clasping her hand, I said I wanted to spend every moment of the next three days with her. No, she said, much as she would like that, she had duties.

I must have dozed off.

When I drifted awake, she was no longer beside me. I heard faintly the water-clear sounds of Debussy.

I felt suddenly desolated, beyond anything I had ever known before. I had had a vision of what life might be, and in the morning it would vanish.

I could not endure the thought of losing the vision. I opened the bedside-table drawer and took out the phial of sleeping-pills. I wrenched open the lid, and poured the tablets on to the cabinet-top. I picked up my half-full glass of water, put a tablet in my mouth, and swallowed. I gulped another, and a third. Nadia, dressing-gowned, appeared in the doorway; rushed to me. "What are you doing?"

"Peace . . . Peace . . ."

"How many have you taken?"

"Three."

"Thank God, that's all right. They're not very strong. You'll just sleep for about twelve hours." She swept the pile of pills into her hand, and carried them away. Returning, she climbed in beside me.

My eyelids were too heavy to open. Hazily I heard her chide me: "How stupid! Think of Sonia Vinokur's friend, locked in a *psikhushka*. Drugged on sulphur or haloperidol, very probably. Don't you think he'd like to change places with you? Would you like to be 'alone in the forest on the Dnieper's bank'? How ungrateful you are! You think Rozanov would try to kill himself if he were lying here in a warm bed with a passably attractive woman? You want to change places with him?"

"No," I moaned.

Less angrily she said, "In any case, what would I do with a dead Englishman?"

"Welshman," I mumbled. She put her arm around me. Cradled on her bosom, I fell asleep.

T·H·R·E·E

· LIUBOV ·

And the *troika* rushes on . . .
GOGOL

· I ·

One year before, that sphinxlike creature
—Nadia—had shown me round her flat;
I've met George too; he wrote a feature
On me—not wholly accurate:
"'Flu-struck, sprawled out in blue pyjamas,
He traced his ancestry to Thammuz . . ."
Not so. The relative who slipped
Me *Love-Train*, a stained manuscript,
Says ever since that short excursion
To Russia he'd seemed rather odd—
Nervous, and talking about God.
I'd heard, already, Shimon's version
Of what occurred in Leningrad,
And after. Mumbling, "*Cariad!*"

He woke, was greeted with a curt
"It's late! You'll have to hurry." George
Put on a washed and ironed shirt

And left: each step a Cheddar Gorge;
Yevgeni, Pushkin's stricken clerk,
Looked no worse, stumbling through the dark
Funereal streets. He paused beside
The Neva, trying to decide
Which bridge to cross. Over the lap
Of turgid, murky waters, he
Felt his bowels loosen suddenly;
That desperate gulp from Nadia's tap
Last night was probably the cause.
He crouched between a sphinx's paws,

Voiding a putrid Neva slime
Matching in effluence the Nile;
No one was passing at the time;
By Isis, though, the stench was vile.
Once back at his hotel, he crawled
Into his bed; later, he called
His editor—who said to him,
"Stay on, you lucky sod! It's grim
Here . . ." With the mad Falklands slaughter
Still pushing Thatcher up the polls,
Thanks to the simple-minded proles.
Next, Lloyd George tried to ring his daughter
But she was out. He slept—the room
Painfully ghosted by perfume . . .

Nadia, that night, at the Kirov,
Exalted and emotional
After some fine Rachmaninov,
Was bumped during the interval.
The man apologised for spattering
Her dress and then, amid the chattering
Bar-crowd, said she'd done very well

And they intended to "expel"
Her quite soon; they had chosen her
For an important job in Rome.
They'd let the English fool go home;
"He'll sing your praises, cause a stir
Against you here; you'll write about
The Afghans, say. We'll throw you out . . ."

Next day she spoke with Sonia: "Mardian
Fell for the bait." "That's wonderful!"
Said Sonia, picturing the *Guardian*
Eunuch, so exquisitely dull,
Goaded into an act of rape.
"It all seems to be taking shape
As planned; Kushin was so impressed,"
Said Nadia, "that I'm going west."
"*Chúdno!*" "But *is* it? I don't know . . .
Tell me the news about Shimon;
His defeat, surely, means he's blown
His chances? They won't let him go
To England . . ." "No, I'd say he's had
Two victories in Leningrad,"

The guide said, waving to Angharad
Jones, who was by the ladies' loo;
"My English protégée . . . She's married
To someone big . . ." "Did Shimon screw
Her?" "*Da.* And he was so impressive
In helping you; and seemed obsessive
Towards his wife—making it clear
He couldn't bear to leave her here . . ."
They'd liked the way he'd not pretended
Total conversion to the State;
He was a dissident, but "straight",

And it was plain that he intended
To soldier on, with bright hopes of
The new commander, Andropov.

"When he believed he could speak freely—
So they thought—in the train, at home,
He swore he'd fail as an Israeli
Artist," said Sonia. "He'd be dumb,
Like Abram." "Thank you for your warning
About the bugs—" "—Ssh! *Ah! Good morning!*
You had a nice walk, Mrs Jones?
Nadia, a friend . . ." In frosty tones
Angharad said they'd met already.
They saw Lloyd George walk by, a wreck;
He shook like a Kolyma *zek*
On sighting Nadia; had to steady
Himself; while Nadia thought, "Good Lord,
I slept with him! I *must* be bored . . ."

She played a waltz as workmen carried
Equipment from her living-room.
That weekend, Lloyd George and Angharad
Jones sat together, flying home,
And venomously talked of Thatcher;
Militia raided Spassky's *dacha*,
Tipped-off by colleagues who had heard
A love-train tape: a careless word
By someone who could not have known
The youngsters who *hääyöaie*'d and squealed
Were trainees in another field.
Spassky was in the house alone;
No boys—as Barash charged—were found;
Until they spotted fresh-dug ground . . .

While Sonia flew home to her sad
Bed, an old couple who had spent
A quiet week in Leningrad
Embraced their busy son, and went—
As soon as they had dropped their cases—
Along the love-train, scanning faces,
Hoping against hope they would see
The man who so disgustingly
Had spun a tale about vaginas,
Called the Creation of the World.
But though familiar hussies swirled
Brash skirts, and various male diners
Wore a familiar shirt or leer
"Thank God, that dreadful man's not here . . ."

In fact, Shimon was with his parents
—A boring duty. The next day
Sonia came round, and Liuba Charents,
Their friend, the famous singer. They
Talked freely, since the bugs had gone;
Though in a gloomy mood, Shimon
Proposed a toast to Nadia's rape
By which, it seemed, she would escape.
"I'm lost! Explain!" the singer pleaded.
"Someone raped Nadia?" "Yes. Our guest.
The creep you met—George. Masha guessed
He was exactly what we needed.
So Sonia told the KGB
That—if I helped them, naturally—

She thought someone like Nadia could
Persuade him into violence."
"I swore," said Sonia, "she was good;
They thought she lacked experience

And was, maybe, a little cold . . ."
The singer roared as they unrolled
The droll tale; Masha fell about,
And Shimon thought he *might* get out.
"Let's hope so!" his wife laughed. Then Liuba
Spoke of a future world-wide tour;
She'd meet him on some golden shore.
He said, "I promise!" "Where?" "—Not Cuba!
Bermondsey, maybe!" They roared again;
"God!" Masha said. "He was a pain!"

Midwinter. London. Lovesick, troubled
By guilt, George dined with Verity,
His daughter, and a long-haired, stubbled
Student of sociology
In red T-shirt and tartan trews.
"You'll be the next thing Thatcher screws—
The media . . . It's fascism . . ." George,
The nausea rising in his gorge,
Imagining Verity and him . . .
And grandchildren perhaps . . . said, "Right."
Then painted, in a roseate light,
Russia; though parts of it were grim
He'd seen no evidence of fear,
And peace was what they yearned for: *mir.*

His daughter, pausing to unravel
Spaghetti, said it wasn't true
That Russians weren't allowed to travel.
An old school-friend from Hampstead who,
While visiting the States, had been
Swept off her feet, at seventeen,
By a wild Russian in mid-life,
Surkov, and now was his fourth wife,

Was over here again, with Victor.
"They're hardly ever in Moscow,
She says they can just come and go;
Our immigration-laws are stricter!
Next month they're off to Venice," she
Added, a little enviously.

"Surkov's a rather special case;
But—sure—we over-simplify
The situation there . . ." A face
Across the restaurant caught his eye:
Dick Johnson's; plumper, sleeker, bland
As George's sorbet. Johnson's hand
Caressed the shoulder of a chick.
George wondered, was it politic
To tell him of his *alter ego*?
But their bill came, and George's pen
Signed away a small fortune; then
The kids, in Verity's Montego,
Zoomed away, waving, for Hampstead
Through fine March rain, well-wined for bed.

He rode the Tube back to his flat,
Dismal, anonymous; then took
To bed a novel, *Ararat*;
But knew he would dislike the book,
So dropped it on a squalid pile
Of clothes. The author's lurid style,
And themes of holocaust and lust
On every page, aroused disgust.
He'd take it on the train, and skim
Through it before the interview.
He picked a folder up, and drew
Some pages out; he had to trim

His piece about the feminist
Who'd just been exiled to the west.

"Nadia Sakulin," he began it,
"I have described to you before:
A woman with a face of granite
Pride and integrity, who wore
A grey fur hat . . ." He now revealed
What for her sake he had concealed
At first, that one night he had dined
Alone with her, in her refined
Apartment, and so on . . . The news
That Nadia was in Paris had
Brought joyful, painful Leningrad,
Its rapturous talent to confuse,
Back to him with electric force;
Brought longing, grief, desire, remorse.

Through *Figaro* he sent a letter,
Wishing her well; he'd love to meet.
"I'm tired; perhaps when I feel better,"
She wrote back. "I am in retreat."
But no one who observed her buying
Expensive lingerie, or trying
Chic dresses on, would have believed
Her tired, or sick, or that she grieved
For Leningrad. She did the sights,
In weather that seemed mild to her;
Her radiant face beneath grey fur
Turned heads along the Seine. Her nights
Were spent with other émigrés
And exiles: restaurants, operas, plays.

One émigré, with an exquisite
Queen Nefertiti in the hall,

Showed Nadia, on a weekend visit,
A sumptuous room where Braque, Chagall,
And Mondrian amazed the vision.
The connoisseur, with great precision,
Instructed Nadia what to do
When she reached Rome; above all, who
Her target was. She was astonished.
"Impossible!" "We disagree,"
The aesthete murmured suavely. "He
Was once—when he was young—admonished
For carnal acts . . . Oh, nothing much
From our standpoint—a kiss, a touch.

He has a taste for gracious women.
No one has put him to the test.
But see his face—it's only human!
At heart, he is a sensualist . . .
There's talk of a new Polish crisis;
The Church is backing it . . . That's Isis,
From the third dynasty . . . It's not
The time to chance another shot.
I've heard you are the ideal swallow.
'She seemed a pure *eirenikon*
Of flesh and soul'—the *Guardian*
No less! I love that slim Apollo
Found in the Vatican . . . Now we'll
Find you some 'bugs' you can conceal."

The Jeu de Paumes. A lemon-tea.
She murmured, "Que j'adore Renoir!"
To a man posed like Jacques Tati,
Lighting a pipe, behind *Le Soir*.
He casts a glance along the bench,
And says, in very Stratford French,

"C'est bon, oui . . . Moi, j'aime mieux Corot."
Nadia relaxes. He says, "So!
You're free! You took risks at the end;
'Birch' had it sewn up, but this chap
Barash might just have fouled it up;
You were too generous to a friend.
Here's Ivan's number . . ." Nadia scanned
The paper, clenched it in her hand.

"Sorry. The whole affair was hateful . . ."
"I'm sure. It was the only way.
Your husband understands." "I'm grateful."
"We knew the kind of swallow they
Were seeking, and were fairly sure
If you agreed to—bother!" "—whore
For them . . ." "—help them—blast this! You
Would be selected." "So you knew
Their target?" "Yes." "I think it's shocking!
His closest *confidant*! And mad!"
"He has an eye too soon made glad—
By cultured women—by bluestockings."
"Really? How oddly normal! Well,
Thank God, it's immaterial."

"Not so . . ." He stuns her by revealing
Her husband's a much bigger fish
Than she's imagined. While concealing
His doubts, he'd tested the *Kitezh* . . .
The secret fleet must sail as planned,
Only with NATO in command . . .
They'd change the systems if they found
Her husband hadn't really drowned.
She must obey the KGB.
His order seemed beyond belief;

Yet Nadia felt a strange relief;
A mild excitement, possibly;
No, let's be frank, a powerful thrill.
And she had months—at least—to kill.
"What happens if I should succeed?
They'd really let me—disappear?
I can just vanish?" "Yes, indeed;
You'll be completely in the clear;
They'll shrug and think, good luck to you."
"What about Poland?" "The planned *coup*
Is crazy: you'll save lives as well . . ."
Nadia walked back to her hotel.
"My dear, I'm sorry; things have changed,"
Was what the actress wished to say
When, late at night, she rang L. A.;
But Jack—Ivan—seemed so deranged,
So wild, so near the cuckoo's nest,
She thought a gentler break was best.

Then Nadia, brimful of misgiving,
Was greeted by the Kremlin's man
On a spring day, and soon was living
Discreetly near the Vatican.
A *Guardian* article, translated,
Made an impression; she was fêted
By cardinals and feminists.
One day a ring she gently kissed,
And stammered some Mickiewicz, sadly;
Which made the stooping figure turn
From the next soul—"Where did you learn
Polish?" "I speak it very badly.
I'm trying to learn it." "We must see
You're helped." He nodded graciously . . .

In Moscow, meanwhile, at a wedding—
Sergei's "ex" to an oboist—
Shimon saw Lev Selvinsky heading
Towards him, stumbling, clearly pissed.
"How's life, Lev?—You should nurse that cold . . ."
"There's no point—Sergei's *Meyerhold*
Poem was planted in my grip.
It's put paid to my London trip.
Who's got it in for me, Shimon?"
"God knows! That's awful!" Shimon, who
Had known for the past month or two
His journey to the West was on,
Made sure a case of *Ararat*
Walked to his fallen rival's flat.

Recalling George, he grinned with glee
Hearing the news that there had been
A landslide Tory victory.
Then he was in the air, between
Two heavy Writers' Union mutes
In sober and ill-fitting suits;
One of them stirred a flaccid hand
Pointing: the green and pleasant land
Rising to meet them; houses, spires,
A cricket match beside the Thames,
Acres of cars like sparkling gems
In bright sun—but wet tarmac, tyres
Sizzled. The Rubicon was past;
He gulped, for joy, free air at last.

The sponsors of the gathering, ILEA,
Hosted a party where Barash
Saw bearing down a squat, familiar
Figure; he conjured up a blush

As Lloyd George said, "Shimon! You came!"
"Hi! Sorry, I forget your name . . .
George! George Lloyd!" Hearing icy tones,
He swung round and saw Mrs Jones;
"I'd like a word," she snapped; and drew him
Away. "They tried to blackmail you?
Shit, we were bugged." Then someone threw
A playful punch: he hardly knew him,
His bearded brother. "Abram!" They
Laughed and embraced; she moved away.

The brothers, never close, soon parted.
Shimon stood wedged between a bum
Bearing the soulful words *Who Farted?*
And a red vest's *Shoot Tory Scum.*
Then, undeterred, the loathsome Mardian,
Leading a jumpsuit from the *Guardian,*
Boarded and bored him; she had cried,
The female said, when the landslide
Results came in: wept the whole night.
The electorate was crazy, blind.
"Just give them time," said George; "they'll find
What idiots they've been . . ." They might
Be speaking of the day of doom,
The Russian thought; such tragic gloom . . .

So this was England. Scruffy louts,
And women with no style or grace.
His "heavies" in their Moscow suits
Were the Beau Brummels of this place.
Except for one stiff-necked giraffe
Who'd strayed in from the *Telegraph;*
His vowels were choking on an asp.
All round, buzzed jargon, like the wasp

Sunk in his strawberries and cream;
The females spoke of bombs and Benn;
The only flirts he saw were men—
Fairies, as in Mercutio's dream.
England . . . a blind man shuffling by,
A "visually challenged" guy—

As someone—might it have been Ilya?
He had a Russian kind of beard—
Described him. English, that Ophelia,
Simple and rich, had disappeared.
The Purcell Room became quite full
As the Finn, Kauppinen, picked out *Hull*,
A theme unsuited and absurd.
The laureate's speech was thick and slurred
(He'd had a stroke); and his translator
Floundered at times; for instance, "Then
He anointed Väinämöinen"
Became "He dealt the masturbator
A grievous blow"—which brought a laugh
Even from the stately, stiff giraffe.

It seemed to fit a different fiction.
Or fact. In Sergei's mad-house ward
The slip caused by the old man's diction
Would not have seemed at all absurd.
The former head of a museum
Showed people round a mausoleum;
Kravchenko, writing on the floor,
Managed to go on asking for
His Earl Grey tea; an albatross
Kept on attacking a bald skull,
Which claimed that it had murdered all
Jews since the man hung on the Cross—

In fact, he'd worn the yellow star,
And lost his folk at Babi Yar.

Child-killer Spassky was complaining
Because his books from home were late;
A veteran soldier was explaining
How screwing a dead girl felt great.
One who jerked-off to it was coshed;
One cried, "Yanks, bomb us!" and one washed
His face with faeces he thought soap;
One glided down a dizzy slope
On skis; many were like stage-dummies;
Dawn glimmered, and soon "Ilse Koch"
Would burst in like a storm in Blok;
Rozanov comforted two mummies;
Then trembled at the harsh voice of
Ilse, whose real name was Liubov.

· 2 ·

To the faint hubbub of a picket
Of Jewish *émigrés*, Shimon
Plucked out a theme, and murmured *"Cricket"*
Into a moody microphone.
It brought a hush—what wretched luck!
By chance, though, he had learned *svierchók*
Was "cricket", having woken up
To chirrings and a milky cup
Of tea—he'd asked the pleasant maid,
Who'd let him fondle her a while . . .
That Needle brought here from the Nile . . .
Among vague images he strayed,
Then heard the god dictate his theme
And rushed headlong into a stream

Of rhymes, a river-surge of stanzas.
First, he produced a pistol-crack
By flicking at the mike. Then—
                              Danzas

And D'Anthès' second, D'Archiac,
Bent over Pushkin: his face grey
Against the snow, and damp, like clay;
It blended with the leaden sky.
This was more than the shattered thigh
He would admit to; he cried, "Stop!
My shot!" The Frenchman stopped, turned round;
Pushkin aimed slowly from the ground,
And fired; when he saw D'Anthès drop,
He cried in a weak voice, "Bravo!"
Then his face lapsed into the snow . . .

It lurched, a sinister phantasm;
The seconds walked beside the sled;
Agony flayed him, spasm on spasm.
Told that his enemy was not dead,
He sighed, "That's good." Then choked on vomit,
Thought he was flying on the comet,
White in the night-sky, he had seen
Above the Lycée at thirteen.
He talked awhile to his dead mother
As D'Archiac's voice from far away
Spoke gravely to a passing sleigh.
Je viens, maman . . . He tried to smother
A scream as yet another rut
Churned the ball deeper in his gut.

He fainted; came round in a carriage
Soft-springed and closed, provided by
The shadow-demon of his marriage.
Murmured, "I think I'm going to die;
I'm frightened, Danzas." Asked his friend
Gently to tell his wife, and send
His servant out. Through frosted glass

He watched the trees thin, *troikas* pass;
For the last time the city's lights
Glimmered for him; delirium
Swept through him as they neared his home;
"I must complete *Egyptian Nights* . . ."
That line of dots which said you died . . .
Within the poet's house, beside

The frozen Moika, sparkling glasses
Are being set for supper as
Danzas' snowcovered phantom passes
Straight through to where Natalya's
Conversing with the cross-eyed, third
Sister. He doesn't say a word—
The frump and the *krasávitsa*,
Made equal by this moment, are
Flying out to the hall; the dying
Man is dragged in; the women scream,
Natalya flings herself at him,
Sobbing his name, and then is lying
Inert: plain suddenly, and bloody.
Pushkin is borne into his study;

Lies on a sofa. Danzas lights
A lamp. The poet, shivering,
Keeps murmuring "*Egyptian Nights*,"
And asks a weeping serf to bring
Paper and ink. "No, you must rest,"
Says Danzas. "Let's get you undressed."
Fresh-linened, he grows calmer, and
Allows his wife to hold his hand
And fill the cup from which he drinks.
Unkempt, white-faced, she sits there, dumb;
Her light *amour*'s somehow become

Madness and grief. He murmurs, "Sphinx"
Thinking of the embankment steps
Where they've just set Amenhotep's

Stone sphinxes, dredged up from the Nile.
At last a doctor has been found;
Natalya leaves the sick-room while
A bustling German probes the wound.
"Well? Tell me honestly." "It's troubling."
Ringed with black clots, and fresh blood bubbling—
A tiny hole, the price of love.
"A scratch, a scratch"—and yet enough.
Gravely the doctor asks him whether
He'd like to see his friends. His gaze
Moves to a shelf where Shakespeare's plays
And Delvig's poems stand together,
And says, "Farewell, my friends . . ." They came—
His friends; and Spassky—not the same

Spassky who murders kids in play—
The family doctor. Faces bent
Close to him, but seemed far away;
Even his wife's. "You're innocent,"
He told her; then began to retch.
Recovering, he said, "Tell Grech,
If you should see him, that I share
His grief for his dead son . . . Who's there?
Ah, Vyázemsky! And Princess Vera!
My dears! You know I've seen a priest!
Sorry . . . This pain's a fucking beast . . ."
He asked if he might have a mirror,
And took leave of his haggard face
About to vanish without trace.

Along a river-bank he hovered,
The river from which no one drinks;
Lost consciousness, and then recovered;
Asked for—then pushed away—the sphinx,
His wife, exhausted in her grief.
An enema to give relief
From painful swellings in his side
Shot a fire through the tumefied
Rectum, and into shattered bones,
Gangrene and clotted blood. His scream
Woke Mashka from a pleasant dream,
High in the nursery. She hears groans,
Remembers her papa is ill;
Tears gather in her throat, and spill.

At dawn, the pain subsided slightly.
Still warm from bed and sleep, each child
In turn was brought to him, and lightly
He stroked them, talked to them, and smiled.
Then his mind strayed . . . "Gift of Isora . . ."
"It's 1937? What horror!"
"Please, sir, I left it in the dorm . . ."
Danzas, in his soiled uniform,
Lover of women, puns, and food,
Yawned as he heard his friend rehearse
Plans for a novel, play, and verse,
In one; said drowsily, "That's good . . ."
"Go to my desk; bring quill and ink . . ."
Then, once more shot beyond the brink

Of what was bearable in pain,
Pushkin asked for his gun instead.
"Don't let me go through that again."
Leeches were brought in; he was bled.

"I promise you, the swine won't live,"
Danzas, distraught, said. "No, forgive;
Peace, peace . . ." He sucked a cube of ice,
And murmured childishly, "That's nice . . ."
Rambled again, about a *troika*
That he was riding through the sky,
His writing hand invisibly
Stroking someone . . . Outside, the Moika
Stayed frozen. Agents watched the house.
The hooligan was dangerous.

The rogue had never lost his malice,
Though kept from harm by Benkendorf
And even honoured by the Palace.
"They landed, ate, and then flew off"
Had been the fellow's droll idea
Of a Report, from the Crimea,
About a plague of locusts there.
The mutiny in Senate Square
Came back to haunt the Tsar. The city,
Absurdly stirred by this event,
Was no less seething with dissent
Than when he'd had to show no pity—
A hundred exiled for their crimes,
Five executed. Ah, what times!

Elegant carriages belonging
To the St Petersburg *élite*—
Wigs, lorgnettes, epaulets—were thronging
The spacious diplomatic street
Where lived the rather useful stranger.
"Thank God, my Georges is out of danger!"
Cried Katerina, D'Anthès' wife;
Though, when she learned that Pushkin's life

Was ebbing by the hour, she shed
Tears for her sister. His arm bound,
Haughty as when he'd stood his ground,
The Frenchman lightly laughed, and said
To Princess Dolgorukov, "You
Can tell him I forgive him too."

His arm throbbed devilishly, keeping
D'Anthès awake much of the night . . .
Pushkin, who also wasn't sleeping,
Watched a moth burn itself in light;
His agony had eased of late,
Yielding to an oppressive weight,
A kind of anguish, stifling him.
All he had loved was growing dim.
Then suddenly he expressed a wish
For blackberries in syrup, and
Remembered his old nurse's hand
Dipping the spoon into the dish:
Requiring nothing but to live
For him, and endlessly to give . . .

As did Natalya now; transfigured
With joy, she said, "He'll live! You'll see!"
Strangely, her lover's shot had triggered
A change: she was all constancy,
Like Egypt dragging up the weight
Of Anthony . . . It was too late.
He sent discreetly to the plain
Sister a cross on a gold chain.
Why? *Alexandra's revelation* . . .
The story of the bed . . . is seen
As evidence there may have been
A mutual flame or consolation.

I wouldn't trust too much a note
A poet—even Zhukovsky—wrote.

We're told the spinster's face caught fire
When she was given the gold chain.
Another dawn broke. "Higher! Higher!"
He moaned, delirious again.
Then he described to Dahl his feeling
That they'd been climbing towards the ceiling:
Smiling at its absurdity.
A moment later: "Can't you see
I'm dizzy? . . . All right—but together . . ."
The clouds, the Neva, held their breath,
Anticipating Pushkin's death.
He breathed as softly as a feather;
Stars watched, through flurries of white ink,
Petropolis, the *troika*, sink.

Natalya, hearing servants sobbing,
Rushed in, as white as Nemesis.
(And still Georges D'Anthès' arm was throbbing:
Let's not belittle his distress,
Nor what, in different ways, the two
Unwidowed sisters were going through);
Natalya coiled convulsively
Around the ice-cold body she
Had shrunk away from in its heat:
Crying, "It isn't true! Forgive
Me!"—plunging her mouth to his—"You'll live!"
They carried her to her room—her feet
Pulled by convulsions to her throat,
According to Dahl's shaky note.

The poet, grey as Neva's stone,
Was laid out in his "lucky" coat;

A footman baptised with cologne
His master in the open boat.
His face, refusing to be mournful
For the occasion, wore a scornful
Smile. The black priests had come and gone,
The death-mask moulded, profile drawn.
The common people swarmed around
The house, and were admitted one
By one to see the fallen sun
Of poetry. And not a sound.
No one from the *nomenklatura*;
The city grew as dark as Dürer.

The Tsar was firm. At his command
Obituaries were suppressed.
And Benkendorf, the censor, banned
The first performance of *Stone Guest*.
All copies of a portrait bordered
In black were burned; all students ordered
Not to attend the funeral mass;
There'd be a roll-call in each class.
Thank God, when Meyerhold was shot,
We didn't ban black-bordered cards,
Our leaders didn't call the Guards
To spur their horses at a trot!
By *1937*, the news
Still hadn't reached the prison queues.

At dead of night, three sledges trundle
Out of St Petersburg; the corpse
Lies in the second one, a bundle
Rolled up in canvas, tied with ropes.

A sphinx, couched by this northern river
That's so much colder, starts to quiver,
Scenting the raw meat under straw,
And cautiously unsheathes a paw.
But for a sphinx, who lives forever,
Time is no object; it can sense
The building-up of violence
Here, round its new resort, the Neva:
A plenitude, a rich supply
Of blood—and lets the *troika* by.

Blind to the Neva's frozen waters,
Nikita's weeping—not the king,
In Pushkin, blessed with forty daughters
Perfect except they'd not a thing
Between their chubby legs—but only
A serf who's shared his master's lonely
Exiles and house-arrests, and so
Is used to dreary rides through snow,
And doesn't intend to be abandoned.
The old man's—to be honest—pissed.
Turgenev—not the novelist—
An old friend, rides the sleigh behind, and
An armed guard's in the leading sledge
Of the secret, dangerous cortège.

Across the plain the *troika* races.
Torches, commands, at staging-posts.
Fresh horses, tugging at the traces,
Rush onwards through the devilish hosts
Of snowflakes, morning scarcely breaking.
Another night. The next day, making
Mikhailovskoye, the estate;
Turgenev thinks of Lensky's fate,

Seeing the Pushkin house, forsaken . . .
"Shutters are up, and all is pale
And still within, behind the veil
Of chalk the window-panes have taken.
The lady of the house has fled.
Where to, God knows. The trail is dead."

The portly psychopomp's not sorry
The gloomy residence is past;
The trussed-up *improvisatore*
Is carried onwards to his last
Staging-post, where bells are tolling.
Nikita stays; Turgenev's rolling
On to Trigorskoye, some miles
Away . . . The mix of tears and smiles,
A blazing fire, the raw emotion
Of five unknown, warm-hearted girls
And charming widow—his head swirls,
His old heart trembles, in this ocean
Of female tenderness; it's clear
Why Pushkin loved to visit here.

They bring him tea, and he recovers.
They show him, proudly, Pushkin's script
Of Cleopatra and her lovers:
Ten leaves out of a notebook ripped,
And autographed. Around the pages'
Margins are merry *décolletages*,
Soft faces—Zizi's!—tiny feet,
Sketched in that very window-seat
Their friend and songster always sat in.
They smile about the man they mourn,
Their tearful sparkling eyes adorn
Their mournful dresses of black satin.

At length the daughters, aged between
The upper twenties and sixteen,
Have gone to bed. "Another nip of
Brandy?" "I'd better not . . ." Midnight;
He sits with Mrs Wulf-Osípov
By ember-light and candlelight.
She pokes the fire; he reads the story,
Prose mixed with verses, fragmentary—
Yet quite a find. "A riddle . . ." "Yes."
She runs a gnarled hand down her dress,
Then kneels before the dying embers,
Staring into them, sad, remote.
The floorboards creak upstairs. "He wrote
The verses right here—twelve Decembers
Ago," she murmurs. "Late one night . . ."
Her face wan in the flickering light,

She describes how, that day, Arsény
Their cook had rushed in with a tale
Of Petersburg in chaos: many
Deaths and arrests. The poet, pale,
Rushed out; she followed to the garden;
And learned how, hoping for a pardon
From the new Tsar, he had set out
For Petersburg; but turned about,
Oppressed by feelings of ill-omen:
A hare had streaked across the track;
A priest, then. "Had he not turned back,"
Explains the sad-eyed, grey-haired woman,
"He would have been there. So, of course,
He felt a terrible remorse . . .

We made him stay. And I consoled him
That night for missing the revolt.

The girls in bed, as now . . . I told him
The leaping hare was not his fault.
Here, by the fire, we started kissing—
I don't know how . . . Well, I was missing
My husband. I've been married twice.
The fire in me had turned to ice.
Or so I thought . . . His anguish moved me.
I know we did wrong; and of course
I looked at him with sad remorse.
He was so young. He said he loved me:
And then went after Anna Kern!"
She smiles. "We women never learn . . .

I think it pleased him to discover
I was—well, I can't find the word—
Pure? I had never had a lover.
The girls don't know—God! They adored
Him; and Alexis too, their brother.
What scamps they were! I was a mother
For him, that night, I think. Well, then
He wrote those verses, with my pen . . .
I guess I'm Cleopatra . . . Madness!
Why do I tell you this? But I
Can talk to you, I don't know why.
We're of an age, you share our sadness,
And you're as nice as Pushkin said!
It's late; and we should go to bed."

Yet still they lingered; she was charming;
Carnal desires seemed a sin
At such a time; and the alarming
Analogy of Count Nulín
Occurred to him . . . a sweet hostess
Whose eyes are deep, whose fingers press

Lightly, at midnight, her guest's hand . . .
Quite easy to misunderstand
If you're puffed-up with self-esteem;
But, unlike Nulin, this guest's shy,
Won't look his hostess in the eye.
On her pale bosom firelights gleam . . .
Grief makes him shiver; would she press
His hand, outside his bedroom? Yes.

Then offers softly a bed-warmer
That once had warmed the poet's feet . . .
Dark blustery morning threatening storm, a
White-bearded priest rushed to complete
The liturgy. Osipov daughters,
The mother, her two small granddaughters—
Solemn-eyed—huddled in their furs.
Turgenev, gentle man, defers
At the graveside to the weeping
Nikita tottering forward. Dust
Of mother takes her son's weight, just
Like wife and husband used to sleeping
Together in one narrow bed;
Yet only close now they are dead.

Later, Turgenev and Marya,
One of the youngest of the girls,
Visit Mikhailovskoye—see a
Dark peasant-lad with glossy curls
Running alongside, poking out
His tongue at them. "The little lout!"
Turgenev growls. "It's Pushkin's child,"
Murmurs the girl. "Good Lord!" So wild—
What would he breed? (In fact, the poet
Rozanov, proud there's not a trace

Of blue blood in his common face,
Stems from that stock, but doesn't know it.)
Turgenev, sniffing country air,
Remarked, "Our friend seems everywhere."

Marya blushed. "He sowed confusion
Everywhere, yes; but also fun . . ."
Laughter and high jinks, in profusion—
Jumped over tables, fired his gun
Into the trees, the girls all shrieking . . .
She spoke of when he'd last come, seeking
A little peace, two years ago.
His wife, she muttered, seemed a crow,
Unworthy of him . . . They had skated,
She said, together, on that lake.
"His marriage—yes—was a mistake,"
He sighs. "If only he had waited—"
She starts; then stops, and bites her lip.
They clutch hands. The ground slopes. They slip.

"How old is Pushkin's boy?" "Eleven."
"Born in his time of house-arrest?"
Marya nods: "When I was seven."
Everyone cried when he confessed.
His seamstress, called Kalashnikova . . .
"Why do you ask?"—Oh, reading over
His manuscript, that fragment of
Creative joy and fateful love,
Composed in that same era. Only
The verses, she corrected. Then,
Blushing afresh, confessed that when
He came, the last time, sad and lonely,
She'd watched with him the Northern Lights,
And helped inspire *Egyptian Nights*.

She was the tall, aristocratic,
Beautiful phantom of a dream,
Sensitive, haughty, enigmatic
Young lady who had drawn the theme.
He had sketched Zizi—he had told her—
To please her, being plainer, older,
And rather sad. "But it was I,
Not Zizi or Aline." A sigh
Burst from her young breast; he was thinking,
"I'd really like her as my niece,
Or daughter even . . . Well . . ." Some geese
Honked, and the sober sun was sinking
Over the blue-grey hills. He thought,
It's all a mesh, a net. We're caught.

Life's like Madame's stone-jar . . . A snuffling
Old house-serf opened up the chill
Rooms where their friend had languished, shuffling
The cards, or gnawing at his quill;
They almost saw the poet scrawling
At that card-table, with night falling
Outside the frosty pane it faced.
Turgenev shivered; the girl traced
Some letters in the dust. They wandered
Through. The worn mildewed cloth, a shelf
Of cues with which he'd played himself,
Through days and years as he had pondered
Trochees. Loneliness. "Let's go . . ."
Back to Trigorskoye through snow.

"Dinner is ready . . ." A prodigious
Sturgeon. The ladies sombre, he
Spoke of his work in the religious
Affairs bureau, quite solemnly

And at great length, anticipating
His journey back, the papers waiting.
Across from him, Marya hid
A yawn. The conversation slid
By slow degrees back to the scandal
Leading up to the duel, the death.
A freakish draught, a gust, a breath,
Suddenly blew out the candle . . .
A hand slipped off Marya's shoe,
And stroked—as Pushkin used to do—

Her foot! So shocked, she was unable
To speak, or cry out, or draw back
The foot he felt beneath the table!
What should she do? A kick? A smack?
Why, he was older than her mother,
Balding and fat . . . She'd had to smother
Her laugh, with Pushkin, his free hand
Lifting his glass of champagne, and
Talking so earnestly—as *he* did—
She simply couldn't believe it! Still
Blamed modern morals and, until
Someone re-lit the candle, kneaded
Slily her ankle—instep—toes!
Did she imagine it? God knows!

Even while Barash was performing
His piece, so wholly off the point,
Rumours that he was drugged were swarming;
Someone had seen him with a joint.
News-hounds were gathering for the kill;

His marks were as expected: nil.
Lloyd George caught Shimon's arm: "Bad luck!"
The Jew: "I couldn't give a fuck,"
But strode back to the dais quickly
And said "Objection!" languidly.
"'Cricket' was Pushkin's nickname." He
Jumped down and left a rather sickly
Panel of judges to confer
In a demented cricket-chirr.

They'll meet tonight in full committee,
He's told at last; and Shimon nods,
Gazing high over Shakespeare's city
At where serenely sit the gods.
The action has to be much faster,
It's said, they're heading for disaster,
Barely two hundred thousand souls
Are watching—less, even, than for bowls.
Shimon says *Shalom* to his brother,
Then, flanked by his two hoodlum chums,
Strolls out on concrete walks—the Thames
Afroth with rubber sheaths and other
Testimony of summer—clears
A barrier, and disappears . . .

His wife, when she was brought the news
By stern-faced men, burst into tears
And sobs, with pauses to abuse
Shimon and stammer out her fears
That they will make her cross the border
And join him. No, they reassured her.
"I want an immediate divorce
From that—that traitor!" "Yes, of course."
Later, she telephoned a lover:

"The bird has flown. Is there a chance?"
"—Oh God! I'm leaving now for France.
Let's see, when this world-tour is over.
I'd like it, darling. I can't promise . . .
Yes, yes, I'll post your work on to Thomas."

Then Masha wrote a painful letter
To *Pravda*, an outraged attack.
Life for them both would be much better.
With luck she'd get her old job back.
Yet at the end they'd both been tearful,
And Shimon sombre, doubtful, fearful.
They'd murmured tender words, and hugged,
For the first time since they were bugged.
Ten years, even of unhappiness,
Was a long time. Yet she was free,
For physics and for poetry!
Free of domestic cares and stress;
No pile of socks and underpants
To wash! She did a little dance.

If Liuba moved in later—why,
Her cup of joy would overflow!
Late had she found out she was "bi",
And even Shimon didn't know.
Well, time would tell . . . Meanwhile, she sat
And with a glass of Ararat
Toasted their freedom. Then, though tired,
She wrote her Ph.D., inspired.
As if to prove her theory right—
That a carp's fin in Lake Sevan,
Fluttering, affects a New York fan—
George, on the South Bank late that night,

Strolling out from the Purcell Room,
Saw, like a spectre in the gloom,
The florid face of Liuba Charents;
A poster. He went home to Wales
The next weekend, to see his parents.
The Inter-City flew, the rails
Clicked tonelessly; his coach was crowded
With loutish exiles. The sky shrouded
After the Severn. A *svierchók*—
Shimon's defection was a shock—
Clung to the dusty window, chirping
That George, too, glided towards the dead
Like the dead poet on his sled.
A Welsh drunk rolled against him, slurping
From several Guinness-cans at once.
The air was blue with "fucks" and "cunts".

West, to the Valleys, the death-theme
Went with him; he was coming home—
By taxi, slowly, in a stream
Of caravans—to Abercwm;
Father on the harmonium
And mother's welsh-cakes. "Our Lloyd!" "Mam!
Da, how are things?" His cough, much worse.
Same tasteless pictures, pious verse,
Embroidered, on the mantelpiece;
Same china dogs; same musty damp;
Same awful pink shade on the lamp;
Same roast potatoes filmed with grease . . .
He took two packets from his grip,
Late presents from his Russian trip:

Red Army choir, and balaclava.
His frail, declining parents showed

Him snapshots from the Costa Brava.
And yet the sunset sky which glowed
Above the reclaimed slurry-tip
Allowed him poignantly to slip
Into an earlier self as he
Undressed. He tossed uneasily
In his old bed, the mattress lumpy.
Next day, he didn't feel so bad;
Old neighbours called him *cariad*;
He bought his Dad a pint of scrumpy
And chatted, mostly about sport;
The village lived on life-support

Now that its heart, the pit, was dead.
He grieved to see his parents shrunk
In stature; Dad, a fervent Red
When working down the pit, had sunk
Into a stupor; eyes that burned
With anger once, were now concerned
With patterns for a bathroom-suite,
Like Elsie Tanner's in the *Street*.
He can no longer seem to feel
The struggle of the working-class,
The education-cuts, the mass-
Redundancies in coal and steel.
It's old age and lost lungs. Midway
Through George's summer holiday

(There'll be a weekend with the kids,
In Devon, in a caravan),
A battered Ford Cortina skids
Up the grim terrace; a plump man
Climbs out: it's Gareth, George's brother.
"*Cariad*! where will you sleep?" his mother

Wails. But he's just passing through
To Cardiff, where he'll launch a new
Branch of the Council of World Churches.
Bron and her husband come to tea;
Mam has a weep . . . Her family . . .
The table's too small; Bronwen perches
Upon a sofa-arm. She's quiet;
Doesn't eat much; is on a diet—

Or finds the short reunion tiring.
Her husband, a farm-labourer,
Feels out of place, she knows—perspiring,
And trying to talk posh—like her.
Though the stuffed shirt and purple vest—
As Taff will call them—do their best
To put the awkward man at ease,
Coaxing him out, and by degrees
Slipping into their childhood speech—
"Barry John? Bloody brilliant, mon!"—
She senses that it's all a con;
Her brothers are far out of reach.
Gareth drives off; soon Lloyd goes home;
He feels as weightless as the dome

Of Paul's, and tower-blocks of the city.
Plunged into work straightway: a tense
And stormy hour with the Committee
Of Women Against Violence,
The only male among the nine
Muses. He'd pleaded to resign
On grounds of pressure. They'd refused.
From there he rushed off to a bruised
Group. What a flop! At least the scandal
Had kept some interest alive.

They turned their thoughts to '85,
The tercentenary of Handel—
A massed schools' orchestra and choir
Performing, on a barge, *Messiah*.

His summer flew. He dreamt of heaven
One night, and spoke to Gabriel,
A party member. Storms in Devon,
The box-like caravan, was hell.
One August evening, he sprang back
In terror—a gigantic black
Stood at his door, in a *kaross*
Or Zulu mantle. At a loss,
The youth retreated to the hall;
Crept back. "You got some sugar, man?"
A neighbour—gentle Cardigan.
O Christ! The Brixton Carnival . . .
Coincidences come in swarms,
Like bees or ants or summer storms—

George met up with some fellow-members
Of Sanroc, to oppose some tour;
One of them asks if he remembers
A pledge he honoured, years before,
To educate a clever ghetto-
Kid from the shambles of Soweto?
"I think you pledged two quid a week
For his school-fees in Mozambique."
George vaguely nods. "I've heard from him!
Here, read it—he's done brilliantly.
He's got a Soviet degree."
George gives the letter a quick skim
Then lets it drop into his lap.
N'dosi . . . "Christ! *I* killed that chap . . ."

A few nights later, as he slept
Through a tumultuous thunderstorm,
He stole into a house and crept
In darkness towards a sleeping form
In a wide bed. Somehow the room
Reminded him of Abercwm
Where he had uttered his first cry
In 1939—July
17—the very day his knife
Plunged down at throat and breasts and thighs,
Finally rooting out the eyes
Of Meyerhold's unfaithful wife!
George screamed and woke. "Thank God, I'm home . . ."
I hear piano-notes from Rome—

We'd better see how Nadia's faring.
But first—George hears that "*Bozhe moi!*"
The woman struggling up, upstaring,
And he can feel a savage joy,
Plunging the blade into his wife,
Mother, or this Zinaida—life.
Aghast, he stumbles out, makes tea.
"But what has this to do with me?"
He asks himself, as the storm rages.
The link of dates that came to light
During research had caused a slight
Frisson while he'd flicked through the pages
Of Meyerhold's biography—
Then vanished from his memory.

The kitchen's lit up by a livid
Lightning-stroke; the thunder booms.
He sips; his nightmare is still vivid . . .
Nezhdánova Street; the dark bedroom's

More living to him than this grim
Kitchen, its Persil, Ajax, Vim.
A lamp. A magazine. A scarf.
Meyerhold in a photograph.
He wonders, filled with midnight horror,
Was he the woman's murderer?
As if all generations were
Bound by the scarf of Isadora . . .
He finds a biro; writes . . . The cuts.
The door of Zina's bedroom shuts.

And after his attack on Thatcher
Restores his spirits somewhat, Lloyd
Finds in his wallet a white *dacha*,
A creased, nostalgic Polaroid;
A haven on a Baltic cliff
Amid birch-trees; it feels as if
It's known to him, he has been there;
A pure wind's ruffling through his hair,
Stinging his face with salt; he'll write
To Spassky and invite himself!
He grabs a notepad from a shelf;
A disturbed moth flies to the light,
Striking it with a sizzling sound,
And drops unnoticed to the ground.

Elsewhere—a firefly in the night—
A South Korean Boeing strayed
Into a Soviet pilot's sight;
A New York copywriter played
With ads for the Olympiad;
Ben's work for Russian vodka had
Been so good he was in control
Of planning the campaign for Seoul.

A lovely hostess with black hair,
Offering a cloth to wipe his face,
Recalled a mad mid-flight embrace
And Russia—you'd not get him there
Again . . . He took the hot wet cloth
And then was spinning, like a moth.

· 3 ·

The world's unquestionably a sphinx;
With Europe's brutal, abstract head,
Made more oppressive by the lynx-
Eyes, brooding and inscrutable,
Of Russia's Mongol past and present,
The face is not exactly pleasant;
Though, south, it softens towards the crests
Of the dark continent, Sheba's Breasts;
Beyond them, dolphin-like delights
Lead to Dreamtime, the bush. I've seen
Once more the Southern Cross, serene
As in my puberty's white nights;
Yet feel no closer to the truth
Than in my stifling, heat-mad youth.

Take Nadia—why was she in Rome?
Some say she'd been invited to
Work in an orphaned children's home;
That George's view of her was true;

Ivan, they say, is dead—not drowned
But vaporised: now underground,
Kitezh is radioactive. I've
Been told, however, he's alive
By other, more reliable,
Sources than Shimon: who claim she
Used George to gain publicity
So they'd expel her. Who can tell?
Missiles can blow—that's nothing new—
But papal confidants don't screw.

As Shimon spun his tale, I thought,
"He's drunk, he's lonely and depressed;
He's making up a crazy plot,
Partly to entertain a guest,
Partly because his Muse spins lies
(He'd say, she likes to "improvise")
When he's dejected. Mine does too.
And so—this may, may not, be true . . .
Nadia throws coins into a fountain,
The swallow's wished herself good luck.
To get the pure old man to fuck
Challenges Nadia—as a mountain
Challenges mountaineers . . . It's there;
She dreams of breathing its thin air . . .

For Polish lessons Nadia came
To the Pope's ageing confidant
Who had just helped the ageing frame
To rise, in his white circus-tent,
From kissing Polish soil. The swallow
Charmed and diverted him—so hollow
His life's encumbered solitude.
Yet strangely, her Chopin *étude,*

Played with a fierce Slavonic passion,
Made his eyes glitter, glisten, more
Than her blue stockings by Dior;
And as she struck the last chords, crash on
Crash, that wild longing to be free
And boundless, for eternity.

The cleric sobbed. A disbeliever,
She argued with him, like the Fool
In *Lear*; he liked it; wouldn't leave her
In Rome, but took her to his cool
Summer retreat above Albano;
She honky-tonked on the piano
Joplin, and made him cast off that
Ridiculous stuffy little hat.
Became his Feste, earthy, shocking;
Swore like a President; would show,
Relaxing over Veuve Cliquot,
A glimpse of skin above the stocking;
Yet much worse followed; she unzipped
Her silk dress, one warm night, and stripped

Outside upon a patio.
Crickets were clicking, Armstrong played
A trumpet. In the full moon's glow,
Which turned to rainbows the cascade
Falling on nymphs and leering satyr,
Her swaying spirit made of matter
Mesmerised him, he couldn't take
His eyes away. Each azure snake
She made rear up before his gaze,
Half-moons that swayed above the silk
Basque, all her flesh as pale as milk . . .
She pulled a zip—two full moon's rays

Struck him—he flinched, and then a bright
Darkness she bared, like a white night.

She couldn't see if he was feeling
Aroused in an erotic sense:
The circus-tent he wore concealing
All but an awkward innocence,
His skirt outspread like a young girl's
Upon a hobby-horse that swirls;
The nymphs and satyr, Nadia nude,
The house's sylvan solitude,
Servitors at a window, gaping,
Empty ice-bucket, trumpet's blare,
The drag-queen rooted in his chair,
Called up Apollo, leaping, raping
Daphne in laurel-bark, the gropes
Of drunken medieval Popes.

This cleric, with a cry, half-strangled,
However, tore out of the spell
Moonlight and Nadia entangled
Him in; he stopped the jazz; a bell
Tolled through the perfumed night; he stumbled
Away, skirts kilted. Nadia mumbled,
Next morning, that she'd packed her case;
Felt terrible; tears smudged her face.
He smiled, and blessed her. A few rather
Constrained days followed, till she swam
And sunbathed naked; with the calm
Semi-detachment of a father
He gazed at her—with newborn strength
Saw her as brown hills stretched at length.

Her contact calling for results,
That autumn, in the Vatican,

She broke the calm mood, hurled insults:
Was he, she asked, a real man?
What had he got beneath his skirt
That contact with the air would hurt?
She gathered that his life began
Purely, with a caesarian,
Rather than fucking in reverse?
At her obscenity he smiled
As at a poor subnormal child.
"Christ! the whole fucking universe,"
She cried, "was made for love! It's light—"
She struck the window "—fucks your sight!"

"Have you no thought for me? I'm shaking . . .
I'm not your plastic saint from Lourdes!
Look at these breasts of mine—they're aching!"
She hammered out some Chopin chords,
Cried, "Freedom is indivisible—
The body must be free as well . . .
I'd like to bomb to hell that tomb
Next door, St Peter's!" Through the room
The *Hammerklavier* resounded.
"Christ, if you show an inch of tit
Those fucking eunuchs throw a fit!"
The *Hammerklavier* she pounded.
"It's dead! It's dead! It's dead! It's dead!
Send in priestesses dressed in red!

Blow the dome open! give us pagan
Dances and sacred orgies! You
Are wax, like Andropov and Reagan!
Why don't you swop with Reagan's crew,
Or Politburo? Your lot, there,
In fur hats, waving in Red Square,

Would fool the Russians. And they, here,
Electing yet another queer,
Could go on churning out the crap!
Masculine shit! Oh Christ, I think . . ."
"What's wrong?" "I've had too much to drink."
She dropped her head into her lap.
He made her lie down on his bed;
She bugged a Black Madonna's head.

Ringing from a coin-box long-distance,
She said, "At last it's going well,
Darling . . . Still pockets of resistance . . .
Maybe a month—it's hard to tell;
But soon you'll have me, duty-free . . .
Madly! And do you still love *me*?
What's it like there? . . . *Becoming* hot?
Of course, it's spring there! I forgot . . .
A pleasant autumn evening . . . I'd
Love to be lying in your bed:
I'm sorry that I woke you . . . Red
Fishnets—he likes them too!" She cried
Into her pillow at midnight,
Unsure again if this was right.

Ten months had gone by since their eyes
Had met in a quick, anguished glance
While that dull Mass went on. And thighs
Wade the same river only once,
She knew; each time she heard his voice
She knew she'd made the only choice,
And heard Karelian cascades.
Then doubts crept back. And why had AIDS
Struck down Ivan, making it hard
To tell him she had met Shimon

Some twelve months after he had gone,
When, lonely, she had dropped her guard
And found a joyous, strange release
With him? And what *was* this disease?

That end-of-season day at Lord's
In London, Lloyd George watched a match
From the press box. Three hundred words,
He mused, were not enough to catch
This mellow scene, blessed by the Graces.
"Rozanov—would he not change places?"
How true that was. Though just the day
Before, he'd learned his son was gay,
He felt good. Out walked Hermitage,
The last man. Ten to make. George stripped
Then, suddenly, and lightly skipped
Over the fence. He had the edge
On a fat cop; cheers rang; he jumped
On to the wicket, shouting "Stumped!"

The *Sun* showed his back view: "*Hitwicket!!!*"
Their headline shrieked. The *Times* alone,
And *Telegraph*, described the cricket
More fully than his streaking—shown
On TV also, to amuse
After the sober, gloomy news.
So droll! The *Guardian*! Was he drunk?
The *Star* reporter asked his punk-
Haired daughter among ululating
Butch friends at Greenham. She spat, "Pr--k!"
But England, not Lloyd George, was sick,
Said some; his streak was demonstrating
Contempt for Thatcherite aggression.
He entered, in severe depression,

A private clinic, where he penned
His Leningrad confessions . . .
                                    Rome:
"That Chopin made me weep, my friend . . .
Nocturne . . . This world is not our home.
I play a priest, and you, a lover.
For me, the play is almost over."
He led her down into the gloom,
The musty chill, of Peter's tomb.
"As one grows old, one sees more clearly—
Estranged from everything, confused,
Shocked, like ripe apples fallen and bruised—
That this is not our home, but merely
A place of play-acting, a Globe
Where we put on a smock, a robe . . .

Yes, autumn's come, to lay its shadow
On the sun-dial . . ." "And let loose
The wind," she murmured, "on the meadow . . ."
"That's right . . . The summer was too gross . . .
I've grown typecast. And maybe, in
The Maker's eyes, this is a sin.
Nothing seems so important now.
Not even the Church. I think, somehow,
I want that one experience
I always thought I shouldn't have.
And with a woman whom I love—
A Slav—to take my innocence . . .
Or have you changed your mind, my dear?"
A grave, sweet smile. "No. But not here . . ."

"On Peter's rock, yes!" He lay on her,
His robes her pillow, and cold stone;
Far from the cherished Black Madonna
Over his bed, a microphone

Hidden between her tender lips;
These clumsy movements of his hips
Should fly—not to the saints above—
But to the desk of Chebrikov.
Here—silence. But she didn't worry;
There'd be another time. His ring
She touched, silently murmuring
The ice is broken. "There's no hurry!"
She added loudly, for her friend,
Panting, was racing to the end.

That night, her contact came and told her
The Polish terrorists would fail.
Resting a hand on Nadia's shoulder,
Or thereabouts, he said, "Blackmail
Will not be necessary now."
She wiped his spittle from her brow.
"It's been decided that the Pope
Will not encourage them to hope.
They've washed their hands; the Poles are finished."
"Why have they washed their hands?" A shrug:
"They're worried. Freedom is a drug;
Hunger for God would be diminished;
They need a hated Caesar to
Keep the flock faithful—that's their view . . .

You'll have to stay here, as a 'sleeper' . . ."
She went straight to the Vatican . . .
But let's break off; beside the Dnieper,
In the mad-house, Sergei began
To write, at the suggestion of
The chief psychiatrist, Liubov,
His Life, a dismal history;
She had half-promised that if he

Revealed the friends who had misled him
He might be free by the New Year.
"In 1837, my dear
Friend . . ." Then a nurse broke in and led him
At a slow shuffle to a place
Where Sergei saw—a stranger's face.

Yet—he was almost sure he'd met her
Somewhere. For her part, Sonia was
Shocked to the core. "You got my letter?"
He tried to think. He'd had Mama's;
But this was not his mother. Being
On haloperidol, he was seeing
The woman rather from the side—
His head kept twisting. Sonia cried.
"It's someone," Sergei thought, "who cares.
So, what's between us? Marriage? Sex?"
Nina—of course! "You're wearing specs!"
He smiled. "They rather suit you . . . Where's
Sasha?" Then felt a sad remorse.
"You've come to ask for a divorce . . .

I loved you once," he murmured; "maybe
Love's not quite burnt out in my soul . . ."
She said to him, "There was a baby . . .
I'm sorry; I'd no self-control.
I didn't know if it was black."
A distant memory came back.
Sonia wore glasses; it was she.
The Zulu . . . "Well, we'll see, we'll see . . ."
He mumbled. "In Armenia
All will be well." Again he smiled.
She squeezed his hand. "I'd like a child.
Come out, Sergei. They say you are

Much better; give them what they want.
Liubor seems pleasant." "She's a cunt."

They parted. Resting on his bunk,
Later, amid the screams and howls,
The Jackal's shout: "You filthy skunk!"
The flailing cosh, the voiding bowels;
Kravchenko asking for analysis;
Parkinson writhings and paralysis—
Sergei's confusion all but cleared,
Through mad laughs and gross songs he heard
A little black girl, Sonia's child,
Sing from the Dnieper cold and deep
A pure, gay song; he watched her creep
Out of the river, undefiled,
And call to him, as if he were
Her father. Sergei answered her:

"I love you!" then saw Liubov loom
Above him. "*Do* you?" She stalked past.
The Prof was lecturing on the tomb
Where he'd dug out a plaster-cast—
Psikhushka-Brezhnev. He had found it
Rotting in dust and bones; around it
Were grave-goods for the other life:
Three vodka-bottles, a sharp knife
For gouging out the eyes of slaves
In case he had to lick the arse
Of Lenin-Ozymandias,
A god of the pharonic graves.
His face appeared beneath the rust
Of medals buried in the dust . . .

"Confess? Of course, my dear . . . Come closer."
The prelate cupped a hand beneath

His ear. "Unlike the *dolorosa*,
I cannot hear you through my teeth . . .
At least, the image whom I honour
Especially, the Black Madonna,
Can do that!" And the old man smiled.
"You know!" "The Jesuits, my child,
Are older than the KGB . . .
Besides, I've been an actor too."
"Then why . . . ?" "Why did I welcome you?
Because I like you. Love you . . ." He
Tenderly kissed her. "Now," he said,
"Let's give her back her maidenhead . . ."

They made love then, and two or three
Other nights, on his narrow bed.
And Nadia, inexplicably,
Found herself weeping as she read
Augustine's words to heavenly Beauty
(Read carelessly, just as a duty,
At first): Late have I loved Thee, O
Beauty most ancient and most new,
Late loved I Thee . . . And for his part,
The old man read, locked in his room,
The monologue of Molly Bloom,
And felt the rock being torn apart
And life, swimming in roses, sing
Shit or fuck or anything.

One mild clear midnight, in October,
Nadia strolled on the Tiber's bank,
Too drunk to want to sleep, though sober,
And gazed up at the stars to thank—
Everything—life—for being so gifted.
The pulsing sparks, the eyes she lifted,

Seemed to move closer and to touch.
"What's in my soul? Oh, all too much!"
She murmured. "Like a sea, an ocean,
In which I've just begun to swim
Beyond one inlet—thanks to him . . ."
She saw the river's seethe in motion
Round a still point; and in a flame,
Later, back in her flat, the same.

She crouched before a hearth-fire, turning
Charred wood in blackened letters she
Wanted destroyed; impassioned, yearning
Chords of an exile's rhapsody
For Russia fed the pure, Slavonic
Anguish she felt; to the symphonic
Meanders of Rachmaninov
She thanked the ghastly spectres of
Lenin and Stalin and the rest
For making Russian life such hell
Lyrical strains like this could swell
And fill the empty, tortured breast.
The music stops. She lifts the phone,
Heavy as her heart, to call Shimon;

Dialled endless digits to discover
He was engaged . . . In Melbourne's drought
The sweat was pouring from her lover;
His caller, Charents, had to shout:
"I said, the second of December . . .
We're going swimming—you remember?"
"Of course! Where are you? Tokyo?"
"Bombay. It's foul. I'll have to go."
Pacing the flat, he wondered why
His heart was beating like a drum,

Why he hoped Nadia wouldn't come
Just yet; he stared out at the dry
And listless beech-leaves, crucified
By the inhuman heat. He sighed.

Liuba would fit in with Australia—
Bouncy and bronzed—more readily
Than Nadia . . . Four days in Karelia
And two nights by the Baltic Sea
Two years ago: were they enough—
Making love to Rachmaninov—
To build a lifetime's marriage on?
"What do you think, my friend?" Shimon
Asked a splayed-out tarantula.
Yet that first *Cherry Orchard* scene!
Yet Masha! wondrous at eighteen . . .
Eyes, in the love-train's dining-car,
Already aching, merging . . . Why
Did passion like that have to die?

An imperceptible estrangement;
Their jealous and obsessive love
Turning to a polite arrangement;
The girl who'd fumble the right glove
On to her left hand, her tears springing
If he but kissed another—ringing
Nadia for him, to say he might
Not get to her before midnight;
And he would do the same for Masha;
With cynical discussions: "He's
Quite good in bed . . ." "She's a prick-tease;
I had some fun, though, with Natasha . . ."
Now, hoping Nadia wouldn't come
Before New Year. Delirium!

Even if he wished, he wouldn't dare to
Ring Rome and say, "Look, I'm not sure . . ."
He put on an exile's concerto,
Whose chords had echoed there before—
By one of those amazing chances
One finds in life, and old romances,
I'd lived, when young, in Shimon's flat.
He found my early *samizdat*
Lining a cupboard, yellowed, musty.
He wrote me, urged a visit; I'd
Met him when Masha was my guide
In Moscow. Here, watched by a dusty
Beech-tree—how it had shrunk!—I'd found
Myself in dreamtime—underground.

And yet I'd longed to break away . . .
Those were my Russian years, it's clear:
Boredom and airlessness by day,
And night—a time of ghastly fear.
Yet all so lyrical . . . Enough.
The passionate Rachmaninov
Brought love for Nadia back. Shimon
Hummed, answering the telephone.
Rome! Nadia! Conscience . . . It was over.
The chords become a requiem;
They weep. That night—her last in Rome—
She tries to talk about her lover,
While lying with her friend. He thinks
She weeps for him—his Neva sphinx.

He looks at her with warm, shrewd eyes,
And says, "No, you're not acting now . . .
So . . . Your Ivan awaits?" She sighs,
And nods. "It terrifies me how

I've changed towards him. For three years,
Nothing but longings, floods of tears . . ."
She breaks off, thinks I mustn't lie
To him . . . "—but now—I don't know why—
It's not your fault, my dear—I feel
Indifferent." She clutched his hand.
"I'm to be Nadine Peters, and
A blonde! Imagine it . . . Unreal."
Her eyes were moist. He let her talk;
Saw Molly on Gibraltar's rock.

"We'll have a house in Malibu.
It's not far from the naval base.
He says the sky is always blue,
You swim all year, and in your face
Burst breakers all the way from home—
I hurt him when I said, 'From Rome?'
Ivan has some obscure disease;
He says he needs me; I think he's
Dying, in fact. He should have stayed
In his own country. I don't know
What made him drown off Scapa Flow.
It's strange, I still feel he betrayed
The motherland . . ." She feels her face
Cupped by soft hands, and they embrace

For the last time. "Now let the wind
Loose on the flowers," he said. "I can't
Believe that you, or I, have sinned."
"Ah! *Auf den Fluhren*—yes . . ." Aslant
Their narrow bed a streak of light
Fell. With the passing of the night
She whirled into her clothes, and he
Took, from a secret drawer, the key

That would unlock a secret door
Into a secret passageway
Made for the early Popes when they
Let in or out a paramour.
She stands before him in her coat;
He touches brow, and cheek, and throat.

His eyes, for the first time, are sad.
"This is a promise, Nadia: when
We're asked to visit Leningrad—
Which must be soon—we'll meet again.
This is a parting, not divorce."
"You think that's where I'll go?" "—Of course.
You'll not live long in Malibu,
Flirting with Tiger-sharks; for you
Will find the hunger in your soul
Will drive you from that wealth. I know
You'll keep your innocence. Now go,
Before the guards make their patrol."
He'd pulled a rope; a nun had come
To guide her out. She said, "*Shalom.*"

Next morning, packed, and dressed to go,
Even to the scarf around her throat,
She switched her pocket-radio
On for the news. A mere foot-note—
A bomb-blast at a London shop.
The violence would never stop.
The news reminded her of George;
Bile could still rise in Nadia's gorge,
Recalling sex with him. Despair
At Shimon's failure—as it seemed—
The death of all they'd dreamed and schemed,
Had led her to it. A nightmare!

He'd write about this bomb-blast, and,
As always, strive to understand . . .

Where did we leave the Welshman? Rest
Cleansed him like a dialysis;
His Hampstead clinic gave the best
Post-Freudian analysis
In England. There were daily sessions
Based on the sensitive confessions
You've read. He feared, it seemed, a tape-
Recording of some childhood rape.
One day, the leader of the Labour
Party, who lived nearby, dropped in,
With chat, of how next time they'd win,
And *Smoke*, a novel. Lloyd's old neighbour
Was taken aback as he burst out:
"Aha! Turgenev and the Foot!"

And then went back to the election.
The next day, when his brother called,
Lloyd spoke of Christ, the Resurrection,
Most troublingly. The Bishop stalled,
Shaken and sad, when asked if he
Believed in the mythology;
The white-haired, mild-eyed prelate said,
"I'm sure His power isn't dead,"
Then flinched back, seeing a demonic
Expression, like a lurid flame,
Cross George's face, and from it came
A voice which cried in Church Slavonic,
"*Khristós Voskrése!*" and he knew
His mind was gone; "*Voístinu*

Voskrése! He is risen indeed!"
The patient reared to his full height

Then scratched his brow to make it bleed;
But the next moment seemed all right,
Sitting and chatting about Wales:
"They'll bring back Davies if he fails . . .
Remember that Barbarians try . . ."
But as November days went by,
He saw, more frequently, the clinic
As a *psikhushka*—in control,
Sulphur and haloperidol;
Himself, a "sluggish" schizophrenic.
He fasted, kept beneath his bed,
Hidden in a shoe, a crust of bread.

Refused to shave or cut his hair,
Talked to imaginary lags,
Quarrelled with them, refused to share
His daily ration of five fags—
Strangely, he had begun to smoke.
Asked for a paper when he woke
Each morning underneath the bars
Where snow was blotting out the stars;
"I want *Izvestia*!" he cried, thinking
His name Rozanov. He would shout,
"You fucking bastards! Let me out!
He's shit himself again—he's stinking!"
Although, of course, his room was clean,
And *Breakfast-Time* was on the screen.

One night he strolled out, dressing-gowned,
Past his old house; strode on, the rain
Matting his wild locks, till he found
His path barred by a statue. Pain
Seized him, his eyes were sealed by mist;
Trembling with wrath, he shook his fist;

"You wonder-worker, just you wait!"
Then set off running through Highgate
At breakneck speed; but everywhere
The Idol followed, like a hive,
Stinging him . . . Barely half-alive,
Fearful, with lank red beard and hair,
He was discovered by a cop,
Cowering behind a betting-shop,

And brought back . . .
                        But my poor, poor
Lloyd George! Alas! His confused mind could not endure
The shocks he had suffered. His ears still heard
The boom of Neva and the winds. Silently
He shuffled round, filled with dreadful thoughts.
Some sort of dream tormented him. A week,
A month, went by—and he discharged himself.
A stranger to the world, all day he wandered
On foot, and slept at night on the embankment
With other tramps. He fed on scraps from dustbins,
Tattered and mouldy grew his shabby clothes.
Skin-heads lashed out at him, for he could not find his way;
It seemed he noticed nothing, deafened by
An inner turmoil. And so he dragged out his life,
Neither beast nor man, neither this nor that,
Not of the living world nor of the dead . . .

There is a London store, much visited
By foreign tourists and the wealthier English.
A man had driven a ramshackle little car there,
And parked it in a side-street. Christmas-shoppers
Rushed about, on a murky afternoon.
And my poor madman, unnoticed by everyone,
Crouched in a doorway, wrapping up his feet.

The car exploded; and when the pall of smoke
Had thinned, and rescuers moved in, they found
A foot fused with charred letters . . . *Smoke*, Turgenev . . .

It's odd, but on the day he perished
His old friend, the Ukrainian
Kravchenko, by the Dnieper flourished
A non-existent *Guardian*
And said, "Good Lord! Old George!" Dick Johnson
Lit up a Dunhill with his Ronson
And told Rozanov George was dead;
"A nice chap, if a bit too red."
Though coshed by Jackal, he said rain
Had stopped the test at Hyderabad.
I know the world's completely mad;
You mustn't ask me to explain;
Nothing, almost, is a surprise.
The sphinx is moving his slow thighs . . .

Rome froze; yet Nadia, being driven
At speed, the windows down, felt warm;
At Leonardo she was riven
By terrors, an electric-storm.
Feverishly she began to shiver,
Seeing, like arrows in a quiver,
Qantas, El Al, Finnair, Pan Am,
And Aeroflot's deceptive calm.
When she could hesitate no longer,
She joined a stand-by queue . . . She drank
And tried to read, the pages blank.
A calm voice said, "Try something stronger!"
"Thank you." And they began to chat.
He poured nostalgic Ararat;

As Nadia was about to swallow—
Dreaming of Neva and the sphinx,
And striving drowsily to follow
What he was saying about inks,
The black, the white—she felt his hand
Glide swiftly up her skirt and land,
Under her tray; she all but choked;
Her hat—her grey fur hat—was soaked.
Her flight became a whirling *troika*
Which as it dashed through space unfurled
The lost creation of the world.
Nadia sniffed Russia, Neva, Moika—
Yet also an exotic scent,
The southern cunt and continent.

"My God! where are you taking me?"
She cried—the *troika* whirling faster;
The stranger chuckled: "Well, you'll see . . .
'I'm blinded by the blizzard, master!
Can't see the forest—lost the track, sir;
Some demon's got us—that's a fact, sir!' . . ."
" 'A demon's leading us astray;
We're done for—we'll be frozen—whey!' . . ."
"Ah, you know Pushkin!" her delighted
Companion panted; Nadia gasped,
"Of course!" Still fought him; toppling, clasped
Him tighter still; again they righted—
Again she struggled helplessly,
Assailed by demon-fires—*besí*.

This had to be the final curtain!
She ought to know how it would feel.
But this was nothing, she was certain,
Like dying bravely in *Camille*.

Such lightning-strokes! Such bolts of thunder!
Surely the *troika* must go under!
The jolts and jars would never stop;
Everything desolate, snowed-up;
Just mounds of snow, the wayside-stations;
She thought she glimpsed an embryo,
Her child, gape through the pelting snow,
Its cry lost in improvisations
By millions of dead souls—no sign
Of life or meaning or design.

But Nadia cried, "I think it's clearing!"
Saw in the murk pale hints of light
Vanishing and re-appearing;
Then stammered, "Why, it's home!" The white
Night glowed, she saw the candles burning,
The stars' diaspora returning
Like tracer-bullets through the sky.
"Kitezh . . ." And she began to cry,
Seeing that water, in the distance,
Which covered her ancestral home,
A city with more towers than Rome.
She offered, then, no more resistance,
Putting her faith in love, the lake
Made deep and dark for freedom's sake.